T.S. HOWARD

A Gate of Wolves and Winter

First published by Maelan Press 2020

Copyright © 2020 by T.S. Howard

This novel is entirely a work of fiction. The names, characters and incidents portrayed in it are the work of the author's imagination. Any resemblance to actual persons, living or dead, events or localities is entirely coincidental.

T.S. Howard asserts the moral right to be identified as the author of this work.

First edition

ISBN: 978-1-7375377-2-4

Cover art by Warren Design
Illustration by Jake Howard
Editing by Sage Maelan

This book was professionally typeset on Reedsy.
Find out more at reedsy.com

To my two perfect girls,
for filling my life with laughter and light,
even if it made this take a little longer.

Contents

It is my hope that as you continue Faron's journey, you will come to love him as I do—along with the other characters you will come across, both new and familiar.

T.S. Howard

Prologue

In a blizzard that would last a thousand years, a rider on a pale horse forged his way through the snow. The tracks they left led through ice unfrozen for millennia, centuries-old frost, and the fresh crystals that swept the earth here.

On the ground, a band of white marked the line between winter and the rest of the world, stretching east and west as far as a man could see. It was the Veil, and it wasn't where it should have been.

Inside the band, a man dismounted the great white horse. Another soon followed, emerging from the blinding depths of the whistling snows. They wore black leather, except for long, white fur cloaks on their backs.

The snow crunched under their boots in a way that could be felt, if not heard over the shrieking wind. They were silent for a prolonged moment before the first of them spoke.

"I had hoped you were wrong. I'm sorry, Varan, but I had to see it."

Varan, a tall and slender man with long, silver hair answered. "I had hoped as well, Lord Pyre."

"Mid-Augur, and the Veil hasn't fallen even to the Volothin pass. This hasn't happened in…" He paused, searching his memory.

"Never."

A drawn-out moment spanned between them before

Sadagon Pyre asked, "How long?"

Varan seemed to think for a quiet minute before answering. "Soon."

"How soon?" Sadagon pried. "How long do we have?"

"A century, at most," Varan relented. "Perhaps half that." Reading the torment on his master's face, Varan went on over the wind. "It isn't too late, my lord. There can still be hope."

He was met with silence, except for the drowning wail of the wind.

"You can help them, Lord."

"Help them, how?" Sadagon lamented. "If I save them from the wolves and the Veil, they'll only kill each other."

"You know the method I speak of, Vam Sadagon."

"I know that it isn't an option."

Pleading, Varan stepped closer. "Fifteen thousand men are dead in the battlefields outside Murcosta in this year alone. The sands of the Kaor are likewise littered with innocent corpses, wielded by evil men."

"I know the arguments," Sadagon said, interrupting, but was himself cut off.

"In the constant vacuum of power that we've created, there are armies now in every corner. Kearth has fallen to Anveil, her hundred-thousand inhabitants dead. Alpenglow has declared for Anveil, and they march on Empyrion; yet, Murcosta might end them both first. The Men of the Lake will almost certainly ride with whichever force has the advantage."

"I know, Varan," Sadagon said, louder this time. Still, Varan pushed on.

"Great syndicates are rising up over the south, with pirates and pirate kings in Sycele. Istred is all but ruled by raiders and crime lords, not even to speak of the pure corruption of

Blackwood."

"I know!" Sadagon yelled.

"Freedom has had its day!" Varan declared. With the words finally spoken, they were both hushed for an indeterminable moment. Even the wind seemed to respect the temerity of the words. Having said his piece, Varan waited for Sadagon to break the silence. When he finally did, it was with contemplative slowness.

"My father pushed pieces of white ivory around on a table when I was a child, commanding things I didn't understand. When I was old enough to know that the pieces indicated the positions and movements of armies, I was sobered, but I knew that it was for the betterment of mankind. My father was a hero."

Varan looked to the ground.

"Do you know what he was really doing, Varan? Why he moved those pieces where he did?"

"I do," was all he said.

"He was playing games," Sadagon said anyway. "Crashing armies into each other for no purpose other than his amusement, directing thousands of men to slaughter each other so he might play out a realized version of chess."

"That is not the man you are, my lord," Varan countered. "You are not your father. You *killed* your father."

"No," Sadagon said. "You're wrong. That *is* who I am. You refuse to see it, but I have such *anger* inside, Varan—such hatred. If you could see it, you'd run from me and never look back."

"We all fear the darkness inside of us, Lord Pyre. It's what makes us human. What makes you great is how you *resist* that darkness. You're a good man, Sadagon, even if you won't see it."

Pushing his wrists out of his black coat, Sadagon studied the spiderweb of scars on his skin. "Am I even human anymore?" he pondered. "Am I even decent?"

"Vam Sadagon Pyre," Varan persisted. "You are the best man I've ever known."

"I hate them," he admitted. "I *hate* them, Varan. Ever since Vam Bahr, I've felt such a lust for murder in me. No people should be ruled by a man who fantasizes about killing them."

"My lord," Varan began, but then reconsidered. "Sadagon, not a man, woman, or child still survives from the day of White Grave, and not a single one of them was killed by you."

"Then why do I harbor this resentment in me, Varan? Why do I want to *hurt* them?"

"Rare is the man who's been hurt who doesn't want to hurt others in turn. Pain begets pain, Lord Sadagon. Cruelness is its own creator."

"You knew my mother and my father for a long time, Varan. You knew them better than anyone for six hundred years, but you didn't know them before they were gods. If you ask me to pick up this mantle, I will become him. Sooner or later, I will become Olsu in the flesh."

Varan opened his mouth to speak, but Sadagon didn't let him.

"Don't, Varan. I won't do it. I won't become a god. There has to be another way."

"There is," he said, "a possible third option—a way to give men safety from the Veil and her snowbeasts *without* the freedom to kill each other, a way we might take back the actions that led us here." Intensity and sincerity pulling at his voice, Varan said, "There may be a way to reform the godhead."

For a long moment, the only sound was the wind drowning the world in snow.

"Tell me."

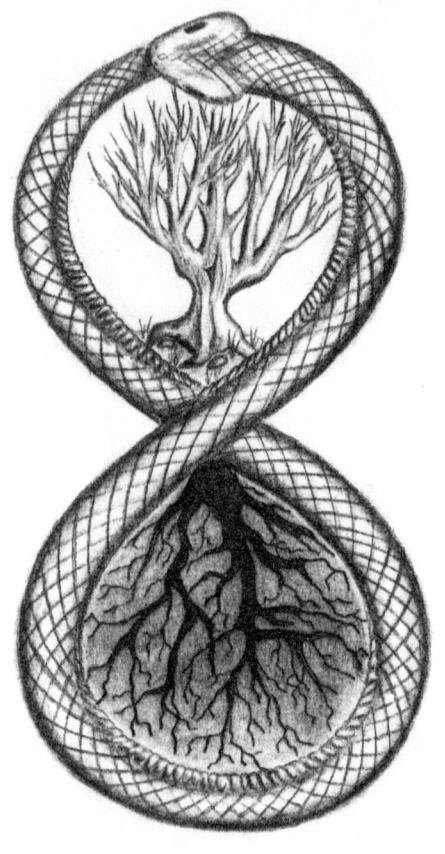

xvi

I

A Gate of Wolves and Winter

ONE HUNDRED YEARS LATER

To Aru'barrahk

Moonlight, weak and pale, filtered in through the slit of a circular tent of tan canvas. In the center was a thick, wooden stake that supported most of the weight of the material, and at its base was a loose section of uncoiled rope. The sinewy, yellow binding was dyed red with blood in more than one place and sliced unevenly with frayed edges.

At the edge of the tent sat a dark figure crouched in shadow, except for a blade of light from the moon and stars. A deep green eye peered back at those stars, waiting for a blackness to come between them.

Silently, just under his breath, the figure counted, starting at one and reaching thirty-two before a silhouette broke apart the starlight. The counting started again at one and ended at thirty-two. The shadow came again.

Over and over, the shadow came, always at thirty-two seconds. The pattern wouldn't become any clearer.

Fifteen seconds after another repetition, the tent flap was pulled farther back, and the eye that pierced the darkness cast around for a wider view. Moonlight revealed a face that was gaunt, sunburnt, and bruised but only fiercer for it.

After a long moment, Faron pulled away from the gap in

3

the tent. He couldn't see any farther into the night. If there was anyone else out there, he couldn't see them, and the odds of a camp of four men having more than one guard were very low.

Gingerly, he felt at his wrists and the skin that had once been there. They were raw now and covered with ever-changing scabs and blisters. They hurt terribly, but it felt good to have a knife in his hands again, even if it was only a stolen table utensil. It had taken time, but it was enough for the rope. Faron had hoped that it would be sharp enough to slit a throat, but it was far too dull for that. It could puncture a pair of lungs if it had to, but that was an awful idea. If it came to that, his escape would be over before it began. Lung wounds didn't kill quietly. With that in mind, Faron picked up the rope that had bound him. It would have to do.

For the past week, he'd been held by these men (no, not men—slavers) and had been subject to their amusements while they bore him toward the slave markets of Aru'barrahk. He hadn't tried escaping before because the desert was hot and vast. There was no water source marked on the map Ulric had given him that night in the tavern, and he didn't have the map anymore anyway. They'd taken that too, along with everything else. They'd even replaced the clothes on his back with wrapping rags that stank of old sweat and blood, but none of that mattered now.

The towers of Aru'barrahk could be seen even at night, soaring into the sky like jagged teeth from a jawbone. Light radiated from the city and filled the sky with a soft glow. There had been no point in running before, but now they were here. He'd arrived where he had intended to go—if not in the manner he'd imagined—but if he could get away now, it would hardly be any setback at all.

There were still just over two months left to find Hadria—time enough. It had to be.

All he had to do was find Jaru'tal—the man who purchased the child slaves from Fayevew—and make him talk. Faron grimaced, then set his jaw. It was a grizzly work, extracting secrets from a person, but he'd done it once before. He could do it again—for Hadria.

Reaching the count of thirty-two once more, Faron peered back out of his narrow doorway to see Jakab'een—the slaver currently patrolling the camp—stride past, right on schedule. He was a lanky man, barely a few years older than Faron himself, with clean-shaven cheeks and a symmetrical face. Faron supposed he might have been considered pretty, but that face hid a sinister disposition. He would often twirl a curved dagger between his fingers and stare Faron down as if wondering what he looked like without his skin.

Faron shivered and lamented for a passing moment that he wouldn't be able to slice the man's trachea. The dark thought surprised him. Faron was no killer, not willingly at least, but he felt a bloodlust for these men that he couldn't deny.

He supposed that was to be expected. They had beat him, starved him, and made sport of it all. It was hardly a surprise that he wanted them dead. He ran over the lot of them in his head.

Besides Jakab'een, there was his brother, Haka'een. What he lacked in his younger brother's looks and brooding intelligence he made up for in over-confidence and bravado. He seemed to stylize himself as the leader of the thieving crew.

Sleeping in a tent across from Haka'een's was Badun'ahl, a man of even lower caste and even less intelligence. He

5

was, however, built like a mountain. The man was a typical mercenary-type, not unlike the collectors Dageran had employed to gather guild dues in that gods-forsaken cave, except perhaps quieter. If his experience with Jakal was anything to go by, this man was more dangerous than the others and should be avoided at all costs.

Finally, there was Harab'kun, the wiry old man who had resuscitated him in the first place. His beady eyes appeared to have trouble keeping focused on any one point too long, and his hands shook with an electrified energy. He seemed the least dangerous of the crew, being the one delegated to the cooking, cleaning up, and with the least acerbic attitude. He fed Faron at nights and always tried to strike up conversation, but Faron didn't give him anything. The less these filths knew of him, the easier it would be to kill them if the opportunity arose.

Four men, all dangerous, all determined to see him sold at the slave markets of Aru'barrahk. Faron grappled with himself inside his tent. He didn't know where they all were. Jakab'een predictably marched around the camp, but was there another on guard? Could he be quiet enough? Quick enough? Did he even have the strength?

He doubted it, but he didn't have many options. He was out of his binds already, and there was no getting back in them. In the morning, they'd beat him unconscious and truss him up for sale. No, he had to get out—now.

Jakab'een passed the tent again, and Faron waited until the count of four before gathering his breath and slipping into the night.

Soft sand muffled his feet, and with the grace of a lifelong thief, Faron fell into step behind his guard. Stooped low to the ground, he took long strides, pushing heel first into the desert sand, then rolling to the balls of his feet before shifting forward. Faron timed his stride with the slaver's.

Growing steadily closer, Faron followed his prey to the distant edge of the camp. If there was any noise, perhaps it would be harder to hear from this distance.

Three more steps—Faron ceased his breathing. Two more steps—he readied the rope. Barely a foot behind Jakab'een, Faron lunged forward with the rough cord and lashed it around the man's neck.

The sound of words formed without air escaped his captor's lips, but they lacked potency. Jakab'een thrashed as he suffocated, his windpipe collapsing. He twisted and tried to throw Faron off, but it only pulled the rope tighter.

"Die," Faron hissed into his ear and then caught an elbow to the head.

The night burned white. Faron cursed as he lost his grip and fell to his knees. His head rang with a high-pitched whine. Stumbling, he staggered to his feet as his sight slowly restored.

Jakab'een wretched before him, coughing bile into the sand. It wasn't quiet. He eyed Faron with murder in his gaze but still couldn't stand.

Faron's instincts kicked in, and he took two frightened steps back, then turned and ran. He had murdered before, but he was no killer. He was a thief, and no thief lived long without knowing when to run.

He barely made ten steps before a tent between him and the horses rustled and belched out a drunken and half-asleep man—Haka'een. They both stopped short, staring at each other for a full second before either could react. In a flash, Faron remembered the stolen table knife in his boot and bent down to seize it.

"Badune'ahl!" Haka'een roared, but that was all the time he had left. In one smooth motion, Faron stood, turned his body flat, and flung the blade with a left-handed throw. It was a crude weapon, but Faron could throw an unbalanced knife. It buried itself deep into Haka'een's eye, and he crumpled like a bag of meat.

"No!" Faron heard Jakab'een scream from behind. He had recovered his voice and was on his feet now.

"Olsu's corpse," Faron cursed, breaking out into a flat run. He heard motion in the other tents as he passed them but didn't stop to see if the others would emerge. He had to get to the horses.

With all the speed he could muster, Faron passed up the first horse for the one with no saddlebags. If it came to a race, the least burdened beast would be the fastest. He jumped into its saddle and whipped at the reins.

Almost before the horse could react, strong hands pulled Faron from the saddle. He slammed into the ground, a stone or root crashing into his back until there was no air left inside him at all.

He tried to fill his lungs but couldn't breathe. The sound that came from his throat was not unlike what he'd just inflicted on Jakab'een.

Gasping for breath, he was dragged away from the horses and shoved face-first into the sand. More than one pair of hands subdued him as his arms were forced behind his back once again and bound with awful rope. It burned like fire where his skin had been previously rubbed away.

"Damn you!" Faron screamed when he had regained the air to speak. "Dead gods damn you all!" Faron twisted to see that it was the old man, Harab'kun, who had caught him. He kicked Faron in the stomach.

"He killed Haka!" Jakab'een cried. "He killed my brother!"

A boot connected with Faron's head, then his stomach. Something else smashed into his side, and he couldn't help but cry out. Tied and bound, Faron writhed on the ground as Jakab'een beat him.

When the ringing in his ears came to a stop, a large hand shoved his face into the rough sand.

"Look at him!" Jakab'een yelled through a hoarse throat. "Look at him!"

A fist smashed into his head.

"Look!"

Faron forced his eyes open and came face to face with the man he'd just killed. His mouth was frozen in an expression of agonizing pain, and a crude iron knife jutted out from the socket of his eye. Blood streamed from that destroyed socket and into the open mouth.

"Look what you did to my brother!" Jakab'een cried.

Faron did look, and despite the knowledge of who he was, guilt crept into his heart—guilt, and disgust. The man was alive before, with thoughts, feelings, and memories. Now, he was nothing.

"Do you see, Aldene filth? Do you see what you've done to my brother?" Jakab'een's hand shoved his face even closer, within inches now. It wasn't the first time Faron had been trapped with his eyes on a skull.

Screams. His vision began to blot out from the bottom right.

"Remember his face," Jakab'een hissed through clenched teeth. "You will beg for a knife in the eye before I'm through with you. You will *wish* for an end so sweet once you know the men who will own you."

Cutting off his own tirade, Jakab'een threw Faron's shoulder into the sand and rolled him onto his back. Faron got his arms up, but they were weak and easily batted away.

Jakab'een wrapped the selfsame rope that had nearly strangled him around Faron's neck and pulled it tight. The stars grew brighter as his vision turned red. A rushing filled his ears as he struggled, kicking with all his might, but he wasn't strong enough.

Jakab'een's furious and rapturous face was the last thing he saw before the world faded from red to black.

Dunestrider

When Faron woke, he was face down on the back of a horse, several yards of rough rope wrapped around his neck. His hands were bound together, and those bindings were connected to his feet. He felt sand in his ears, eyes, and mouth, forced there during his unconsciousness. He gagged, and a wet lump fell from his mouth.

A searing pain exploded across his back, punctuated by the sound of cracking air. Jakab'een held a short whip in one hand and contorted hatred on his face. He whipped Faron again, adding a sharp line across the ocean of bruises and welts that was his skin. A sharp inhalation of breath marked the strike, sucking half a mouthful of sand down Faron's throat. His gasp transformed into a fit of vomitous coughs.

"Murderer," Jakab'een said. He cracked the whip again. The horses whinnied at the familiar noise and trotted nervously to the side.

"Put it away," Harab'kun said, wrestling with the reigns for control of his mount. Faron was tossed from his position behind the saddle and fell unceremoniously to the ground. "Akwin damn. There is enough pain in his future without needing to startle the horses."

11

Leaning over the side of his horse, Jakab'een scored another three stripes in quick succession across Faron's side before putting the whip away. Faron screamed and writhed on the ground.

Hardly conscious and deep inside his own agony, Faron didn't notice Jakab'een dismount from his horse. He kicked a wave of sand in Faron's face and open mouth as he approached. Faron wretched, unable to breathe for a long half-minute before finally vomiting bile onto the sand. It was acidic and terrible. He gasped for a lungful of air, then wretched again, the horrible stench and taste of stomach acid almost causing him to throw up a second time.

Sand in his throat, bile in his mouth, and pain *everywhere*, Faron took a deep, stabilizing breathe. He was certain that if he tried to speak, he would be sick again. Jakab'een laughed above him, and Faron felt a hatred he didn't know he was capable of.

"Get up," the man commanded. "You walk from here."

Bound as he was, Faron had no chance of standing on his own, and both of them knew it. Jakab'een kicked him in the gut anyway.

"Stand up, murderer," he said, then dragged Faron to his feet with strength that far surpassed his own.

Faron had never felt so much pain in all his life. He took long, steady breaths to manage it, but it wasn't enough. He stood under the hot sun, every inch of exposed skin a deep shade of red, and focused on not falling over. While he did that, Jakab'een looped a long section of the yellow rope through the bindings on his wrists and tied the other end to Harab'kun's saddle pommel.

"Keep up," Jakab'een commanded. "Or we will drag you."

With no choice but to obey, Faron walked behind the slavers and attempted to manage his pain.

A few hours later, Faron and the men who owned him came to the city of Aru'barrahk.

After so many days, it was a palpable relief to finally see the city, even though it was where he was meant to be sold. Even if he couldn't possibly escape, being sold to anyone else meant getting away from Jakab'een.

With a nervous anxiety, Faron was pulled inside. Soaring walls of sandstone broke into the sky—old, weathered, and crumbling in more places than not. Various hues of white, yellow, and red stone made up the bulk of the great buildings behind the walls, fading paint showing on most of them. Round towers and massive arches dominated the landscape.

Even in his beaten-down state, Faron couldn't help but notice the exotic beauty of his surroundings. If the desert was the crown of the world, then this city was its jewel. As far as the eye could see, there were structures so large and grand that it boggled the mind. Faron stared, open-mouthed and wide-eyed at the great work before him. At what seemed the absolute edge of the desert, the city was built right up against the rim of a jagged, sheer range of mountains. They were a red sandstone at the base but transitioned into a dark gray granite somewhere high above. The peaks of the near-vertical granite slopes were white-capped and covered in snow, a great dissonance from the heat that beat down on the dunes so many tens of thousands of feet below. Faron had never seen such a high peak in all his life.

Despite the heat, the city flourished with life. Tall green cedars and trees with long trunks and fan-like leaves decorated every roadway, every street corner, and every door.

Magnificent arches and grand colonnades supporting massive temple-like structures were many and worked intricately with staggering amounts of gold. Most opulent of all, however, were the wide reflective pools that spanned large and flat across courtyards between buildings. Some blazed with dazzling reflected light in the open, and others sat in the shade of great pavilions supported by thick columns. Shocking as the city itself was, this was the most surprising—beautiful, unguarded water. Boys and girls of all ages played in the fountains and pools, casting water into the air and onto the sand. In a land of such intense dryness and heat, it was a truly decadent thing to see.

Faron had never seen anything so magnificent in all his life. He had heard that Alden's capital, Empyrion, was an imposing and majestic sight, with its many keeps, castles, manors, and long-abandoned chapels, but he was certain it couldn't compare to this. He was so caught up with the massive bronze-capped towers, he hardly even noticed the multitudes of people staring at him.

Every street, alley, and storefront was filled with the dark people of Kaor. As Faron turned his attention to them, he found that many watched him with what could only be described as curiosity, except for those who looked as if they wanted to stab him. Gold, silver, and glass jewelry adorned the wrists, biceps, necks, ears, and heads of nearly every man and woman he passed. These people valued adornment, it seemed, and it was in abundance.

Previously, Faron had harbored a hope of escaping and hiding among the people of the city, much like he had in Fayevew, but that had been well beaten out of him. Now, though, seeing the vast differences between himself and the

14

Kaorn, any vestigial remnant of that hope quickly evaporated. It would take more than a hood to hide among these people. Nearly every person he passed stared openly at his light skin and muttered, "Oathbreaker," or something to that effect. He had no idea what oath he had broken.

The farther they went, the more opulent the city became. The yellow sandstone structures began to appear painted with black or white ceramic, reflective and smooth. Open markets sprawled along colonnades, men and women sitting on rugs and pillows, hawking their goods. They even passed a few long wooden platforms where, not even attempting to hide what they were doing, men and women stood in brass shackles, and the people down below bid for the auctioneer's attention.

A slave market, Faron realized with a sick feeling, out in the open, like they were selling and buying potatoes and turnips. Faron didn't see any children in the crowd of people waiting to be sold, but he still itched to throw a knife at the man orating on a stand. He swore a silent vow that he would—somehow.

"Do you see that man?" Jakab'een asked with a grin on his face.

Fatigued, Faron looked where he indicated, seeing a tall man with a white streak in his beard. He was dressed all in gold.

"That is Larac'kal. He is known for buying boys about your age. He... enjoys them, you see." His grin grew wider. "Perhaps I will sell you to him."

"He is not pretty enough for Larac," Harab'kun cut in, speaking for the first time in a long while. "And too old. Besides, we are not selling the Aldene here."

"Then where?" Jakab'een's brow pulled into a narrow V-

15

shape.

"To the Dunestrider," the old man answered with casualness.

Even the towering Badune'ahl hesitated half a step.

"They will not let you into the King's Market," Jakab'een scorned. "They may kill a 'Kun for even trying."

"And an 'Ahl and an 'Een," Harab'kun replied. "But we have him." He yanked on Faron's ropes, making him stumble forward. "And Akwin favors the strong. We could sell him here, or we could get five times the rate from the king's favored."

Exhausted, Faron was almost too tired to wonder who they were talking about.

"Or the damn 'Tal will take him and cut off our heads."

Harab'kun opened his mouth to reply, but the hair on Faron's neck stood on end. The part of his consciousness that retreated like a kicked dog woke with a start, heedless of the pain that might come from wakefulness.

"'Tal?" he asked. "As in Jaru'tal?" The desperation must have been evident in his voice because Harab'kun cut off his reply and stared at him. Jakab'een placed a kick between his shoulder blades.

Hands and feet bound, Faron landed hard on his side.

"Outsiders do not speak of the Dunestrider, and murderers do not speak at all." Jakab'een's voice was immediately tinged with bitterness and contempt.

"No," Harab'kun said. "Let him speak. He has told us nothing about why he is here, and I wonder what he knows."

Taking that as permission to proceed, Faron asked again, "Is it Jaru'tal? Please." He was so determined that he didn't even flinch when Jakab'een wrapped his fingers around the handle of his whip.

"It is not for a slave to ask," Harab'kun said, but then he went on. "But… yes. The very same. Jaru'tal Dunestrider is the king's favored, the ruler of a great merchant house, and the richest man in all the Kaor. What does that mean to an Aldene boy who won't tell us how he came to the middle of the desert and why?" He cocked an eyebrow as if no answer could surprise him.

"I'll go," Faron declared. "I won't fight you."

"You'll what?" Jakab'een asked.

"Please," Faron insisted. "Don't sell me here. Take me to Jaru'tal."

The old Harab'kun raised one eyebrow into a sharp arch. "What could an Aldene possibly gain by selling himself to a notorious slaver? How could you even know his name?"

"I won't fight you," Faron said again. "Sell me here, and I'll attack you until you're forced to kill me; but, take me to Jaru'tal, and I'll go willingly."

"How do you know his name, Aldene?" Harab'kun repeated.

"Absolutely not," Jakab'een intervened. "I intend to sell you to rapists or mad physickers. You will wish for a slavery as mundane as hard labor."

Harab'kun ignored him. "Tell me how you know of Jaru'tal, and I may consider."

Jakab'een interrupted them again, losing his cool. "Do you not see how this is dangerous? He *wants* to go! Why would you take him where he asks? So he may kill another of us? He knows something that you do not, Harab."

"Most men do," the old man said offhandedly, eyes focused on Faron. He contemplated for a long moment. "Tell me why you came to this desert. I might listen to you if you do."

"I'm here," Faron finally said, "for him—Jaru'tal." When the older man waited for further explanation, he added, "He has something that I need."

"You cannot be considering this, Harab," Jakab'een said. "If they do not hang you in a gibbet for entering the King's Market, they certainly will when this son of oathbreakers tries to attack the Dunestrider."

Harab'kun's eyes were still intently searching Faron's. He didn't respond.

"Listen to me!" Jakab'een yelled. "Do you not see you are doing what he wants? He'll see us all hanged in cages."

"He doesn't know that," Harab'kun finally answered.

"Please," Faron begged, whispering only to Harab'kun. Finally, the old man nodded.

"I will do this for you, son of oathbreakers, but first, you must do something for me."

"Anything," Faron promised, almost lightheaded with relief. He was going to Jaru'tal. Even captured, he could still find Hadria.

Harab'kun only nodded before turning away. "We are taking him to the King's Market."

"You don't command us!" Jakab'een yelled at Harab'kun as he got back on his horse and led Faron away. "You do not lead us!"

"Neither do you, Jakab."

"You would deny me my brother's vengeance?" No one answered, except to continue leading Faron away.

It took every modicum of self-control Faron possessed to not turn around and look at the man. He felt his eyes boring into his back and wanted to run.

Standing alone, Jakab'een yelled, "I want half!"

The procession stopped again, and irritation flashed in

Harab'kun's eyes so briefly, Faron almost missed it.

Turned around to face his younger companion, Harab'kun said, "There are three of us here, Jakab."

"He killed Haka," Jakab'een said, throwing a murderous glare at Faron. "I want my brother's fourth and my fourth. That's half."

After an uncomfortable silence, Harab'kun replied, "Very well. For your brother's wife and daughters, it will be." He turned to the mountainous man beside him and placed a few small coins into his palm. "Badune, if you are swift, you can find a length of steel chain for our oathbreaker. It doesn't matter what price, so long as they are clean and large enough to cover the rope-burns on his wrists, and find him a tunic with full sleeves."

Without a word of question, the thick-shouldered man strode away into the setting sunlight.

"What are you doing?" Jakab'een interceded. "You do not give orders to us."

"No, and Badune'ahl understands that he is not being ordered." The big man didn't turn around to confirm Harab'kun's words. "His share has just been reduced from a third to a fourth, and he understands that to earn anything near what he was, we'll have to get as much as we can for our oathbreaker. That means making him presentable… and docile."

The two men looked at Faron, dark eyes speaking a shared understanding. Faron wondered what he'd just agreed to.

"Badune," Harab'kun called, turning the big man around. "Meet us at the old temple to the Lesser Kindred. We won't want anyone to hear the screaming." Jakab'een raised an eyebrow but said nothing, apparently resigning himself to witness whatever torture the older man had planned.

Faron swallowed hard.

A Knife in the Back

Through the city, they pulled him—away from the reflective white and black columns, statues, and buildings and toward an ancient and collapsing place. Massive sandstone bricks crumbled one on top of another, and abandoned temples had fallen into disrepair. This portion of the metropolis was quiet, far removed from the bustle of markets and busy families. Faron glanced over his back warily. He knew places like this—places where thieves and murderers were more common than not—and the sun had finally set.

"Why are we here?" Faron asked, the darkness growing deeper every moment.

"For privacy," Harab'kun said, "for answers, and for obedience. You will tell us what reasons you had for coming to our desert, and then we will... convince you to abandon them. I think, for once, Jakab would agree with me." The younger Kaorn grunted in a way that told Faron of the wicked smile on his face. Cold plastered his insides.

"Before that, though, I want you to understand that I'm helping you. Do you know how very much harder it would be for you to survive as a lesser slave? If Jaru'tal rejects you, you will be worked nigh until your death in a mine or as a quarrier or puller of stone—or something worse if Jakab gets his way." Harab'kun turned to Jakab'een. "We tie the horses here."

They came upon a large crumbling building that appeared several thousand years old. The doorway was long gone, but the wall itself had since disintegrated, exposing dark, extensive hallways within. Harab'kun gestured them up, and they climbed.

"If this is done, you will not only languish under Akwin's eye; you will lose any chance you had at vengeance upon the Dunestrider."

Faron blinked. He hadn't told them that.

"That is why you are here, isn't it?" It was hardly a question.

Faron didn't answer.

"So, do you see how a little restraint could serve you? An easier life and close proximity to the man you hate. Above that, I will receive my payment and won't need to kill you."

"*Our* payment," Jakab'een corrected from behind. Faron shivered to think of him at his back, even if the only light came from his torch.

"Yes, of course, you know what I mean."

They approached a large, fallen column which they climbed to a higher level. Harab'kun paused to help Faron make the climb with bound feet. He seemed to know where he was going.

"Do you see how both of us can benefit? All I ask is that you do not kill the Dunestrider."

Beaten down, exhausted, bound, and walking like a sheep to the slaughter, Faron sensed a trap, but not in the broken temple. The trap was in Harab'kun's words.

"I never said I wanted to kill Jaru'tal," Faron hedged.

"You do, though." Even in the dark, Faron could sense

Harab'kun's veiled expression.

He didn't answer.

"It will be better for you if you give up your intention, son of oathbreakers. Tell me why you are here."

Faron kept his mouth shut.

They entered the exposed hallway, high above the ground and far from other people. Jakab climbed the last of the stone steps and leaned against an open archway, arms folded in a longsuffering manner. To one side ran a long hallway, black and lightless; to the other lay a massive opening into the night. It looked to have once been an elevated hallway itself before crumbling and falling a hundred feet to the ground below. The old man stopped them here.

"When it comes to coin, there is no place for question. You must know how serious I am about receiving payment from Jaru'tal. I will not allow you to keep me from it." He tossed the midsection of Faron's rope over a rusted iron sconce and pulled on the other end, hauling his arms into the air. The motion jerked Faron's back against the wall and took most of the weight off his feet. Harab'kun tied off the rope on another empty wall-sconce.

"Do you have your knife, Jakab'een?" he asked. "The sharp one?"

He nodded with a wide grin, then drew it. Faron's stomach dropped when he saw it glint in the moonlight.

Harab'kun interrupted his shallow breaths and panicked thoughts. "You will be docile, young Aldene, if I have to carve the heroism from you. I will have my coin from the Dunestrider, and I will have no interference from you." He brandished his own knife, smaller than Jakab'een's and with a wider curve. "Now, you will admit why you have come to

23

this desert." He pointed the knife at Faron. "You are here to kill Jaru'tal Dunestrider. Confess it."

When he didn't respond, Harab'kun nodded to Jakab'een who turned to face Faron, then punched him in the gut.

"Why are you here?"

No answer. Jakab'een backhanded him across the face. His already swollen lip broke open again.

"Why are you here?" Harab'kun asked again.

No answer, except for shallow breaths. Another bruise was added to his stomach, then face again. An involuntary tear slid down Faron's face. The beating continued. Jakab'een threw his head against the stone wall, drove a knee into his gut, choked him, and hurt him however he could until, finally, Harab'kun spoke again.

"That's enough," he said. "Our friend is nearly ready." He brought his knife to Faron's throat, seemed to think better of it, and lifted it above his head, singling out Faron's pinky finger against the stone. "Last chance. You will be honest, or you will lose a finger, one at a time until you confess."

Faron remembered issuing a similar threat to Garad and how it had not been taken seriously. He had cut off the man's hand. Faron trembled. He didn't even know why he held back so fervently. All he knew was that Harab'kun *wanted* him to break.

"So, one more time, young Aldene. Why are you here?"

Faron didn't care anymore. Shivering, he admitted, "I came to find Jaru'tal, question him… and kill him." He slumped in defeat. The years he'd spent in Dageran's service had equipped him to lie, steal, cheat, and hurt others, but he wasn't well prepared to withstand beatings and torture. Already, he had been abused half to death. He could withstand no more.

Harab'kun backed away. "Good," he said, breathing almost as hard as Faron. "Good. You can be honest. Now I can help you."

"I don't want your help," Faron cried. "I want you to let me go."

"I can't do that," Harab'kun said. "The only thing I can do for you is remove your thirst for violence. It'll be better for you—to be more docile. Aggressive slaves don't last very long, I'm afraid." He hesitated. "I am sorry for it, but I am going to have to remove your manhood."

Shock filled Faron's expression as he realized what Harab'kun meant. He had heard stories of tame half-men that walked the desert as servants or punished criminals, but he had never actually considered the possibility that it was real. It was a thing simply not done.

A wide line of a grin splayed across Jakab's face with dark satisfaction. Faron lowered his brow and frantically considered how to kill the men. With Badune still gone, he might have stood a chance if he could get his arms lowered and if he hadn't been repeatedly beaten and half-starved. He didn't have his knife, either. The only thing he could do was bring both feet up together and try to get in one solid kick.

Jakab'een slid his torch into the sconce above Faron's head.

Hefting the knife as if testing its balance, Harab'kun said, "Cut off his trousers."

Icy dread flooded Faron's gaze as Jakab stepped closer with a glimmer in his eye.

"This is for my brother," he said.

Faron tensed, breathing hard, and readied himself to kick with his whole body, his back against the wall. Jakab's glare became a sneer as he neared Faron. A heartbeat before he was within kicking distance, Harab blurred into motion. With a flash of steel, he struck like a coiled snake and sank the curved knife deep into Jakab'een's back. Metal parted flesh with a wet ripping noise.

Confusion and surprise overcame his cruel smile as Jakab'een coughed blood, splattering Faron's cheek. Stumbling, Jakab turned to face his betrayer, eyes growing with terror. He coughed another lungful of red blood, spilling it all down his front.

"Half?" Harab'kun spat in his surprised face.

With a strong twist to his shoulder, Harab'kun turned the dying man and wrenched the knife from his back. The deep wound erupted with blood.

Before Jakab'een could fall to his knees, Harab'kun kicked him and sent him tumbling through the open archway, hundreds of feet to the stones below. His body landed with a sickening crunch.

"Akwin favors the strong."

Faron's eyes flicked between the man and the empty archway, trying to process what had just happened. Instead, he managed only panicked, shallow breathing.

"I am sorry you had to see that," the old man crooned, wiping the blade on his trousers. "But his greed was insurmountable, and he was not trustworthy. I could not allow him to ruin this for me, and as a bonus, you now fathom how very serious I am about receiving that reward."

"You killed him," Faron stated simply.

"He has labored hard for it. Come, young Aldene. We climb higher."

Tentatively, Faron ventured, "Why?"

"We must wait for Badune."

Through long, dark hallways and up never-ending flights of steps, Harab'kun dragged Faron. Eventually, they came upon a staircase above the crumbling temple, exposing themselves to the cold night air and twinkling starlight. No railing or banister adorned the steps, except a small, nearly knee-high stone guiding. It looked to have all been carved from a single stone. At the top of the steps was a small square platform, no more than four feet across, and an old but tough-looking wooden chair—a thief's perch? A great swath of the city could be seen from this height, even in the dark.

By Harab's order, Faron sat. An additional length of thin rope was used to secure him to the legs and back of the chair, though not tight enough to cause discomfort. For nearly twenty minutes, he sat that way, staring at the stars and attempting patience. Each time he tried to speak, he was hushed and told to sit in silence. Hope and confusion flickered inside his breast, but all he could do was wait.

He allowed himself a small smile to think of Jakab'een dead with a knife wound in his back.

For the first quiet moment that day, Faron let his mind wander, if only slightly. Harab'kun had said Jaru'tal paid five times the going rate for some specific slaves. Faron made a confident guess what the requirement might be: his age. Between that and the fortune he offered, Faron was certain that Sadagon was involved—somehow. Who else would pay so much for young slaves if not Sadagon, ruler of a city dependent on young blood? Faron was on the right trail. He could feel it.

With deceptively quiet steps, Badune'ahl ascended the staircase and came into view.

"At last," Harab trumpeted. "What took you so long?" The

man flicked his gaze between Faron and the older Kaorn, an inordinately dense mass of iron chains and balls in his arms. Though he tried not to show it, he breathed heavily from the exhaustive climb.

"Where is Jakab?" he asked, motioning for Harab to take the heavy manacles. He made no move to receive them.

"On the adjacent tower," Harab lied, pointing into the dark night. "He holds a torch aloft for us. Do you see?"

The man squinted into the dark. "No."

"Then look where I am pointing," Harab chastised, gesturing emphatically. Extending his neck, the large man stepped to the edge of the high platform, toes brushing the knee-high remnants of the ancient railing.

With a wiry finesse, Harab placed a two-handed shove between the larger man's shoulder blades, tripping him on the curb. It might not have been enough by itself, but the heavy chains pulled him over the side, and with only a light grunt, he tumbled over the edge into the darkness.

Faron looked away as the man began to scream.

With a long sigh, Harab'kun slumped to the ground. "What a shame," he proclaimed. "I liked that man."

"Then why did you kill him?" Faron felt oddly sick. He, after all, would have done the same thing given half a chance.

"To demonstrate my resolve to you for one, because I owed him much coin for another, but mostly because Badune is a loyal man, regardless of his caste."

"Was," Faron corrected. "You killed him because you owed him money?"

"No," Harab'kun sighed. "No, I did not. I would have happily paid my debt to him, but Badune simply cannot be trusted with what we are going to do. He would have betrayed me without a shadow of a doubt."

Quietly contemplating, Faron asked, "And what are we going to do? There were four of you before, and now it's just you. If you think you can still sell me like property, you're wrong."

"I'm not going to make you a slave, son of oathbreakers," Harab'kun said. "Because you are going to do that yourself."

Faron didn't dignify that with a response.

"The reward for a slave of your age and lineage is somewhere between four and six thousand foals." In response to Faron's bewildered look, he replied, "It is a silver coin, not a young horse."

"Why would I care," Faron asked, "how much you're likely to make from selling me?"

"Because it is no small amount, but I think it is not nearly enough, don't you?"

"Get to the point."

"I have, in my possession, a body that is worth a few thousand foals to some, but do you know who is worth ten thousand times that? A hundred thousand times?"

"You want me to kill Jaru'tal so you can rob him," Faron said.

"Believe it or not, I am not a slaver by trade. In fact, I don't have any form of trade at all. Finding you was simply happy chance."

"Not for Haka'een," Faron cut in. "Or Jakab, or Badune."

Harab'kun laughed. "Indeed, no, but I am not unaccustomed to one man's misfortune being another's good fortune."

"You're a thief," Faron said.

"An old thief," he admitted. "One who's growing tired."

"So, what do you want from me?" Faron asked.

"You want Jaru'tal dead, and I want coin. If, by unfortunate fate, the Dunestrider were to purchase the wrong slave and if he were to come to an untimely end, there would perhaps be an opportunity for a man like me to liberate a few things from his home and place of business."

"So, you'll help me kill Jaru'tal?" Faron asked.

"I do not help anybody with anything. What I am proposing is a trade."

Faron's brow furrowed deeper. "How so?"

"You are obviously a dangerous foe," Harab explained. "And the Dunestrider does not purchase violent slaves, so I propose this: Allow the Dunestrider to believe you are tame until I have received my payment. This will position you close to him. In return, I will give you an advantage over Jaru'tal."

"What kind of advantage?"

"The kind that involves a key and violent bowel movements. Perhaps a weapon."

"How do I know you'll deliver what you promise?" Faron said suddenly. "For all I know, once you're paid, you'll slip out of the city without me."

"I could do that, but if you can't trust me, perhaps you can trust my greed. You're not the only one who stands to gain from a fallen 'Tal."

Faron nodded. There was infinitely more money to be had in robbing Jaru'tal than from selling one slave. It was the kind of point Synick would make.

"I did," Harab'kun continued, "dispose of two of my friends for you already. If you do not believe I am resolved to work together to make a giant bleed, then you will never be."

Faron grimaced, eyeing the older man up and down. It turned his stomach to even think of allying with the would-be-slaver, but he didn't see that he had any other options. The fact of it was that Harab'kun was right. They both stood to gain by standing together. That didn't make it any easier.

"Do you see, young Aldene, how our interests are aligned?"

"You want to use me," Faron said, "to kill someone you wouldn't dare, so you can rob them."

"Someone you already want dead," Harab'kun argued. "But yes, I am using you. Does that mean we can't both help each other get what we want?"

Finally, Faron nodded. "No."

The wiry, muscled man dropped his thoughtful expression and adopted a smile. "Then we are no longer enemies, but allies!" He leaned Faron's way and, with quick dexterity, sliced the bonds that dug into his skin.

With great relief, Faron stretched his arms. It nearly brought him to tears. Harab'kun, now the image of joy, pulled him into a one-armed embrace, though Faron noticed he gripped his knife with care.

"And it is the most unlikely of allies who are favored by Akwin Ashamat, is it not? Come," he continued exuberantly. "There are none here to deceive."

Shocked at how quickly and unexpectedly his fortune had turned, the two of them looked out over the city as they began laying plans.

Karan'dal

A few days later, when the most obvious of Faron's bruises and cuts had been given time to heal, they were back on the city streets, surrounded by Kaorn who wanted to kill him. Faron ignored their whispers and stares, and all told, it wasn't too difficult. The ropes were on his wrists again, and despite the time they'd been given and the looseness of the knot, they still ached at the contact. The scarring would probably mar his arms forever, like the brand below his collarbone and the flame-scars on his chest, shoulders, and palms. Harab was surprised when he saw them, but Faron declined to discuss them.

Harab'kun led the way through the winding streets, keeping people at bay with his eyes like a hawk with a kill. They passed through destitute districts, where the buildings crumbled around them, to wealthy places, where even the stairs were coated in thick slabs of white paint. Harab took them through grand bazaars, markets, and a hundred staircases, climbing ever higher into more and more prosperous sections of the city until the foremost mountain-cliff came into view, a grand yellow sandstone palace at its heart.

Large circular towers melded directly into the vertical wall of the incalculably huge mountain as if it had been carved centuries before, and sunlight glittered powerfully off the circular bronze rooftops. The size of the palace was mind-boggling, though entirely dwarfed by the mountain behind it. It was undoubtedly, Faron thought, the tallest mountain in the world.

At the end of the last staircase, a pair of scarlet-clad guards eyed them suspiciously, but Harab'kun didn't even make eye contact. They looked for a moment as if they would block the path, but between Harab's confidence and the Aldene slave in tow, they were allowed to pass unchallenged. If there was any nervousness in the old man's demeanor Faron could not read it.

A grand courtyard filled with glittering water and gold splayed out before the palace, colorful tents filling the spaces between long lines of black columns on either side. It was a market, Faron realized, reserved for a higher social caste than the markets he had passed below. The men and women here wore bright and colorful silks and far more gold than silver, with true gemstones in place of glass. The palace courtyard displayed wealth like nothing he had ever seen. It would have been enough to make Synick's eye twitch and fingers itch for years after.

Flaxen rope tied to his wrists, Faron was pulled to a purple tent on the west columns. Harab'kun rapped his knuckle on a post between the two flaps, and after a moment, a man appeared from inside. He was short with a bald head that reflected the sun and garbed in red silk that glistened like morning dew. Large golden hoops fell from his ears, and the smell of powerful perfumes wafted from the interior. He eyed the two of them critically.

"I do not deal with your caste here: a 'Kun or a 'Kan.

Regardless, leave before I call the guard."

"Fortunately for you," Harab cut in. "I'm here to offer a gift to the Dunestrider, and you need not deal with me."

"I could have you hanging in a gibbet," the man said. "And it's where you would belong."

"It's a good gift," Harab went on after a slight pause.

Casting his eyes around, the bald man sighed. "Very well, bring him in."

The inside of the tent was an even deeper purple than the outside, with all edges trimmed in gold. Large chests and cabinetry were pushed up against the outer edges, with stacks of fat pillows in seemingly random locations. Large fur rugs covered the stone floor wherever possible.

"What may I call you, coin keeper?" Harab'kun asked.

"I am Karan'dal," he answered in an offhanded way. "Now, come to me, Aldene," he demanded. His voice was higher than Faron would have expected, but his force of expectation was not at all lessened by it. With strong fingers, he pinched Faron's cheeks, forcing open his jaw. He peered inside like he would to determine a horse's age. "Hm," he grunted to himself. Surprised, Faron tried to pull back, but the man tightened his grip, hurting Faron's cheeks even more.

"Uh, uh, uh," he tsked as Harab yanked on Faron's cord and tugged him to the ground. The appraiser took it in stride, though, and bent, pinching Faron's hamstrings. The numerous bruises had gotten better over the past few days, but they still lanced with pain when prodded.

Faron let out an involuntary grunt.

"You've been beating him," Karan'dal said.

"Yes," Harab'kun admitted, somewhat slowly. "It was necessary when I found him, but he has offered no resistance since."

"You would lie to me, caste of 'Kan? To a 'Dal, servant of house 'Tal?"

"Your guess was right the first time, servant of 'Tal. I am Harab'kun, and there is no lie. I beat the boy when I found him in the sand but not since."

Faron tried to look diminutive if that were possible. After a few more pokes and prods, the bald man spoke again. "Why did you think the Dunestrider would buy this boy?" His voice was full to the brim with arrogance.

"He is the proper age," Harab answered honestly. "Even I have heard the tales of how the great Jaru'tal pays handsome rewards for Aldene children under the age of eighteen."

"Do you know why the Dunestrider only deals with those under a certain age?" Karan'dal asked.

"It is not my place to ask," Harab said obsequiously.

"Because the young are largely more meek and willing to obey. In truth, any Aldene around twenty would suit if they weren't all so aggressive."

"As you can see," Harab began. "He is well mannered enough for you." Karan'dal cut him off with a sharp tongue.

"So, you understand then? If I make this bargain on behalf of the Dunestrider, Akwin give him glory, and your goods prove to be unruly and troublesome, your bargain will be worthless to me."

"Wise keeper of coin," Harab'kun began with a servile bow. "I—"

"I cannot accept this one." He shook his bald head. "There is far too much fire in him. But the point is moot, anyway. Jaru'tal is not here."

Faron tried to hide his worry, but Harab spoke up on his

behalf.

"I can make all the promises in the world to you of this one and his supposed fire, but none of it will matter if the Dunestrider is not here to buy. Where is he?"

"Away," Karan'dal said with deliberate obfuscation. "On urgent business."

"When will he return?" Harab'kun asked with a furrowed brow.

"A month's time," he answered. "But that does not matter to you because this one lacks the right temperament. You've wasted my time," he declared. "Now, get out of my tent, and consider yourself lucky I don't call for the guard."

"There is still my gift to consider," Harab offered. "And a new gift besides."

Jaru'tal's servant considered for a quiet moment before conceding. "You have half a minute," he said.

"First, I will take an entire third of the purse and return it to you, as a gift."

"You're offering me a lower price?" Karan'dal said with a level gaze. "On stock I refused to buy?"

"If you see it that way. That, and a month of hard labor."

That piqued his interest. He arched one bald eyebrow and asked, "Whatever do you mean?"

"You say Jaru'tal will not arrive for a full month. I sense an opportunity."

Faron felt worry creeping into his chest. Where was Harab going with this? They hadn't planned on this.

Harab went on. "Could you not, in this time, loan him to the mines or quarries and earn some small value? And if that revenue found its way into your palm... the Dunestrider need not know." Harab took the fact that he wasn't being thrown from the tent as an indication to continue. "A little income for you and a chance to test the Aldene's fortitude and temperament. A month of hard labor would be plenty to determine if he is made of the proper stock." He turned his palms face up in a half pleading, half suggestive way. "If he is up to your standards and if, by the time the Dunestrider returns, you have a proven slave to present to him, would he not be well pleased?"

A long moment of silence extended in the opulent tent. Finally, the bald man said, "'Kun's and 'Kan's are thieves, one and all. I can offer you half the traditional rate, a sum of three thousand foals, if at the end of one month his temperament is proven." He cut off Harab's objection before it could be voiced. "Three thousand foals and not an eye more, to be paid in gold."

Faron's shoulders tensed. Could he afford to wait a whole month for Jaru'tal to return? He mentally counted the days before his and Hadria's nameday—a little over two months—and he still didn't know where she was. It was close, but what other choice did he have?

"It is agreed," Harab'kun declared, pushing the first two knuckles of a fist onto his forehead, crossed by a thumb. The man returned the gesture and offered a small engraved stone tablet to the aged man, which he called a chit.

Faron's mood was dark, but he did and said nothing. One month—one month to find the monster who could lead him to his sister and the man who had taken her. He could endure that.

Picking up Faron's rope, Jaru'tal's coin keeper said, "Come along now. I have just the place for you."

Tossing his chit in the air with one hand and catching it

with the other, Harab'kun said, "Farewell, son of oathbreakers. It was my great fortune to have found you."

A Fifth of Rose

Smoke and dust filled Faron's nostrils in equal measure. With laborious effort, he swung a pickaxe at the dark wall before him, where it bounced off stone and reverberated painfully in his hands. He swung again. Blisters had long since covered his palms and fingers, opening and reopening, but now he paid them no mind. The soft skin on his hands, callused only by the hilt of a knife and at the tip of the fingers, had been covered with a thick layer of calluses and dirt. His scars were harder to ignore, burning with each twist of palms upon the pickaxe.

Ruddy light cast from a pale torch illuminated the forms of two Kaorn boys beside him—Raor'taa and Nath'ahn. Thin and scrawny, the pair were bullied the most in the small band of slaves, and so they were given the worst position in the mine: at the tunnel's head, breaking the untouched stone. None were as low as Faron, though—an Aldene—who was positioned between the two at the forefront of the new tunnel.

Ore—that was what they sought. If they found it fast enough, they would avoid being whipped or branded or beaten—except Faron, of course. He was never touched. Being the prospective property of Jaru'tal, he was given special treatment—comparatively, of course. He wished he wasn't.

Other boys worked down the length of the narrow shaft in the earth, widening it, searching for the gray-orange that meant raw iron. Beside the torches, though, everything looked orange. Still, Faron's sharp eyes watched carefully as he broke apart the rock in front of him. He wondered if this was how many of the tunnels in the guild had been formed? He shook his head. Taskmasters or no, things were still not so bad as to daydream of his previous master.

Through the darkness behind him, Faron became aware of a team of five or six shadowy figures towing a barrow by harness. They shrugged off the leather straps and set about with shovels, flinging the loose dirt and rocks into the four-wheeled contraption. When it was filled, they turned about, donning harnesses, and tugged the barrow back toward the surface of the mine. There, it would be sifted for ore, gems, schists, and other valuable stones before being tossed onto the ever-growing pile of tailings. Even that job was denied Faron and the two slaves beside him—since you could walk back with an empty cart.

Sweat stung his eyes and slicked his skin, though his throat was dry and parched. He could only imagine how the others must feel. He was given water twice as often as they. He would be expected to be in good health when the Dunestrider came for him. This only made the other slaves hate him more. Once, a handful of older boys had cornered him, wielding stones, branches, and fists, but they had all been beaten with iron clubs by a watching guard before they could land a blow. If they disliked him before, they hated him after that.

If that wasn't enough reason to hate him, he was fed better food too, and more of it. Harab likely had a hand in that. While others became thin, he grew lean, forming muscles he'd lacked previously. He'd tried sharing his bread with Nath'ahn before, weeks ago, but it had only gotten the boy beaten and robbed by the older, stronger boys.

Watching the others eye him as he ate his fill might have been the hardest part for Faron—that and seeing the guards whip and beat them and not being able to interfere. Despite how they despised him, Faron couldn't bring himself to hate them back. He looked in their hopeless eyes and only saw himself. These boys were even less free than Faron had been during his slavery. He couldn't fault them for how they viewed him. The hatred he did feel, though, was for the taskmasters, the slave owners, and the slave guards. His blood boiled with seething anger each time he witnessed a slave beaten for raising his eyes or collapsing from hunger, and it took everything in him not to murder the slavers. He could have killed them—with a cord, a rock, or even his fingers—but not more than one or two, and not without losing his chance at Jaru'tal. He breathed deep, releasing the crushing pressure from his jaw.

Jaru'tal—he had to remember why he was here. It wouldn't do to lose Hadria's trail to save one or two slaves from a beating. That truth tore at him, but it stood.

To his right, the crack of a whip splitting the air lashed across his ears, and he winced as he heard the resulting grunt it elicited. The short, bearded man who wielded it barked something at a boy who widened the tunnel Faron made, and Faron had to stop himself from glaring at the man with contempt. He wanted to kill him, but no, not now—not after all the work and all the waiting he'd done. Today would be the end of it. Jaru'tal would send for him, and he'd leave these tunnels forever.

Even that provoked a spark of guilt in Faron. He wanted to save these slaves, not escape them. Could he bring them with him? He didn't see how, but he promised that one day, somehow, he'd come back for them and assassinate the men who lorded over them. Faron allowed himself a small grin. He could bear the weight of their deaths. After everything he'd seen these men do to the young boys around him, their souls would be a pleasure to carry.

Soon the horn was sounded, and the digging crew shrugged off harnesses, rubbed blisters, and deposited their tools in neat racks along the walls. As the team of sweaty slaves ascended from their tunnel, they rose into the early morning light. Already the earth had begun to bake. They were given water freely then and scraps of food too, though mostly just bread and dates—as Faron had learned they were called.

Today was the thirtieth day since he'd been sold off to Karan'dal. Today he would meet Jaru'tal, the man who would lead him to Hadria. Anticipation filled him from head to toe, making him feel both alive with alacrity and sick to his stomach. He rubbed the fading tan line on his finger, where Hadria's ring used to be. There was barely more than a month left until her nameday—barely more than a month before Sadagon consumed her to fuel his twisted immortality. Wherever this trail was going, he had to get to the end of it—fast.

The line of slaves made their way to their yellow stone barracks, under the watchful eye of the tall, whip-wielding Kaorn. Once inside, they were more or less left alone, except for a guard to keep fights from going so far as to keep them from work. They were valuable property after all. This man was the opposite of the one in the mines—tall, thin, bare-chested, and without a scrap of hair to be seen. Despite his familiarity with the slaves and the slim chances of a fight breaking out so quickly after exhaustive labor, he glared at them all witheringly.

Faron lay down on his too-small cot amidst the mass of tired young boys. It smelled of blood and sweat, and the thin straw mattress poked him through the threadbare cloth, but he was too tired to care. The majority of the others did the same. They would sleep and be roused in six hours for another shift.

Through the familiar lumps and scratchy stalks of his sweat-stained cot, Faron felt a slightly irregular form pressing into his back. Making sure no one was watching, he slowly reached underneath the piled mass of hay and felt something hard and small. It was metal. Carefully, he extracted a small brass key and slipped it into his pocket. He smiled to himself. Harab'kun had come through. For a few minutes, he breathed deeply, trying to master his pounding heart. Before he could take ten breaths, a key rattled in the lock, and the door swung open. What little sound there was faded away.

Keeper Karan'dal walked through the short door, stooping to enter and wrinkling his nose in his fine red silks. He scanned the dimly lit room quickly, as if eager to be gone, and pointed at Faron when his eyes found him.

"You. Aldene. Come with me."

All eyes turned toward Faron, some inquisitive, others angry. He ignored them all. Heart racing, Faron stood and crossed the room. He gathered no possessions and wasted no time. He had neither. The opulently dressed man gripped him by the arm with predatorial force and slapped a pair of iron manacles around his wrists. Faron was so infuriatingly familiar with the devices that he had calluses where they rubbed against his skin. When he was properly secured, the silk-garbed man seized him with strong, thin fingers and pushed him through the doorway. Once on the other side, the beak-nosed man looked him up and down a few times.

"You look better for the wear since the last time I saw you," he noted, almost as if to himself. He pinched a sore bicep, but Faron allowed it. "Perhaps some time under Akwin's eye has taught you some humility?" Faron did not respond. "Or perhaps not. It is no longer for me to judge. You are to be inspected by the Dunestrider himself."

Again, Faron said nothing, though he bubbled with anticipation. After a quick once over like an inspection on a loaned packhorse, Faron was dragged to the building just across the sandy street, where they were met by a fat, greasy-looking man. Faron knew, just from the look of him, that he'd never swung a pickaxe before in his life.

"Barnu'kar," the keeper addressed. "Akwin's eye has shifted, and our pact fulfilled. I've come to settle your debt." He held out a pompous smooth hand.

"For the boy?" he questioned. Faron could not yet determine a man's caste from his accent, but this man was certainly among the lowest there was.

"Yes, for the boy," Karan'dal spat. "For one month's service."

"Very well," the pudgy man acquiesced, gathering a small number of coins in a palm.

The way Karan'dal appeared while receiving them was similar to how another man might look while reaching into a barrel of fish guts. Faron suppressed the desire to strangle him.

Before long, the two of them had left the unpainted and unrepaired slums and entered the magnificent opulence of a wealthier district. As before, the grandeur of it all staggered him. Gold, silver, and pearl had been worked intricately into massive pillars that supported unfathomably heavy stone roofs. Each one had the magnificence of a temple, but the temples were grander still.

At the entrance to a small building attached to a far more lavish one at the side, Karan'dal pulled open the door to let them in, but before he could usher Faron forward, a man with a tall hood stumbled out and nearly fell on the keeper.

"Akwin damn you, filthy cur!" Karan'dal yelled as the man supported himself on the keeper's arms.

"Apologies," the stranger said with a deep bow, never lifting his face. "A thousand apologies."

Karan'dal sniffed loudly and waved a disdainful hand in dismissal, but he was already gone. With frayed patience, the keeper shoved Faron through the door where the smell of steam and fragrant soaps wafted over them. It was powerful and foreign after so long without a bath.

"In," the keeper urged. "I won't present you to such as the Dunestrider smelling like an entire pack of camels."

Another windowless room. It took a long moment for his eyes to adjust to the dark, but when they did, he noticed a low-burning fire on the far side, tended by tall, dark girls in white work shifts. Closer was a deep depression in the stone floor, filled near to the brim with steaming water.

Kneeling by the fire, one girl with short woven hair pulled large iron balls from the embers with long tongs, loading them into a green basket. Another dropped them into the pool. A man, waist-deep in the water, unloaded the heavy, cooled balls to the side, where they were collected and heated again. It was an impressive system, and Faron took it in over several moments.

Karan'dal tossed a coin to a man who sat cross-legged in the corner, long braided hair piling in his lap, somehow managing to make even that simple gesture appear arrogant.

"Scrub him down with a fifth of rose," he ordered. "He must be made presentable."

The man in the corner stood, pocketing the small coin. "He is covered in filth, keeper. I will have to change the water after him alone."

With a harangued look, Karan'dal threw another coin on the ground and fixed his gaze on the ceiling. The sitting man nodded.

"Disrobe," Karan'dal ordered, looking at Faron.

Suddenly flustered, Faron realized he intended for him to disrobe here, without even a screen of mist for privacy. He cast his gaze about and noticed the two girls had waded into the steaming water, clutching baskets of towels, scrubs, and soaps. They eyed their feet in a way that suggested it was more out of exhaustion than respect for his privacy. Faron dismissed his foolish embarrassment. He didn't have time for it.

They were slaves too, he realized, and they were waiting to serve him. Faron glared at the man who must own them and felt his nails nearly pierce the skin of his palms. Even these young girls weren't spared from a slaver's greed.

"Disrobe," Karan'dal commanded again.

Don't snap now, Faron told himself. *There's nothing you can do for them.* He grit his teeth and swore he'd come back for them—somehow.

Finally, he undressed, careful to remove the key from its small pocket and hide it in his palm. He couldn't risk the keeper going through his pockets and finding it. His manacles were removed to allow his arms out of his stained, ragged shirt. Clenching both fists, he waded into the pool. It was hot, but not like the stifling heat of the mine tunnels or sweltering sun. It was a heat that worked knots from his hard muscles and seemed to lend him strength. Standing on either side of him, the two slave girls each took an arm in sodden, wrinkled hands, and washed away the filth that had accumulated from a month of hard labor.

Water came away black where it touched him, webbing throughout the pool and revealing pale skin underneath. His sunburns had long since peeled away, replaced by soft pink skin, which soon after turned pale in the darkness of the tunnels. Whatever was left of his tan—accumulated from long days of travel through forests, plains, and desert—was now gone. So tired were the slave girls that they didn't even seem to notice his pale skin, something everyone who passed by remarked at either with their eyes or with stones.

Soon he was clean, and Karan'dal procured a new set of clothes—long gray and white wrapping cloths in the style of the desert people. Grateful for his foresight with the key, he tucked it in a fold in the cloth, a makeshift pocket, and allowed himself to be ushered outside. His heart skipped a beat as they went up the grand staircase that led to Jaru'tal's purple and gold tent.

He had a plan.

A Message

L ike a goat on a lead, Faron was tugged to the entrance of the tent. If Karan'dal's grip had been tight before, it was fierce now. With a twist, he brought Faron about, facing his sour expression.

"You will bow under Akwin's gaze before one as great as the Dunestrider." Faron didn't respond. "You will prostrate yourself on the ground of this temple. You will speak only to answer. You will maintain your gaze upon the ground. Do this not, and you shall return to the mines." Again, Faron did nothing by way of response. "Do I make myself understood?" Finally, Faron nodded.

With an impetuous nod in return, Karan'dal stepped aside and opened the tent flap. A tall man in deep purple silk with gold trimmings faced the opposite wall, hands clasped behind his back. A long, silvery sword of the finest steel hung from one hip, naked and exposed without a scabbard. A belt of three daggers hung from one shoulder and across his waist, each sheath encrusted with jewels and gold.

Jaru'tal.

"By the grace of Akwin Ashamat, defender of the strong, giver of foals, I present a nameless one for the pleasure and consideration of the great Jaru'tal Dunestrider, bringer of wealth, trader of souls. May he find pleasure in this offering."

After the flowery introduction, Keeper Karan'dal prostrated himself upon the shaded marble inside the tent, forehead and nose pressed to the earth in Jaru'tal's direction. Faron did not fall upon the floor, staring a challenge into the back of the slaver's head. Finally, the tall man turned, and Faron saw his face.

Fire—fire and dark shadows erupted in his mind. Fury filled him as he saw the man who'd certainly had a hand in his sister's disappearance. Anger boiled and bubbled within him as the flames of his mind's eye licked higher and higher. The convoluted scars on his chest and shoulders pained as if being branded once again.

Jaw clenched and cold green eyes intense, Faron met the slaver stare for stare. The dark man had a long, thin nose and impressive jaw. He might have been handsome, but Faron took no notice. He only resisted the temptation to bludgeon this man with his shackles.

Jaru'tal raised a thin eyebrow, almost curious. "Kneel," he commanded.

Faron did not kneel. He had one chance to play his hand, and his heart pounded with anticipation. If he were wrong, he would soon find himself a slave once again. He took a moment to breathe. Keeper Karan'dal took notice of Faron's disrespect and stood like a coiled viper. With long fingers, he grasped the back of Faron's neck and pushed, forcing him into a bow.

It was now or never. Faron threw an elbow into the man's gut, and the wind rushed out of him. Murder filled Karan'dal's eyes as he coughed and lunged for Faron again. The man clearly wasn't accustomed to his victims fighting back.

Never breaking eye contact with Jaru'tal, Faron said in a clear voice, "I have a message from Sadagon."

Jaru'tal's expression didn't change, and for a moment, Faron felt a cold stone in his gut; but, then he saw Karan'dal's face contort from fury to wide-eyed shock, and it gave him the lie.

"How dare you utter that name!" Karan'dal burst, stretching his hands toward Faron again, but Jaru'tal was faster. He struck out with the back of his hand, and Faron flinched; but, it wasn't meant for him. With a powerful strike, he slapped Karan'dal across the face, leaving a raised mark on his skin. He fell to the floor and made only the slightest whimper.

In the blink of an eye, the fire was gone, the dark spot fading away, restoring his full vision. He was right! Jaru'tal *knew* that name. Conjecture and hope had led him here, but *he was right.* It was a struggle not to laugh and let the smile spread across his face.

"I must apologize for my keeper of coin," Jaru'tal intoned in a deep, strong voice. He was younger than Faron expected—in his early thirties at most. "He can be without thought when his passions rise." Karan'dal rose to his knees and fell on his face repeatedly, bowing and begging pathetically.

"What is a messenger from the north doing in my city with shackles around his wrists?" Faron's heart nearly stopped beating—*the north.* That's what he needed to know. How far north? Where? Was Vam Aranath in Anveil? A hundred questions flooded in all at once. He needed more answers.

Jaru'tal seemed to catch himself. "No, don't speak of it," he said. "Not here. There are ears here. Come with me to my home. There is a place we may speak in the utmost secrecy."

"Good," Faron said, trying not to let his relief show. That was exactly what he had hoped for. With the deft fingers of a practiced thief, Faron reached into his makeshift pocket and procured the key to his manacles. Reversing his wrist, he quickly turned the lock, and the shackles fell away. Jaru'tal raised one black eyebrow in a way that was either surprised or impressed. When Karan'dal heard the shackles strike the polished marble floor, he jumped reflexively and continued bowing, although this time perhaps toward Faron as well.

"Come, Karan," Jaru'tal said. "Accompany us."

"No," Faron said, attempting to sound self-important. "I have waited a month under the guise of a slave to ensure this message is delivered safely, and if I trusted your pet, I would have left it with him the night we met. He stays here."

"You can trust my keeper," Jaru'tal insisted. "Though he may be slow of thought, he is my most trusted property and the only man living in Aru'barrahk who knows the name of the World Steward—that is, besides myself and you. He is trusted with the great secret of my wealth, and I trust him with whatever missive you may carry."

Faron continued the lie. "The message I carry is for you only, from the direct command of Sadagon. I would not disobey him in such a direct order, would you?"

That did it. Turning away from the bowing Karan'dal, he was all compliance. "It is not for me to dictate the whims of the World Steward."

World Steward—was that another of Sadagon's names?

"There is a place we may speak in confidence one with another. Come, and I shall take you there." He held the tent flap of the door open for Faron, ushering him out onto the grand temple amidst the massive black colonnade.

Ducking his head, Faron noticed a flash of snow-white fur in the corner of the tent, hanging out of a partially-closed chest—fur so white and pure he had only seen it's like once before, on the man who killed his father and stole his sister. Stooping away from the opening, Faron strode to the trunk, opening it to reveal a full white cape, except for two dark gray stripes that ran parallel down its center. It was identical to the one worn by Sadagon all those years ago, but beyond that, it was familiar. It reminded him of something, though he couldn't remember quite what. He held it in his hands and glanced wordlessly at the Dunestrider.

"Do you require my cloak, messenger? Has Lord Pyre not gifted you with one of your own?"

Searching for something to say, Faron replied, "I lost it, I'm afraid. Thank you, but no. I only recognized it is all." So caught up with recollection, Faron stared still, running the fur through his hands.

"Are they not all, more or less, similar to this?"

Realizing the scene he was making, Faron lied, "No. You do not know how much Sadagon honors you. Did you know that this was his very own cloak years ago?"

Jaru'tal's eyes brightened. "I, in fact, did not know this. I shall hold it in ever-higher esteem from this day, in honor of our friendship." He held the tent flap higher, Karan'dal still prostrated on the ground before him. "Shall we depart?" Dropping the heavy cloak, Faron turned and exited the tent. It was time to find out what Jaru'tal knew.

Across the city, he was led, until they finally approached a massive stone structure that looked more like a temple than anything else, except not decrepit and abandoned. Crowds whispered and parted for the slaver, some even going so far as to bow before him. Jaru'tal paid them no mind.

The door to his home, if it could be called that, was large

enough for four men to walk abreast. Two guards stood, holding naked spears by their sides, staring dutifully across the street. Their leather and cloth liveries were dyed a deep purple, including the veils that draped across their hidden faces.

"Welcome to my home," Jaru'tal said jovially, as an old slave opened the door from within. There were more guards inside. This was going to be difficult.

"I trust there is somewhere we may speak?"

"Indeed. In the rooms above there is such a place, but first, we must refresh." He slapped his hands together in one loud clap, and an older man in a white robe answered, stepping carefully from a hallway across the entry. He bowed his head without words. "Coffee, Mika'rul. My journey has been long and cold. Bring cream for my guest."

The man nodded by prostrating his head even lower and darted back into the hallway he'd come from. Jaru'tal motioned for Faron to follow, and they moved up a flight of stairs. Through a narrow, windowless hallway lit by red torches, they went, until they came to a heavy wooden door. Strips of iron ran across its length, staggered by thick metal bolts that bound the planks together. Pulling a large key from a pocket, Jaru'tal opened the lock.

"You may be at peace here. There are only two keys to this door—one is with me and the other with my keeper, who will not enter unless I command."

So Harab'kun had been right about that. Faron nodded, and Jaru'tal strode across the room, leaving the door open behind him. The chamber was large, with a single ironbound window draped in maroon cloth. A tan wooden table sat in the middle of the space, two chairs placed across opposite ends. Jaru'tal let himself in the far chair, sitting with an easy demeanor. A young boy with deep skin and shoeless feet entered, balancing a silver tray in his arms. He placed the platter on the table and poured two cups of a steaming black liquid. Jaru'tal frowned at him.

"Boy, where is my manservant, Rhana'ahl, and why does he have you carrying his tasks? I will have him buried if he thinks he can shirk his duties when I'm away."

In a soft voice, the boy said, "Missing, Dunestrider. He wasn't in his bed this morning."

Jaru'tal shooed the boy away with an arrogant hand. "I will serve us, boy. Leave." When the door closed, Jaru'tal said, "Perhaps my manservant has been buried already, but I jest, of course. He can be replaced and this moment cannot be. Have you ever had coffee, young Aldene?" Faron shook his head in the negative. Its smell was pungent and earthy.

"You've traveled far and labored long to speak with me. Come, drink and be revitalized." He poured cream from a small saucer, turning the black liquid a deep brown. "Many of those who have never had coffee find it too strong for their liking and weaken it with cream. Perhaps you will find it refreshing." He offered the pewter cup.

Faron eyed it dubiously, attempting to appear casual. Could he refuse without causing suspicion? He accepted the cup. Under Jaru'tal's watchful eye, he pulled a small fraction into his mouth, careful not to swallow, then coughed the liquid onto the floor. The taste was far stronger than the smell, and not nearly as pleasant. He coughed and grunted, not needing to embellish the act. Still, he was careful to get it all out of his mouth

Jaru'tal laughed. "You Aldene are always so weak on the

tongue. If you can acquire the taste, it will be good for you. Coffee strengthens the body." He took a long pull on his own before grimacing slightly. "Though, I see Akwin does not favor your timing. My manservant's replacement does no justice for the drink. It is easily turned bitter. Perhaps he will have to be replaced as well." He took another sip before shaking his head with a frown and placing the cup back on the tray.

"But enough of that. Tell me, dear friend, what is this message you carry?"

Faron's mind whirled through his options. He had been given a lot of time to think during the past month, and he'd settled on a safe enough lie; but now, other options tempted him.

Going against his previous decision, Faron said, "Two things: The first is that he's looking for someone—a girl of seventeen, with blonde hair and blue eyes, by the name of Hadria. Do you know her?"

"I know several people who would fit that description but none by that name, I'm afraid." Jaru'tal's eyes were beginning to fill with suspicion. Perhaps he was overcoming the surprise of having Sadagon's name thrown in his face. "Have we met before, young messenger?" Jaru'tal asked.

"No," Faron answered, recovering from having his hopes dashed. It was time to get the conversation back on track as he'd planned. There wasn't enough time for deviations. "The second item is a summons. Sadagon requests a meeting with you. As it happens, I need to return to him as well." Now came the important part. "If you will permit it, I would hope to travel with you."

Jaru'tal smiled a wide, knowing smirk. "Of course! Allow

me to take you to the most guarded secret of my house, without any proof of who you say you are." To Faron's surprise, the Dunestrider slid one of the curved knives from his knife belt, and his smile faded away. "I think not," he said. "You see, I was right before. I do know your face. I know that I've seen it before. I just don't know where."

Faron slinked back into his seat, his false smile slipping.

"I also am very curious why the World Steward would send a messenger who isn't one of his archons and why that messenger would summon me when Vam Sadagon could have done it himself in person while I was a guest in his home not even a month ago."

Faron's stomach dropped.

The slaver pointed with the beautiful blade. "Now, you will tell me how you came to know the name of Sadagon and which of my enemies you are working for."

Faron frowned, still seeking a way to turn the situation around.

"Tell me," Jaru'tal prodded, "before I invite my guards to find answers through other, messier means. I promise you, they will not be so kind."

Faron swallowed hard.

False Alarm

Harab tugged the white kitchen robes off his back and tossed them aside. What kind of maniac insisted that his kitchen help wear white? A large brown coffee-stain adorned the front, proof that he was better at infiltrating than brewing and serving. He traded the clothes for the deep purple cloth and leather that lay piled neatly before him until he was a completely different person. He twisted his right arm back and forth, trying to get the cloth to fit the right way. Why was this material so blasted stubborn? He pulled at the wrist, and it finally smoothed out. He sighed with satisfaction. He was becoming particular in his old age—well, *near* old age. He still wasn't so old he couldn't take part in a robbery or two. Some people might argue with that, but not the man who lay unconscious at his feet, tied up and naked.

He'd been guarding the outside door to the kitchens all by himself—the amateur—not once suspecting that an attack might come from the door he guarded and not the courtyard beyond. Slamming him with the door and cracking him over the head with a club had been laughably easy as well as satisfying. He would recover—probably. The man was from a higher caste than Harab, though, so he didn't much care one way or the other.

Harab donned the leather cap, completing his stolen dis-guise of purple guards' armor. Everything was purple—from the cheaply stained cloth that must have bled like a pig when washed, to the cracking leather breastplate. The Dunestrider couldn't help but flaunt his elevated birth, could he? In part, this was why he had made a deal with the Aldene boy to begin with. To get rich was the main goal, but reminding the high born that they, too, could bleed was always a worthy endeavor.

Neatly dressed now, Harab dragged the hamstrung guard to the wide cellar doors and tossed him inside. Maybe he'd keep the manservant company. They'd be found in there, sooner or later, but Harab didn't need long, and if the pattern he'd witnessed over the past weeks held, he had until nightfall.

Dusting off his hands, he walked away from the courtyard and fiddled with something in his pocket. It was warm from his palms and heavy, too. Rounding the corner, he raised his veil. How incredibly convenient that these imbecile guards chose to wear them—for intimidation purposes, most likely—but it made infiltrating a breeze.

Paying no attention to the guards, he rose to the next level, slowly up the staircase, and through an ugly, narrow hallway—making a point to hit his borrowed spear on each step as he had seen other guards do—until he came to a heavy door. He could faintly hear someone talking inside, though not enough to understand what was being said. With a soft whistle, he pulled the item from his pocket—a large iron key, previously in the possession of an irritatingly arrogant keeper, Karan'dal. With a casual turn of the wrist, he inserted the key and locked the door. It made a nice, satisfying click.

He also dropped a small brown bag and scooted it under

the gap in the door with his foot. It didn't really fit, so he pushed a few more times until it got far enough through that he was satisfied. He smiled to himself.

Now for the fun part, he thought. Turning and running down the stairs, he hollered at the top of his lungs, "Alarm! Alarm!" and sprinted out the front door. Like a mother duck with her ducklings, the inexperienced group of guards roused themselves and chased after him, spears raised and ready. Out the door and down the street, he led them, turning at random. They'd likely run with him toward nothing for miles before they realized he wasn't going anywhere, wasn't a part of their group, and was just leading them on a merry chase to distract them.

"Alarm!" he continued to yell as the disgruntled guards chased after him for who knows how long. Eventually, they'd catch on and he'd have to lose them, but until then, he'd see how far they'd go before realizing they'd been duped. Harab smiled to himself—*highborn idiots*.

Bloodlet

Faron heard a small click in the door behind him and a soft scuffing sound. He turned to see a small brown piece of cloth being awkwardly toed underneath the narrow slot at the bottom of the door. Jaru'tal noticed it too and rose to his feet, putting the knife on the table.

"What in Akwin's nine glories?" he began but was cut off by the sudden cry of alarm from beyond the door. If he wasn't distracted before, he was now, and that was enough for Faron. Harab had come through.

"I will deal with you—" He clenched at his stomach, a look of confusion crossing his face. Confusion turned to pain, and without warning, he doubled over and heaved the contents of his stomach onto the table.

Finally.

Standing so quickly that he toppled his chair, Faron kicked at the heavy table. The lip of it drove deep into Jaru'tal's gut and knocked him back into his seat. With muscles newly formed between a pickaxe and stone, Faron threw his weight behind the table, lifting and shoving all at once. The dagger clattered to the ground. A small ruby popped out of its setting and bounced off the hard sandstone floor.

Arms splayed out before him clawing for something to hold,

Jaru'tal tipped over as the table legs groaned their protest and shattered. The edge came down hard on Jaru'tal's chest, and Faron heard ribs crack. The Dunestrider cried out in pain for his guards but scarcely made more than a whisper, no breath in his lungs left to expel.

Flipping it the rest of the way, Faron sent the table crashing a hair short of Jaru'tal's head. The platter and cups clanged as they were tossed across the floor, the steaming, poisoned liquid splashing everywhere. Before Jaru'tal could move the arms that shielded his head, Faron tore a second gem-encrusted dagger from the belt at the slaver's chest. Wasting no advantage, he plunged the knife into a shoulder. Jaru'tal found breath to scream then. Lifting it again, he struck, but this time Jaru'tal caught the blade with both hands, his left arm shaking violently.

With a snarl, Faron forced the blade down, using a knee to pin the wounded arm, but he was still outmatched. Jaru'tal was far stronger than he. Changing tactics before the slaver realized he had the advantage, Faron swung the knife around and tried to stab it into his opponent's side. It barely grazed him.

"Guards!" Jaru'tal cried. "Guards!" None came. Harab had led them away.

"No one will come to save you, slaver," Faron spat, still grappling with the knife. "You're already dead." Jaru'tal wrested the knife away, but Faron let it go and landed a quick punch on the man's throat. He stood and backed away. Breathing or not, Jaru'tal had the knife now. Scrambling away from the blade's arc, Faron tore the splintered table leg from its base. He hefted it with uncertainty. It was heavy, with a wider reach than he was accustomed to. Faron had trained long hours with a dagger and crossbow, but not with clubs or staves.

Panting hard, Jaru'tal swung to his feet with a grimace—knife brandished in one hand, stomach held in the other.

"You are every bit as caged as I, little assassin." He swung the blade with a long arm, closing the gap between them in an instant. Faron danced out of the way but not far enough to avoid the tight fist that came after. The skin on his hands might have been soft, but Jaru'tal's bones were hard, and for a moment, Faron saw nothing but black.

Staggering away and blinking, Faron fended off a downward slash with his table leg but took a boot to the abdomen. Sensitive muscles tensed as pain coursed through him, and Faron backed the rest of the distance to the door. When his vision refocused, Jaru'tal was on him. Blood dripped from a gaping hole in his shoulder, and he stooped in obvious pain, but still, he came with fire in his eyes.

Reaching out with the wounded arm, Jaru'tal seized the far end of Faron's makeshift weapon. The knife came soon after. Faron leaped back the small length left to him as the knife whistled past, just where his stomach had been, but he didn't let go of the club. Awkwardly, they wrestled with the carved length of wood, Jaru'tal trying to work the knife between them and Faron twisting the club to ward it off.

Jaru'tal snarled and slashed at Faron's fingers, forcing him to let go. Lithe as a leopard, the slaver reached up with both hands and shoved with his superior weight, forcing Faron against the door. Air rushed from his lungs, leaving them constricted and empty. His vision dimmed. Stars swimming before his eyes, Faron felt the hairs move in his ear as Jaru'tal whispered, "I could sell you—for more gold than you would ever guess—but this time, I will take more pleasure in slitting your throat myself."

Faron's vision dimmed further, even the stars beginning to go dark, but still, he struggled against the man's superior strength. Between the table leg and the door, Faron was completely suspended, suffocating from the pressure on his lungs.

Screams.

Faron's heels slammed against the door as he tried to find purchase to lift himself away from his constrictions, but he found nothing.

Screams.

His sight fled entirely.

"May your soul find rest."

Faron's foot swung wildly in a final, desperate kick, and it connected with something soft. He heard a hard grunt and slipped to the floor. Color immediately returned to his pounding head as his lungs filled, just in time to see Jaru'tal drop both the table leg and the knife. He was on his knees. The slaver gripped his stomach before heaving once, twice, then three times, ejecting bile and stomach contents onto the floor.

He was a pathetic sight, retching and prostrated, completely defenseless. Faron seized the advantage. Still weak from lack of breath, he turned into a backward kick, delivering all the force he could muster. Jaru'tal sprawled across the floor and coughed when he landed hard on his side. He tried to talk, but his lungs were empty.

Faron grimaced as he stooped to pick up the table leg, half-covered in bile, then crossed the distance between them.

Jaru'tal staggered to his feet, wiping at the corner of his mouth with a ruined sleeve. "Who are you, assassin?" he spat.

"I'm not an assassin," Faron answered, breathing heavily. "But I am here to kill you." He swung and was rewarded with a sharp crack as the wood landed against the slaver's forearm. Jaru'tal registered the blow with a sharp intake of breath, then stumbled backward.

"I can pay you. I have riches I can give—gold and emeralds, land! I can pay you five times what you'll get for this. Ten times!" His voice was thin and his words quick.

Faron struck again, this time toward the legs. The club made solid contact, and Jaru'tal fell with a cry. He remembered the last belted knife then and struggled to free it from the sheath. Faron didn't give him the chance. Jaru'tal's hands shook violently, and knocking them aside was an easy thing. Faron stole the dagger and plunged it into Jaru'tal's thigh, narrowly missing a major artery. Still, blood surged from the wound like a market center fountain in Blackwood.

Jaru'tal screamed, and Faron stabbed his arm, a shoulder, anything that would weaken him without killing him—instantly, at least. Kneeling atop the man's chest, Faron brought the blade to the slaver's throat, perhaps with more force than was necessary.

"I have gold!" he cried. "Mountains of it! Take it, please. Take anything!"

"I don't want it."

Something large crashed into the door, and Faron shot a nervous look over his shoulder. It wasn't wasted on his victim.

"Help!" the man cried, nearly sobbing. "Help!"

Faron cuffed him hard, pinning one arm with a knee, a knife to his throat. "Where is Sadagon?" he yelled through his bloodlust. Another blow shook the door.

"Faster!" Jaru'tal yelled.

Cursing, Faron threw the knife across the room and grabbed a chair, throwing it under the latch, effectively leveraging the door closed, in case there really was another key. It rattled as it was slammed again.

He turned around to find Jaru'tal scrambling to pick up one of the fallen daggers. He seized it with weak fingers and swung at Faron but was easily dodged. The blade fell from his fingers as it missed its mark, and Jaru'tal fell to his knees, retching again. Nothing came up this time.

The door shook in its hinges.

"What did you do to me?" the man yelled, terror touching his voice.

"Poison," Faron answered. "But not enough to kill you. Still, I have an antidote for if you tell me where Sadagon is."

"Why are you doing this?" He gasped. "How do you know that name"

"You provide Sadagon with young slaves. I want to know where they go."

"It is my cousin, isn't it? Is he the one paying you?"

"Nobody is paying me," Faron said with a shake of the head. "Nobody is conspiring to steal your wealth. All I want to know is where the slaves go."

"If I tell you that, there is no future for my house, no future for my son."

Faron kicked the Dunestrider in the side of his head. "Don't talk to me about your son," he spat. "Do you think you can use the protection of families as a defense? You don't protect families, Jaru'tal; you destroy them."

"The sin…" Jaru'tal began. "Is on the buyer."

Faron dropped a fist into the man's exposed neck. "The sin is on you. I'm putting it on you. And now, I'm giving you a chance to redeem one of those sins. Where is Sadagon?"

The door shook.

The Dunestrider gripped his stomach. "Give me the antidote so we may talk."

"Is he in Vam Aranath?"

Jaru'tal's eyes were wide and not just from pain. "What do you know of the God City?"

The words hit like a wall of water. He knew it was real, now, and that it was north. He had to find out more.

The door shook.

"If you want to live, Dunestrider, you'll tell me everything you know."

The slaver groaned in agony as the poison ran its course. "Give me the antidote!" he cried.

"Where is Sadagon?"

Blood dripped from silk onto the hard stone as Jaru'tal managed to regain his footing. When he did, he was gripping something in a chest pocket. "If you have it," he said. "I'll kill you and take it off your corpse." He lunged forward, but between the poison and blood loss, he was slow. Seizing a fistful of sodden purple silk, Faron swung around the larger man—using his own weight to knock him off balance—and slung him into the ironbound window. His face slammed into the glass, and it cracked from the force.

Another massive blow struck the door from behind. Faron's pulse quickened.

"Where is he?" Faron pried, pressing Jaru'tal's face to the window.

"Help!" he screamed, louder than ever. Jaru'tal got one hand up, far enough to grasp at Faron's face. His grip was weak, but he was still fighting back. Faron drew the man's head backward and drove it into the glass again. The window splintered with a sharp crack, and shards came away in Jaru'tal's face. He screamed. With a fistful of sweaty hair, Faron did it again.

Time was running out.

"Where is Sadagon?" Faron yelled, grappling with the man's flailing arms as he pushed him into the window. Another blow shook the room, and Faron began to panic. "Tell me!"

With increasing force, Faron crashed the Dunestrider's head against the window and its iron frame—once, twice, three times, four. With each concussion, the glass filled with cracks, webbing out higher and farther, and the iron squealed in protest.

"Where is Sadagon?!" Faron screamed. He got no answer. Jaru'tal was growing unresponsive, except for the hand on his chest pocket.

"Where is Vam Aranath?!"

The door shook.

Jaru'tal began to laugh. Faron punched him in the gut. When he regained his breath, he said, "Your time is running out, son of oathbreakers."

The door shook.

"Tell me what I want to know, or I'll kill you!" Faron shouted in his bloody face.

"Do it," Jaru'tal laughed. "And you will have learned nothing." Faron punched him in the stomach again, sending him to the floor where he laughed still. He kicked him in the gut, hard.

"Where is Sadagon?" Faron repeated, just as the door shook

again. This time, an axe-head split the wood, and a hole was left where it came away.

"Your time has run out, son of oathbreakers," the man wheezed. Through the hole in the door, a man leveled a crossbow. Faron threw himself to the side just as the bolt was fired. It exploded through the window.

Teeth clenched and spittle flying from his mouth, Faron grabbed Jaru'tal's head and threw him at the window with all his might. Glass exploded and rained down on the street below, shearing the skin on the man's neck.

That stopped his laughing. His screams broke out across the great buildings beyond the window and grew louder when Faron yanked him back through. Another axe strike hit the door, widening the hole. He could hear the panic of the men on the other side and the clicking of the crossbow reloading.

"Tell me where Sadagon is!" Faron screamed. "Where is Vam Aranath?"

He didn't answer, except to clutch at his chest and yell, "Shoot him!" Faron glanced up and noticed the crossbow back in the hole, pointed straight at him. He barely managed to get out of the way before the bolt was loosed, burying itself in the sandstone wall.

"Kill him!" Blood pulsed down the slaver's neck, drenching his torso almost entirely. His face was unrecognizable.

The crossbow was clicking again, and the door shook. There was no way out. Faron lost any semblance of control he had.

Holding his head against the glass, Faron punched the back of his skull. Jaru'tal screamed with what faculties remained to him.

"Where is she?!" Faron screamed in return.

With both hands, Faron slammed Jaru'tal's head against the glass again. The iron frame shook in its holdings, the sound of sandstone coming loose and grating underneath.

"Where is my sister?!"

He didn't answer.

Screams.

Faron threw the slaver with all his might. The entire window exploded from the sill, shards of glass flying through the air, reflecting the dazzling sunlight. It crashed to the ground far below amidst terrified screaming—whether at the falling window or the bloody man hanging out of its place, Faron didn't know.

"Where is she?!" he yelled. "Where is my sister?!"

Jaru'tal was delirious.

Faron pulled him back in by his silk robes and screamed the question again; but, his eyes were glazed, and Faron knew that he had beat him too hard. Jaru'tal was beyond words now, though he still clutched at his robe, as if protecting something precious. Suspicion rose in Faron as he realized the clicking of the reloading crossbow had come to a stop.

With instinctive force, he tugged the barely conscious slaver in front of him just as the quarrel was loosed. It struck Jaru'tal through the hand and square in the chest. The slaver's eyes shot open wide, and he released a massive exhalation. The fingers on his pinned hand tightened around something in his robes. Someone screamed from beyond the door.

With a soft curse, Faron yanked Jaru'tal's hand away, the arrow passing through it with a sickening, wet crunch. Keeping the dying man between himself and the door, Faron parted the robes on Jaru'tal's chest and reached inside. He deftly found the pocket and pulled out a small, golden length of metal—another key. His hand came away bloody as another blow slammed the door.

Seizing the brown bag Harab had forced into the room, Faron shoved the key inside. Acting on instinct, he ripped away the fist-sized emerald that hung around Jaru'tal's neck as well as a dark velvet coin purse, then added them to the pouch.

"No," the Dunestrider gasped, surprising Faron. "You cannot… do this to me." He coughed blood.

The door split almost in two as the heavy axe slammed it again. One of the purple-garbed men beyond shoved an arm through, searching for the lock.

Faron took the dying man and shoved him halfway through the window. People below gasped in horror at the brutalized mess of the Dunestrider's face.

"One last chance!" Faron lied. "Tell me where the slaves end up, or I'll let you go."

Jaru'tal was silent for a short moment. "I can't!" he whispered through ravaged lungs and throat.

"Tell me!" Faron screamed, shoving him out further.

The door opened. He was out of time.

Jaru'tal wheezed on the stone sill with an arrow puncturing a lung and his face covered in lacerations. There was nothing more Faron could get from him now, but it wasn't enough. In a flash of vindictive spite, he whispered, "Dead gods damn you," and shoved him through the window.

He didn't even scream on the way down.

Faron stole a glance over his shoulder to see the veiled guards forcing their way inside. He heard the sharp sound of glass shattering under the weight of a corpse and leaped onto the sill himself. They were nearly on him.

Up above was a thin ledge—old and crumbled away in places. It was not the sort of thing men trusted their lives to, but he was out of options. With a sick feeling in his gut, Faron jumped into the air, hanging for a long moment before seizing the ledge with strong fingers. He pulled himself up and away from the window.

A purple-veiled guard leaned back through the open space and reached out to pull him down, but he was already gone. With the practiced fingers of a thief, Faron climbed from ledge to ledge, scaling to more stable and sure footings. Gold, pearl, and black jet worked into the ornate walls offered plentiful handholds. Another man leaned through the window with a crossbow, but Faron pulled himself over the top and disappeared.

On his feet, Faron slung the bag over his shoulder and broke into a run, cursing himself. A key—a single key. The one man who could lead him to Hadria was dead, and he had nothing but a small gold key. A knot of anxiety pulled at his stomach so intensely, he almost fell to his knees. Another man dead, and he was no closer to finding his sister than when he'd begun.

Maybe Harab'kun would know what to do with it.

Guards called from far below, and he could spy some climbing ladders; but, he leaped over a street onto a lower roof—and then another and another—until he was quickly lost, leaving his crime and pursuers behind.

Murdered Hopes

Twelve hours later, Faron emerged at the top of the abandoned Temple to the Lesser Kindred, where Harab'kun sat, legs folded, apparently ignoring the chair. Somewhere below were the corpses of Jakab and Badune. Faron briefly wondered if they were the only ones to meet their end in such a way when Harab'kun's eyes fluttered open.

"Young Aldene! It is good to see you alive," he said, standing and pulling Faron into an awkward embrace. "Though I wonder what kept you so long?" I would have thought you had been captured, if not for the many patrols searching for the pale demon."

Thirsty and exhausted, Faron managed to croak, "I had to wait until dark on the rooftops. I wouldn't have made it five feet in broad daylight, even if no one was looking for me. Do you have anything to drink?"

"Your skin *is* peculiar," Harab admitted, pulling out a fat waterskin from his belt. He handed it over, and Faron drank greedily, letting it splash over his lips. The water was warm, but his relief was palpable. "But that's enough of that," he continued. "I see you made good use of the bag I lent you."

Faron nodded. "It helped."

"I go the extra mile." He nodded toward the bag. "What did you get?" His eyes sparkled with anticipation.

"A few things," Faron said. He pulled Jaru'tal's intricate pendant from the bag.

Harab's eyes widened in awe. "That is even bigger from up close."

"And this." Faron tossed him the coin purse. It was filled with thick pieces of gold.

"You could have kept this yourself, and I would never have known," Harab commented.

Faron shrugged. "I don't really need it. Just give me a cut." Harab nodded emphatically, counting the coins. "You're satisfied, then? With our deal."

"Between this and the chits I stole from the keeper's tent, more than satisfied, certainly."

"I also found this," Faron said, revealing the little key. "In his pocket."

Harab inspected it keenly. "It seems to belong to a vault or safe."

"Do you think it's a safe in his home?"

"Quite possibly." He nodded. "The keys to the barrack vaults are iron, with Akwin's Eye affixed to the handle, and the Dunestrider is not a man to occupy a storeroom below his caste."

"Was," Faron reminded him.

"Ah, yes. The great Dunestrider brought low at last. He fell from a window, I heard?"

"Yes," Faron sighed. "Among other things."

"How many ways is it necessary to kill a single man?" Harab inquired comically.

"I wasn't trying to kill him," Faron snapped, his anger and

frustration rising to the surface. "I ran out of time, and it was his own guards who ended up shooting him."

"He had eleven stab wounds."

"Not fatal," Faron grumbled. "I suppose there's no chance I'll be able to quietly slip out of the city now, is there?"

"Indeed, no. You are a very wanted man. Tell me, though, did you learn what it was you sought? Are you satisfied with your vengeance?"

"No," Faron growled. "Not really. He wouldn't tell me anything—to the very end."

"A brave man."

"A coward," Faron retorted. "An eel who dealt in the lives of children for profit."

"The fate of slaves is a weight on the soul of the buyer, not the seller," Harab argued. "A man cannot control what another might do, good or evil."

"Jaru'tal said much the same thing," Faron said levelly. "He was wrong, and he died for it. The sin is on both, and they *can* be controlled, both buyer and seller. I've done it before, and I will again."

"How so?"

"By killing them."

Harab'kun raised his thick eyebrows. "I suppose there is that. Is that how you intend to live out the rest of your days? Slaughtering the buyers and sellers of men, all through the world?"

"No," Faron began. "I have to find someone. After though…" He trailed away as he thought. Faron had been far from the only slave in this massive city. Every street, shop, and pit was packed with them—young, old, man, woman. It made Faron's skin crawl to see them and not help. "After… yes. Yes, every damn one."

Harab laughed. "You are like a flame of white flash rock—so very interesting, but one must be careful not to get too close and be burned." He laughed at the joke Faron did not understand. "So, what is it you plan to do next, young Aldene?"

Sighing, Faron lifted the key into the waxing moonlight. "I need to find what this opens. Jaru'tal seemed to want to keep it safe when I was… questioning him. Maybe it leads to something that will tell me where the slaves are sent. Do you think Karan'dal would know?"

Harab swallowed awkwardly. "No. I don't think he could tell you."

"He knew the name of Sadagon," Faron realized, feeling a modicum of hope. Perhaps there was another way to find where the trail of slaves led. "If I can get him alone, I can make him tell me everything." He noticed, with a little surprise, that he relished the chance to squeeze the pompous man's neck.

"No," Harab insisted. "You can't."

"And why is that?" Faron snapped, frustrated.

"Because," Harab clarified. "He is dead. I slit his throat while you dealt with his master. Already, I have sold his chits and claimed my new wealth. It seems in doing so I have robbed you of your goal. Forgive me, young Aldene."

The feeling of realization left him more deflated than before, and he groaned, frustrated. "There were two people in this city who could have led me to Sadagon, and we've killed them both." Potent regret filled him from head to toe.

"I'm sorry," Harab said. "I will repay my debt to you if I can."

Not answering, Faron said, "That's it, then. I have to find out what this key opens and pray for… something."

"And how will you do that?"

"By breaking back into Jaru'tal's home and shoving it into every lock until it turns one."

Harab whistled softly. "That is a great risk you take upon yourself, young Aldene."

"I have no choice," Faron replied. "If I don't find out where those slaves are sent, someone close to me will die—if she hasn't already."

"It is a great secret you hunt," Harab whispered. "Men have been killed for asking too many questions of this nature. The Dunestrider has accrued vast wealth by keeping this knowledge to himself, and his home will be filled with the Office of Inheritance, sorting out his belongings between inheritor and the Great Akwin Ashamat. Temple guards will be there as well to keep out the likes of you and me. It is no easy thing you are proposing."

"I'm no stranger to this type of thing," Faron insisted. Still, he grimaced. Where was Synick when you needed him?

"You have Jaru'tal's pendant," Faron acknowledged, changing the subject. "Can you sell it?"

"As fast as I am able. Between this, the gold for your sale, and the chits I have stolen, I will be rich as long as I live. Perhaps even my children will be rich if I manage to procure any. Who knows, money has much power."

Despite himself, Faron chuckled. "Harab," he said seriously. "I might need your help to get a few things."

"I owe you no small amount of coin either, my foreign friend," he exclaimed jovially. "Though, not enough to kill you for." He laughed as if at a grand joke. Faron only gave him a flat stare. "Speak, and it is yours."

Faron gave him the list. As Harab'kun made to depart, he

stopped himself and said, "I nearly forgot! I have kept this for you for no small amount of time." He reached behind the legs of the old wooden chair and procured a large linen bag. In it were his old belongings—faded blacks, dagger, crossbow, bolts, and at the bottom, his silver ring.

Faron exclaimed in genuine joy, donning the leaping wolf on his finger in a flash. Hadria screamed but not loudly. How odd that he could find that comforting after a month of mostly silence. He clenched a fist, feeling the silver around his index finger, and nearly shed a tear in pure relief. With a small smile, he buckled the dagger onto his belt and handed everything else back.

"Will you hold onto these for me? I can't take them where I'm going, but I'll be back soon."

"It would be my pleasure, my young friend, and if you do not, it will be my great pleasure to sell them."

"Get me the items on that list, and if nothing goes wrong, I'll be back before sunrise."

The Lost City

Everything was silent. Faron, garbed in a soft black cloth, lowered himself carefully down the precarious ledge until he could feel his toes in their sanded pigskin soles make contact with the three-inch ledge below.

With the deftness of a practiced thief, he pushed back and traded the ledge to his fingertips. He didn't have quite the strength to stop himself completely, but he didn't need to. With reduced momentum, he swung in toward the empty window frame and landed on the stone sill. He exhaled softly, turning back and peering at the street below. A group of three guards stood beneath the window dressed in a deep scarlet, the color of the king. They didn't seem to have noticed anything.

Faron shook his head. This was stupid. He murdered one of the wealthiest and most influential people in Aru'barrahk, narrowly escaping, and now he was sneaking back in? He groaned inwardly and patted his pocket for the hundredth time, making sure the gold key was still there. With gloved hands and a veiled face, he stepped properly into the room. Blood still stained the floor, the table, the chairs—everything. It was a grizzly sight, and the smell was no better.

Light from the setting moon filtered in through the empty

window, but the room was otherwise dark. The door at the far side lay swung open, tilted unnaturally on destroyed hinges. Small slivers of wood littered the floor where the axe had strewn them, and a gaping hole was visible as a deeper patch of blackness against the dark door. Very little had changed since Faron's escape—and the murder. Tilting his head around the doorway, he peeked down the hall and came almost face to face with a guard. If not for the faint light he carried, Faron would have missed him. Just outside the candle's gentle nimbus, Faron threw himself back, soft shoes keeping his silence. Crouching, he spun behind the battered door, barely fitting between it and the wall.

Sure enough, the guard walked in, scarlet cloth glowing dimly in the weak light. His boots were hobnailed and made a distinct sound as he did a round of the room. Faron could see him through a crack where the hinge had fallen away from the door, but he averted his gaze. The feeling of another man's eyes on your back was a very real thing.

As quickly as he'd come, the man left, returning down the hall toward the stairs. Faron went the other direction. Without the moon and the guard's candle, it was dark as pitch. Not a single window illuminated the hallway, as he had previously noticed, but there was another door opposite the stairs before the corner. He would try it. Tracing his hand along the wall, he stepped noiselessly on the long, soft rugs.

It was locked. Cursing to himself, he reached into a pocket and retrieved his lock picks, courtesy of Harab. Normally, the hardest part about picking locks in the dark was finding the keyhole in the first place, but this time, a small trickle of light fell through the tiny hole. Perhaps someone had left a lantern on? He hesitated. There could very well be someone on the other side. Perhaps he should try another room first. He heard a hard leather boot scuffing the bottom step from across the hall—no time to consider.

In a flash, he had his pick and lever in the lock, twisting and lifting the thick pins simultaneously until the door opened on oiled hinges. He slipped inside just as a faint light came into view, and the door closed with a soft click. He cringed. There was no way the guard didn't hear that. If he locked the door now, he certainly would hear and raise the alarm, so instead, Faron did the next best thing. Removing his gloves, he grabbed the handle and pulled with all his might, rendering it immovable.

On the other side of the door, Faron could hear the unknown guard's footsteps. They were slower—cautious. He pulled for all he was worth. From the hall, the handle attempted to turn, but Faron held fast. The pressure stayed for a brief moment and then abated. He heard a satisfied grunt, and the footsteps fell away. Faron breathed a sigh of relief, turning, and nearly had a heart attack.

Suspended in the air, not five feet before him, was the body of a purple-clad guard, hanging upside down from a hook in the ceiling. His heart leaped into his throat, and the only thing keeping him from a scream was his utter lack of breath.

"Atha's desiccated corpse," Faron cursed to himself when his shock wore off. "Blood and ice."

A single, small candle flickered on a desk, deep in a pool of wax. The light it cast fell harshly across the suspended body, and Faron felt he recognized it. The house guards all wore similar purple armor, but for some reason, this one seemed distinct. He eyed the corpse with his back to the wall, regulating his breathing when it hit him. It was the guard who had fired the crossbow and impaled Jaru'tal's chest. Had the others killed him for that? Was it these red temple guards? Was this some sort of ceremonial punishment for unintentionally slaying their master or for being unable to save him?

Faron swallowed hard. He had pulled Jaru'tal into that arrow's path. He recalled the bloody, broken figure splayed across the street below the window. That was a weight he could carry—for Hadria—but this? Was he responsible for this? The man had been garroted and savagely beaten.

Without the veiled leather cap, Faron could clearly make out the man's face, and to his surprise, he was handsome—and young. He averted his gaze, surveying the rest of the room—simply to look at anything else—and fell back on old habits.

A thin bed lay adjacent to the desk, and a cabinet occupied another corner. There was no casket, safe, or coin purse to be seen, though thin lines of dust indicated where a chest had recently been. Opposite the door, he found a tall window, closed by a latch that opened to a small, round balcony. He undid the latch and noted it as a possible escape route if need be.

Outside the door, he heard the guard pass by again and felt a wave of nauseous heat as he realized he had forgotten to lock it. He froze, but the footsteps passed by, continuing back toward the stairs. Faron continued on. There was nothing to help in this room, and the corpse was making him more than uneasy.

Taking the candle with him, for brevity's sake, he stepped out into the narrow hall and rounded the corner. There were another two doors here—a light wooden door on the left and one occupying the full end of the hallway, made of solid iron. Now that he had turned the corner, he could hear voices coming from the sturdier of the two doors, though faintly. That was likely where he needed to go.

He slipped into the room on the left first, it being unlocked and unoccupied. Inside, the sandstone walls were pocked with small shelf-like holes, filled with parcels of paper, scrolls, and ledgers. Curious, he set the small candle down and flicked through the numerous parchments. He found ledgers of payments, both made and received; personal messages, one marked from the king; notifications of shipments, though it didn't specify what or where; and other miscellaneous things that taught him nothing remotely helpful or incriminating. The only room left to reasonably suspect was the one at the far end of the hall, and the voices could still be heard inside.

He had considered searching through Jaru'tal's bedroom, but his gut told him it would be fruitless. Jaru'tal didn't seem the type to keep important things anywhere but behind a thick iron door. Sliding back into the hall, Faron padded closer to the quiet voices. Sure enough, at least three men could be heard debating or arguing about something indiscernible.

Pushing his ear to the metal, Faron debated about how to get inside. Should he come back the next night? No, he had wasted far too much time in this city already, and his eighteenth nameday was drawing near—Hadria's nameday. She had very little time left.

No, he would have to find a way to clear the room—tonight. Pressed against the wall, his mind raced. He hadn't anticipated needing to clear out a room and didn't have the materials to start a fire. Nothing in this sandstone home would burn anyway. If he had some sulfur and noxweed, he could mix an odor bomb that might do the trick, but he had neither. All he had were his lock picks, his straight knife, a thin but strong rope about fifteen feet long, and the oil-black clothes on his back. Could there be something of potential use inside the home itself? The rooms seemed to have been scavenged for anything of use or value already—seeing as the only thing he'd found was a hanging corpse. Faron froze, struck by a morbid idea. He checked the hinges on the door—inward-facing. It could work.

He paused for a long moment, considering, but the approach of boots on stairs spurred him to action. There was no time to consider the morality of what he was about to do and no other conclusion to come to. He had to act.

In a flash, he was back inside the first room, careful not to let the latch click this time. The man in the hall passed by, did a round of the long hallway, and went back down the stairs. Faron shook his head in annoyance at the diligence of guards who didn't sleep through their shifts, then got to work. First, he opened the window and stepped into the cold night air. The balcony was ringed by a stone railing that seemed to have been carved from the original structure itself. However ancient, it looked sturdy. He tied his rope to this and left it spooled on the ground. With luck, he wouldn't need it, but Faron didn't leave things to luck.

Next, he unsheathed his knife and cut down the suspended body. It fell to the floor with a muffled thump. He waited several moments before continuing, but nothing stirred beyond the door. Faron dragged the corpse across the room, where he remained several minutes for the guard's eventual return and departure. As quietly as he could manage, Faron opened the door and dragged the dead man across the long rugs that adorned the stone floor. Even after his forced time in those dank mines, he had a difficult time of it. He cursed to himself. If this were the first or even fifth time he had been forced to desecrate a corpse for a job, he would've been grateful, but it wasn't, and it didn't seem to get any easier. At least he hadn't had to dig this one up.

With a shrug, he slumped the body against the iron door as well as he could. Luckily, the way he had been hung locked his knees in place, and Faron was able to keep the corpse standing—or maybe it was just *rigor mortis*. Either way, the dead man stood. Faron felt his stomach turn but pushed it aside, along with his guilt.

Unable to shake off his grimace, Faron reached past the body and knocked on the door. The arguing stopped. Suddenly, a more discernable voice flowed from inside.

"Captain, if you've come to ask after our timeframe once more, I will have you strung up and drawn for interfering with temple business!" The voice was aged and impatient. Faron didn't answer, except to knock again, harder this time. He was met with an exasperated sigh and shuffling movement. Dodging back, Faron slipped into the adjacent room and peered around the edge from the safety of the dark. The door opened inward, and for a brief moment, Faron could see an old Kaorn garbed in white and red, a white beard adorning his face. The corpse fell directly on top of him.

Terrified and surprised cries split the quiet home as the man who had opened the door fell to the ground, a body pinning him down. He hit his head in the fall but flailed and backpedaled to escape even faster. Another man nearly trampled him as he fled the room, eyes in a feral panic, yelling, "Naien Anuit, Naien Anuit!" Faron recognized the name as the devil of their archaic religion.

Another two men fled the room, blubbering something similar in their terror. Finally, the fat man who was pinned under the corpse got free, kicking and nearly tripping in his haste. He vanished around the corner, calling for the guards.

Dashing across the hall, Faron sprang into the secure room, pushing the corpse across the ground and out of the way of the door. With a set jaw, he turned the lock, effectively barricading himself inside. He would have to grapple with escaping when it came to that. For now, he had to find the lock to his key. Whatever secret it kept, Jaru'tal didn't want him to know it.

Turning, Faron gaped at the interior of the room. It was large, and stacked from wall to wall were chests, coffers, bags, safes, and all manner of valuables. Faron was wrong. Everything valuable in the home hadn't been stolen or scavenged. It had been collected and brought here.

A mountain of coins filled one corner, and rich tapestries and paintings covered the walls. Bowls of crystal fruit that looked unbelievably intricate sat atop piles of gold-bound books. In one corner, a large silver basin spilled over with jewelry fine enough to make Synick apoplectic to see it unstolen—not to mention the gilded candelabra. Ingots of gold and silver lined the ground next to jeweled weapons, far too fine to ever see any actual use—except the bloody knife Faron had stabbed Jaru'tal with. Chests and caskets lined the walls wherever there was space available, and at the base of every pile, lay a paper label. Were they inventorying the Dunestrider's possessions?

There were at least nine chests in the room and four or five smaller caskets, though half of the chests were already open. Faron took a deep breath and cursed himself for the tenuousness of his hope. There was no real surety that the lock to his stolen key would be in here or that it would teach him anything if it was, but he couldn't forget the way Jaru'tal reached for it when he mentioned Sadagon. It was related—it had to be.

Knocking over an ornate candlestick, Faron jumped to the nearest chest, fitting the key inside. It was far too small. He tried another with the same result. He heard someone gasp and curse from the hall. They had found the corpse. He didn't have much time.

He seized an ornate casket—the kind meant to lock coin on a storefront counter—and slipped the key inside. It fit but didn't turn.

"It's locked," drifted a weak voice from outside.

"Impossible," said another. The handle rattled. Faron heard a harsh whisper but couldn't make out what it was. His heart seemed to skip a beat. He cursed and tried another lockbox—gold plated this time. The key didn't fit. The pounding on the door increased. He nearly dropped a ruby-encrusted jewelry box as he slipped the key into it, but it didn't open.

Nearly in a panic now, Faron lunged for the last casket—an ugly wooden thing, more of a miniature chest than any-thing—and tried the key. It turned. His heart leaped into his throat as the lid sprung open, revealing two small pouches and a folded piece of paper. Inside one pouch was a pile of gold coins, minted in the currency of the desert people.

He winced as someone once again pounded on the door, yelling something inaudible—or perhaps he was just too panicked to interpret it. Cursing silently, he closed the lockbox and shoved the entire thing inside the bag that slung across his shoulders.

Through the clamor that continued beyond the door, he heard the jangle of keys, and his mind snapped to attention. His time was up. Pushing two fingers to an eye, he spun to the far side of the room and extinguished the candles. Stooping as he passed it, he scooped up a crystal orange from the bowl of crystalline fruit. It was heavy and the kind of thing Synick would have kept as a curiosity.

The room went black as tar as he extinguished the lamp on the opposite end. He crouched beside a desk piled with silver plates, wrapped in the darkness.

Soft candlelight and a light scrape marked the door opening inward, and he stayed poised, ready to leap but completely still. With his one open eye, he made out the figures of men holding weakly trimmed candles designed for length of use and not brightness. Compared to the lanterns he'd just extinguished, it was still dark and hard to make them out. He felt toward his knife but stopped himself. He wouldn't kill innocent men—not while he still had a choice.

"We know you are in there!" a guard called through a veil. He held a candle that illuminated the hallway, which he lifted higher to try and see into the room. Faron smiled. That weak, undirected light only served him, both illuminating and blinding the men outside. A dark figure on the floor told him they moved the body.

"The dead are walking," a man whimpered. "Kalan'lin, there is no living thing in that room—only demons."

The captain put a hand behind another man's back, pushing him forward. "Light the lantern inside."

The man stammered and pushed back. "You cannot make

us go in there. It will kill us all." Fear was thick on his voice.

"Are you temple guards, or are you sniveling mules? Ganak'hav," commanded the first. "Give us more light. It may just be nothing."

"Great Akwin, protect us with thy holy gaze. Make us strong both night and day. Grant us—" He was cut off by a slashing voice.

"Be silent! Where is that light?"

Finally, Faron heaved the crystal orb through the air. It exploded in a fantastic crash against the far wall, where the third guard let out a small scream as shards of glass stung his face through his veil.

The two guards nearest Faron whirled around, the captain staggering backward into the room as he did so. Faron lunged from his dark corner, finally removing the fingers from his eye. As it opened, the dark-adjusted eye showed him the hallway in perfect clarity, and he lunged forward, grabbing the staggering captain and throwing him into a pile of something expensive. His candle sputtered as it struck the floor, and he cried out as if he'd seen a ghost. Before the second guard could react, Faron was upon him, shoving fiercely into the small of his back with a shoulder.

He heard the man's extended exhalation as the wind rushed from his body, and he curled on the floor, trying to scream. Without air, though, he only retched. The third man whipped back around now and noticed his fallen brethren. Quite unexpectedly, he fell back, hands raised to defend himself from the nameless shadow. Faron passed him by, uncontested. He had terrorized them enough.

He was acutely aware of the guard captain tossing coins about the counting room as he rose to his feet and charged down the hallway. Faron slipped into the first room and slammed the door shut as he sprinted past. No time for locking, he leaped out onto the balcony. The man burst through the door behind him, but Faron already had the rope in his hands, and, trusting the knot he'd tied beforehand, slipped off the edge of the terrace.

Increasing his grip on the rope to slow his fall, he slid along its length faster than he could control, the black cloth gloves not providing the same level of resistance as leather. He was moving too fast. At the end of the rope, he slipped off, body gyrating awkwardly. He fell ten feet to the ground and landed—poorly. A spike of lancing pain shot up through his thigh, and he couldn't help but cry out. The three men guarding Jaru'tal's window jumped in near unison but recovered quickly.

Ice, he cursed. He had forgotten about them.

The commander of the guard appeared from over the balcony. "After him!" he shouted. If not for his veil, Faron was sure there would have been spittle flying from his mouth. Not subject to the same terror as the guards in the hallway, these guards promptly obeyed. One thrust a spear at him, which he barely managed to roll away from as he sprung up from his knees into a run. Pain lanced up his leg with every step of his right foot, but he ran anyway. At least it wasn't broken, he realized. He could put weight on it, even if it hurt.

Half running, half limping, Faron raced down the street, red-clad guards not far behind. Normally, Faron might have lost them near instantly. What he lacked in strength, he made up for in speed, but now he was barely able to maintain his lead. A knife clattered against a wall near his head, and he leaped to the side reflexively. Perhaps he wasn't maintaining that lead so well, after all.

Another five or six guards barreled around a corner from the front entrance of the house, directly blocking his path. Cursing, he threw himself down a small alleyway between massive temple-like structures. Hopefully, it let out somewhere. Full tilt, he ran, the bob of his head illustrating his limp in plain view of the guards in the thin alley. If even one of them had a bow, he was a goner. With only a few stars for light, Faron nearly ran headlong into a wall before getting his arms up to redirect his momentum. He noticed a break in the complete darkness where the alley turned and let out into the open, and he pushed off, desperate for speed.

Faron erupted from the dark alley and into the open air of the road. He made a sharp right, only to be tackled from behind. He landed on his lungs in the sand, and air rushed from them, leaving him half winded. He felt, rather than heard, a blade drawing across leather, and he rolled, tossing the man slightly to the side.

A dagger stabbed the ground where he had just been. Throwing a knee, Faron sank it deep into his attacker's gut—another red-garbed guard—and kicked him off with his good foot. More guards poured in from around the corner, and Faron scrambled back to his feet, running for all he was worth. His limp was lessening.

Climb—he had to climb. He cast his gaze about for a way to reach the rooftops, but these buildings were massive, monstrous things. No wagon or stacked barrels would do the trick here like on any corner of Blackwood, and the walls were coated with a slick ceramic black or white paint, besides. Trying to climb them at speed was certain death—but not in the older district, he realized. Many of those buildings were smaller and had long since crumbled away. They would be perfect for an escape, but he was running the wrong way.

A patrol of over ten blue-clad guards turned a corner, walking casually until they spotted him running, the fastest of the scarlet men still giving chase. They shifted spears, halberds, and maces off shoulders and pointed them directly at him.

"By Akwin, stop!" they commanded. He did no such thing, instead, turning down another small alleyway, this one with a faint light at the end. He tripped over something that grunted angrily in the dark—a homeless man? He staggered back to his feet and sprinted on. How far could they chase him, he wondered? His ankle pained him, but Faron was an excellent runner. That was the primary reason he had survived to become such a skilled thief. He could almost always simply run away if caught.

A pursuer slammed a shoulder into the wall, not bothering to slow down for the corner. He screamed angrily as he regained momentum. Faron threw himself to the side instinctively. He heard the whistle of splitting air as an invisible blade flew past, combined with the sound of someone tripping and falling flat. The man had also tripped on whatever was sprawled in the alley, and it had thrown his aim off.

Faron heard bells ringing near and far as he burst from the alley, turning again toward the poorer district of the city. More men appeared, bearing all manner of colors and insignias. Faron ducked away down dark alleys and curving roads to avoid them. Like a madman, he ran until the buildings around him became coarser and chipped, massive stones the size of small houses lying near the edge of toppled structures and sometimes in the road. He peered behind and realized he had lost his pursuers. His foot was pulsating with pain, but not in-time with his steps and not as severely as before.

Not stopping to feel relieved, he hobbled up a fallen column and pulled himself on top of a roof—then a taller one, and a taller one still—before he allowed himself to collapse. He panted clawingly amidst the angry ringing of the bells and sprawled on his back, exhausted. His throat was raw with thirst. After several minutes, he sat back up and felt at his ankle. He pushed a thumb into the throbbing section and was pleased to find that the pain lessened instead of increased—not broken, it confirmed. He massaged it tenderly and noticed a fire springing up from a rooftop.

A puzzled expression on his face, he watched as another fire leaped into the night, then another and another. All across the city, flames lit the night, illuminating both street and rooftop while the bells tolled. The streets below buzzed with activity, men marching in all directions, out in incredible force. They were looking for him, Faron knew. He had to get out of the city.

Anxiety twisting his gut, he released his ankle. It was already feeling better—just a bad fall, was all. He unfastened the linen bag on his shoulder and, once again, opened the box inside, making out what he could in the dim starlight. He opened the bag of coins and set them aside, then opened the other pouch. His eyebrows rose when he saw what lay within, disappointing as it was—gemstones, finely cut and of various colors. They clinked together softly, catching and refracting the twinkling starlight. Those he pocketed—out of habit more than anything. They might prove *very* useful.

Last of all, he unfolded the parchment, squinting to make

out the words. More fires sprung up about the city, and for the first time, Faron noticed great braziers mounted on the corners of many buildings for the purpose. Tilting the parchment toward the crescent moon, he was just able to read what appeared to be a notice of payment fulfilled for the gems in the strongbox. Frustrated, he flung it aside. Why bother locking up something so innocuous? And why keep the key on his person? Certainly, the gems were worth a fortune, but no more than the vast expanse of treasures Jaru'tal already possessed. There had to be something else.

He looked back in the empty box, frustration rising. There *had* to be something else. The trail couldn't just end like this! Angrily he picked up the box and smashed it against the stone roof of the tower he perched upon. It clattered almost to the edge where he heard a sharp snap, and a thin, flat piece of wood fell away, skidding across the roof.

A hidden panel? Suddenly his curiosity was ravenous, desperate. He pulled open the box, and sure enough, the wood paneling had been a false bottom, so small he hadn't noticed. Synick would have—nothing got past him—but Faron wasn't quite as experienced. A large folded piece of stretched, yellowed leather lay in the bottom. It looked ancient. Gingerly he reached in and extricated it from its resting place. Each corner fit so well into the box it was difficult to remove. So perfect was the fit, Faron believed the box to be constructed specifically to fit this item—whatever it was.

It crackled as he pulled it out, dry and neglected. Carefully, he opened it in the dim light. It was a map—a regular map, he realized—not a treasure map, not a travel map, but an old, massive, decorative map that might once have hung on a self-important man's wall.

What was so important about such a mundane thing? Why hide it so carefully, and why would Jaru'tal keep the key on his person? What about these contents prompted the man to think of them when Sadagon's name was mentioned?

Frustration rising again, Faron studied the map. It was old. Borders were wrong, and cities that had long since been destroyed by the revolts of the Supernal Dusk were marked. How could this possibly be important? Tempted to fling it away in his anger, Faron turned it around and found a message on the back, written in a wide hand with faded black ink:

> *Praise to Lord Olsu, God of Judgement and Might. Long may He reign over all that is, was, and will be. May He grant us safe passage in life, as in death, and may He find this tithe pleasing.*

It sounded like a prayer, and the script was large and flowery. Underneath the incantation was another script, written smaller and only slightly less extravagantly:

> *May this gift reach our Lord in grace and serve as a reminder of His loyal servants in Empyrion, who wish only to serve and obey.*

Faron's eyes widened as he read. Had this map once been a gift to Olsu, the fallen god? How much would something like this even be worth?

He looked up to see more braziers had been lit, lighting up the night. The city shone like a thousand exploding stars, red flames reflecting off the bronze domes that topped most of the taller towers. How long would he be safe here?

He flipped the map back over. Hopefully, Jaru'tal had secured this relic for more than its monetary worth. There had to be *something* that would help him. As he studied the ancient leather, he noticed something he had never seen before.

To the north, far beyond Anveil—north higher even than the veil itself—was another city. That was impossible, of course. Nothing existed in the Frozen North. It was a land of horror and frost, controlled by the ever-present snowbeasts who prowled the eternal winter, always searching for meat to devour. Monsters and ice—that was what the north was—but despite this, a black dot representing a city lay beside a name. He squinted.

Kearth, it read. Faron frowned. He had never heard of a city named Kearth. Perhaps the map was simply incorrect. Several of the cities' names were misspelled, and Anveil was named Anvale. The map was so old it was completely obsolete. Similarly, there wasn't even a line depicting the Veil.

Above the mysterious city of Kearth, Faron noticed two more brushstrokes, each higher north and farther east than the last. Vam Bahr sat nestled in a range of artistically rendered mountains, clearly far above the Veil but still below the dot that represented the final city. The last dot lay below fine brushstrokes depicting an archaic temple, beside which was a delicately penned name:

Vam Aranath.

Blood rushed from his face as he paled in shock. Vam Aranath—the God City, City of Temples, City of Light—now known only as the Lost City.

Maps had been destroyed. Libraries had been burned.

For hundreds of years, even the name had been lost as the Twinborn Gods faded from the memories of those who survived them; but, here it was, the same name that Ulric had whispered to him that fateful night that felt so long ago, inked onto a page where it could not be destroyed. He stared hard, a lump in his throat. The Lost City, defying all reason by existing where nothing could—The Frozen North. Faron's heart sank through his stomach. That was not a place he could go.

A land of eternal winter, snowbeasts prowled the North, haunting the ice and snow. No man set foot above the Veil and lived—except Jaru'tal. In winter, he had come to Fayevew and dealt in an illegal slave market with the lives of children. Somehow, he had crossed not only the great desert but the vast plains and forests in the White, where winter beasts haunted and hunted. Years before, Sadagon himself had come to and disappeared from Alhalow in the dead of winter, taking Hadria with him.

Long had Faron wondered about that, and today still, he desperately questioned how it had been possible. His stomach turned. Winter beasts were not a foe he wished to contend with, or even witness from behind the tallest wall in the world, but still, it must be possible. Ulric had guessed at it, and here was further proof.

Vam Aranath lay in the North. No wonder it had been lost. The true wonder was how it had been built in the first place. How even would he find such a city, assuming he wasn't torn to shreds by hungry beasts? He peered back down at the map and located Aru'barrahk. It was called Aru'barow on the ancient leather but accurately depicted, as far as he could tell. The city was backed by an unfathomably high mountain to the north and an impassable desert to the south. He may not have Sadagon's ability to travel through the winter, and certainly not above the Veil, but he couldn't stay here.

He gazed into the darkness where he knew the great sands would be. Last time he had tried to cross it, he had been captured and eventually rescued by Harab'kun. Now, without a horse or any form of supplies, he wouldn't last three days in those sands. If he had more time, he could buy what he needed, but no one in this city would sell to a foreigner. With all the hundreds of men who milled about down below, he doubted he could steal what he needed either.

He realized there was no way to reach the edge of the desert alive. Beyond that, there was nothing but grasslands for weeks in his desired direction. No, he couldn't go that way.

He changed his view to the north mountain—the supposedly sacred seat of the grand palace of Aru'barrahk. It stretched high into the sky, blotting out stars and casting a shadow, even at night. That monolith was the literal edge of the desert. Beyond those peaks lay the empty plains, dancing the edge of the Frozen North, and just beyond that lay Anveil.

He had to go north. Vam Aranath was north. Hadria was north. They were beyond his reach above the Veil, but he could get closer, and maybe then, he'd know what to do. Anveil—he had to get to Anveil. Yet, he couldn't cross the sands alone. He ground his teeth, flicking his eyes between the mountain and the map.

Along the traditional route through the desert and plains, it would take nearly a month on horseback to reach the mountain city. That was far too long. Hadria had barely more than a month before their nameday, and by then, it would be too late—and he didn't have a horse. His eyes drifted to the great mountain of black against the cloudless night—a sheer, straight monolith of red and yellow sandstone below razor peaks of granite and caps of ice. Could he climb it? Looking back to the map, he estimated that if he did, he could make the trip to Anveil in ten days, maybe twelve.

The High Seat of Aru'barrahk was supposed to be impassible, but he wasn't sure if that was because of its sheerness or the fact that it was included in parts of their religion. Touching the great cliffs was considered blasphemy, he had learned, as much as killing a Kaor steed. He stared at the cliffs for a long time before setting his jaw.

It was the only way.

Escape from the Desert

The sky began to gray as stars winked out. The sun would rise soon. Had he been out all night already? It was long past time to go. He would visit Harab to collect his clothes and supplies, then—

He heard the low thud of wood against stone behind him and whirled around. Hundreds of feet in the air, atop the yellowish sandstone tower, a ladder had been put down, and it vibrated with the motion of climbing men. He swore and stuffed the purses and ancient map into his bag. He heard it crack like paper as it went in, and winced.

A man's head appeared above the edge of the ladder, veil unattached under his chin so Faron could see his face. His nose was large, and his cheek was scarred heavily on the left side.

"The pale demon!" he cried, spying Faron. "He is here!"

Cursing, he cast about. How had he not noticed the guards clambering onto the rooftops? Systematically, they had been flushing him out, and he had been pondering over a three-hundred-year-old map. The blue-garbed guard mounted the ladder and charged Faron. He made a split-second decision. To the north was the High Seat and the mountain he would have to cross to reach Hadria in time. To the east was Harab with all of Faron's supplies, including his warm leather clothes. He couldn't get to both while being chased, and every moment he spent in the city increased his risk.

He went North.

Faron turned and leaped over a small alleyway toward another rooftop. He sailed through the air and landed in a rough roll, springing out into a run. His ankle was feeling far better, he noticed. A contingent of bow-wielding men arrived on the rooftop behind the first scout and took aim. He spun to his right as arrows whistled through the air, some clattering off the rooftops and others sailing deeper into the gray morning.

He peered off the edge of the temple-like building at the street below. It, too, was busy with men. When would they give up searching for him? Just how important was the man he murdered? A bell behind him tolled a different chime, and he instantly knew what it meant. Down below, the men scrambled to attention, redoubling their search. A rooftop ahead of him spilled with men carrying bows, and he jumped for a higher building on the left. He gripped its edge and almost slipped as he slammed into the wall but managed to get his feet flat and push up, scurrying higher.

Let's see them follow me over that, he thought appreciatively. Men rushed toward the most recent of the frantically chiming bells as archers peered around edges of towers and distant rooftops, trying to figure out where he had gone. Few men alive could climb like a boy raised by psychotic thieves and a sister without a fear of heights. Over rooftops, he flew, back toward the richer district where he had been only a few hours earlier. He avoided rooftops lit with braziers or mounted by men as often as he could but was still shot at a few more times as he made his way to the High Seat and the mountain it was built into.

Eventually, when the sun was risen, he found himself before the sprawling grounds of the magnificent palace. He eyed the cliffs speculatively. Those walls *were* incredibly steep, with very few perceivable handholds. He wasn't able to spy out a potential path until about halfway up the structure's height, where the cliffs began to lean back and the palace with it.

No buildings came near the High Seat, except for the colonnade of gigantic black pillars supporting what Faron's mind could only perceive as a walkway, though with no way to reach it. Under these pillars were the lines of colorful tents that came together in the marketplace where he was bought by Jaru'tal. He would have to approach from down there, and it was full of guards. Men in scarlet armor and livery were scattered all around the massive courtyards, some going about their business, others clearly searching for someone—him, he didn't doubt. The city had gone on full alert.

His heart pounded with anxiety and frustration. Who was Jaru'tal that he commanded the mobilization of an entire city?

The rising of the sun presented a new challenge. How was he supposed to make his way past so many people when he was dressed all in black and they were looking specifically for him? The sweeping staircases that led up to the palace were littered with guards, all facing south. Frustrated, he searched for another path. Why would they even suspect he would come this way? Farther along the grounds and very near the palace were lines of great black statues of prancing horses, just off a raised platform and stairs. If he could climb one of them, perhaps he could jump up to the very base of the palace without alerting anyone. From there, he would find a path, or, failing that, climb the palace itself.

Setting off toward the mountain, Faron stayed a few rooftops in from the outer edge—both to keep a low profile and because there were archers on some of those roofs, scanning the crowd below. Hopefully, they wouldn't be a problem. As close to the mountain as he could get, Faron descended by leaping onto a domed roof below. He dropped to a balcony and finally lowered himself far enough to fall safely. There was a small but thick patch of fan-leaf trees here, giving shade and shelter from the eyes of sentinels.

Peering about the wooded area, he approached the last of the massive black statues. Facing away from the palace, it had one knee bent, raising a leg in the air. It almost appeared to be in a cantor, if not for how high the leg was raised. He examined it from below. There was no way he could scale the thing. It was tall, smooth, and slick looking. He frowned. Maybe he could get up if he climbed one of these strange, branchless trees?

He tried but slid down them with nothing to hold on to. Frustrated, he stabbed his knife into the porous looking wood and attempted to use it as a handle. If he could just get high enough, he could use the tree's natural bend to reach the top. It didn't work. The knife just pulled out chunks of the wood, refusing to stay properly imbedded.

How was it possible that he could scale a building but not a deformed, branchless tree? He wished he still had his rope. Abandoning all dignity, he wrapped his arms around the tree and hugged it with his knees. He managed to gain a foot of height by shimmying up it. He kicked down with his feet and gained some altitude. Slowly he slid his way up the trunk until he reached the bases of the giant, fern-like leaves and pulled himself on top.

"There," he groaned. The raised knee of the horse statue was nearly level with him now, still slightly elevated, and about seven feet away—a long jump for no running start. He examined the retaining wall that made the difference between the raised palace courtyard and the lower land beyond. Sure enough, it was smooth and painted. There would be no climbing it. Sighing, Faron resigned himself to the jump.

Springing from his crouch, he threw himself toward the statue. He landed on the leg, which was longer than he was tall, and stumbled, arms pinwheeling. A loud crack rang through the area as his weight bore down on the ancient statue. He half-seized, half-fell onto the long mane of the horse's hair, thankfully carved with plenty of detail, and held on for dear life as the leg fell away and shattered on the statue's base twenty or so feet below.

He cringed. They would have heard that halfway across the city. Getting his feet on the smooth black stone, he managed to pull himself up with his finger grip on the long, flowing mane and pulled himself up over the shoulder. No time to catch his breath, he balanced on the statue's back and hopped up onto the raised tail. Would this break too? He leaped as hard as he could, fingers stretching for the top of the sheer retaining wall.

He slammed into it with full force but managed to get his fingers and palms around the sharp edge of the end of the courtyard. Winded, he heaved and pulled himself up. The massive grounds of the palace were ornate and beautiful, but they provided no sort of cover. He was completely exposed near the base of the monstrous mountain that held the palace, and every single man and woman was staring directly at him, looks of horror on their faces. He got the impression he had just committed some form of blasphemy or other.

A scarlet group of guards, standing under a sculpted sandstone arch, immediately began yelling. *When is this going to stop!?* he screamed in his mind, breaking into a flat run. He made for the sheer mountain, searching frantically for a way up. He wouldn't make it, though, he already knew. These guards were fresh, and he was long since tired out. If he tried climbing now, they would just shoot him down, and that's if he even made it to the base.

Nonetheless, he ran. The mountain was smooth and near completely free of crevice for several hundred feet. Like a polished knife, it jutted into the sky, no serrations along the bottom of its blade.

He traded his bets for the palace itself. Unlike everything else in the wealthier district of the city, the palace was free of paint and had seemingly been so since its inception. Ancient cracks ran up the foundation, bricks the size of doorways crumbling around the edges, creating possible finger holds, but none were near the base. The first three levels of the palace looked to be carved from the mountain, smooth as polished stone with hardly a flaw—save for a crack. If he could reach the upper levels, maybe he could make it higher. From there, he might be able to get to the mountain, but there was no way to feasibly make that climb—not quickly, at least. He needed a way up.

There. He spied a tower made up of sandstone bricks, only separated from the main structure by a few feet. That could work. He dashed for it, scanning for the best way up while puffing hard, in desperate need of a rest.

The tower door opened. From its belly poured tens of

guards in red, bearing halberds, axes, and a few great curved swords. Faron stopped dead in his tracks as they pointed the weapons at him. He looked back the other way, where more guards were closing in. To the left, there was nothing but cliff. To the right was more open courtyard. He turned that way when more tower guards stepped in his path. He was surrounded.

Faron reached for his small knife. He wouldn't go down without a fight. One of the guards laughed.

"This is the one they are searching for?" he asked through a veil, humorously disbelieving. "The one called the Pale Demon? I see nothing demonic about him." The other guards snickered.

"Surrender to us or die," another declared. Faron flicked his eyes wildly, searching for an escape. There was *always* an escape. He didn't see it, though. He was in an unfamiliar place, surrounded, and exhausted. There was nothing left to do. He lifted his hands into the air.

"Taka," the same man commanded. "Take him to the tower to be hung from a gibbet. We must know why this infant killed the Dunestrider and how." Prodding his heaving chest with weapon points, they marched Faron toward the palace.

Faron, terrified and exhausted, allowed himself to be shoved along, breathing hard to catch his breath all the while. His head spun with fatigue and anxiety as they came upon the grand palace. He noticed, for the first time, a series of man-shaped iron cages suspended over the second or third floor and shivered. Is that where they would put him? A sort of claustrophobia gripped him as the yellow-brown walls swallowed them, cutting off any chance of escape.

If the palace appeared ancient on the outside, it was opulent beyond imagination on the inside. Large arches, rimmed in gold, outlined glassless windows where three men could stand abreast. Crystal chandeliers hung from intervals in the silver worked ceiling, and gems of all colors sparkled in the light that streamed through the open windows, glancing off the ceiling. How they kept thieves away, Faron had no idea. Synick would likely have a seizure seeing all this wealth un-plundered.

Spear points at his back, Faron ascended a winding staircase. He peered to his right as he passed a long hallway, just as ornate as the last. The windows on this level were smaller than the one below, but they had no panes, letting in whatever cooling wind might come. Faron itched to dash for the window and leap out, but he remembered the smooth exterior of the first three levels of the palace. If he jumped out now, there would be nothing to scale. Could he potentially climb the palace fast enough not to be shot down anyway? He didn't know. For now, he allowed them to shepherd him higher. There was no other choice.

With no prompting to stop, he climbed another flight of the ascending staircase, winding round in large spirals. Even here, he breathed deeply to regain his breath. The third level was nearly all white, every surface painted in a thick ceramic coat. They shoved him to the far end of the hallway, where an iron lever and set of gears protruded from the wall. He could see the gibbet through several open windows before he reached it. In sharp contrast to the rest of the palace, it was rusted, unadorned, and ugly. It seemed incongruous next to the image of wealth and power that the palace exuded, but it was anything but unused. Several more cages hung down from higher levels, some with clean skeletons inside.

"Open the cage," the commander ordered, stopping the

procession. A soldier with a curved sword at his hip reached out and fiddled with the great lock on the door. Faron took mental stock of the men around him. On his right, a man wielded a heavy club, lethal and devastating, but slow. Similarly, on his left, a man held an axe. The point of a spear touched his back as if the man wielding it knew what he was thinking. That was the most immediate threat. Others filed behind them, barring the way back, but Faron didn't want to go back. He had to go forward—for Hadria.

Without warning, Faron twisted and seized the haft of the spear in a backhanded grip, throwing his feet below the soldier holding it and pivoting with his hips. It threw him completely off balance. Faron yanked on the weapon with all his might, but the man didn't let go. He should have. Using his own weight against him, Faron shoved the spearpoint into the ribs of the swordsman working the gibbet. He screamed and fell from the open arch, and the spearmen fell with him, loosing a chorus of terrified screams.

The other guards leaped into motion, except one who abruptly stepped back, but it was too late. Faron jumped onto the windowsill, kicked off the wall for extra height, and leaped, twisting back toward the palace. For a single moment, he was weightless, suspended in the air outside the window—nothing below him and nothing above—until he seized the side of the cage and held on for dear life as it swung violently.

The two guards landed with a wet crunch. No time to think about what he'd done, only climb.

"Stop!" a guard called. "In the name of Akwin!" His voice was high and ragged, disturbed by the sudden death of his companions.

Blood pumping through his ears, Faron heaved and pulled

himself up until he was standing on the anchor that pinned the gibbet to the wall. The line of painted stone ended here, replaced by ancient, weathered, sandstone bricks. He jammed his fingers in the large cracks at the corners and pulled himself up as only a thief could.

Now free of the window, he risked a glance below. The men he'd thrown to their deaths lay in dark pools of blood. Other armed men, who stood by massive columns, looked up from the bodies and directly at Faron. They rushed inside with a vengeance. From inside, he heard another voice.

"He touches sacred stone!" a man shrieked. "Kill him! Kill the pale demon!"

Another man looked up through the window, a spear in his hand. He jabbed it onehanded at Faron, but he managed to shy to the side just in time to deliver a swift kick to the shaft. It tore from the man's hands and fell to the grounds below. Faron hoped it fell on someone.

"Kill him!" he heard the voice scream again. "Akwin demands blood on the stones defiled!"

Leaping up, Faron found sure footing in the ancient bricks. Another man leaned out with a bow, but Faron strafed along the massive palace's rounded wall toward an adjacent tower, making the angle nearly impossible.

The voice was more panicked than before. "Do not strike the stone!" The arrow loosed, and Faron felt a red-hot tearing in his arm, but it whistled past. Looking back, he saw a long rip in the black cloth, blood seeping out. He had taken off skin above the elbow, perhaps slightly more. Grinding his teeth, Faron scaled higher. His arm still worked, thank the dead gods.

The bronze dome of a tower came level with his back as he

climbed, and he pushed off, landing on the short flat area at the base. The metal was hot. Faron half dodged, half stumbled, as another arrow buzzed past him on the bronze-capped tower, stained green with patina. He rounded it to put something between him and the bowman.

He heard screams and cries as women below noticed him on their sacred palace—or maybe they finally noticed the two bodies on the stone. Guards turned and frantically began pouring into the large arches. One man raised a crossbow and fired a bolt at him. Faron stepped to the side but didn't need to. It struck the sandstone under his feet. It was a long shot from the courtyard below. He heard bits of stone shatter and pelt the underside of the dome on which he stood.

To his shock, another man, perhaps his captain, unsheathed a curved dagger and buried it in the archer's back. Faron could hear him cry out as he writhed on the ground below. They truly believed that this palace and mountain were sacred, didn't they? Shaking off the surprise, Faron turned, took a step back, and ran for a shorter tower, the base of which jutted out from the second level. If it kept them from shooting more aggressively, he would desecrate their precious stones and piss on them too. He leaped off the edge and heard the sound of bowstrings.

Tossing his head to the side, he found more guards aiming through the windows. They were waiting for him. Three arrows split the air around him, one less than a hand's width from his neck. They screamed past. Faron landed hard against the tower dome and rolled quickly to the far side. Flustered, he stopped in its relative safety. That had been close. Faron didn't know anyone that could have made that shot, but these archers had gotten very near to it. They were good.

He would have to be smarter. Peering over the dome, Faron inspected the palace wall. Maybe fifteen feet to his left, a far larger tower rose into the air, connected by a corner to the palace itself down to the base. It was another staircase, just like the one he'd ascended with his armed guards. He spied a window in the rounded stones, and an idea struck him. He could not climb to the top through this hail of arrows. He could, however, climb from the inside.

Sticking his head around the corner and then whipping it back, Faron braced as arrows punctured the air where he had just been. Good. As quick as he could, he peeked around the rounded corner, hoping no other archers were waiting for him to mess up. They were nocking new arrows. He wouldn't give them the chance to draw.

Taking a running step, Faron jumped back toward the palace and straight into an archer-occupied window on the fourth level. The man looked shocked to see Faron flying toward him and tried to get his bow up in time, but he wasn't fast enough. Faron slammed into him with a knee to the chest and elbow to the throat. *He would survive that*, Faron thought. *Probably*. The other archers were barely pulling in from windows as he rolled, the man's body absorbing most of his impact. Fast as a lynx, he hopped around the corner and darted up the massive spiral staircase, hoping to the dead gods that there would be no guards already there to stop him.

Though he could hear half a battalion filing up the stairs from below, he ran into no one as he took the steps three at a time. One level he passed, then another, and another until he came to the top of the tower. It let out on a sunny, open rooftop, where two guards stood sentinel to the tower entrance. Faron, though, came up from behind them.

Not slowing down, he leaped with all his force and seized the necks of both unsuspecting guards, throwing all his weight into them. He swung his legs forward for extra momentum. Their helmeted heads smashed into the stone with satisfying force, and Faron landed on his backside.

Not bothering to check on the status of the two men, he jumped back up and ran across the patio. They may not have been knocked unconscious from his attack, but they wouldn't be getting up too soon either. He heard swearing as a woman in blue silk noticed him. She didn't try to stop him, so he just ran right past.

From here, the palace ascended in tiered terraces, matching the subtle curve of the mountain. All that was left was to ascend these terraces, and he would reach it. He trembled with exhaustion but was nearly there. A small pair of short towers containing spiral staircases stood against the wall of each terrace, and Faron fled up them as quickly as his shaking legs would allow.

Men streamed onto the open rooftop below, but thankfully, Faron could see no more guards ahead. Good. He was surviving purely off adrenaline now, and it would run out. He had to get away.

His lead dwindling, Faron stumbled up one terrace and then the next. His breathing came hard and ragged, and his limbs were leaden; but finally, he approached the last obstacle. There was no tower at the end of this terrace, only a slightly reclined wall made of the same yellowish sandstone as the mountain. He looked back. There was barely one platform between him and his would-be killers now.

Puffing hot air in and out, Faron braced himself for another exertion and ran straight for the wall. With its shallow angle, he made four vertical steps before losing momentum and throwing his arms as high as they could reach. The very tips of his fingers clasped around a hard edge, and he dangled there for a long moment. His lungs felt wet and cold.

A line of scarlet men began filing from the dark alcove behind, and one man leveled a crossbow. Wheezing, Faron got one knee under himself and pushed, the other leg dangling and exposed to the men below. He rolled forward instead of standing and pulled it away as fast as possible. Good thing, too, as he heard metal striking stone where his leg had just been. Would that man die for touching the temple, too? Or did different rules apply on the inside terraces?

He didn't stay to find out. Finally, the magnificent cliffs stretched above him, an unbelievably massive wall of stone in a sea of sand. The top appeared miles away, extending into the sky, but he didn't need to get to the top. He only needed to reach the cracks where the other mountains split apart, hopefully leading to the edge of the great winter north.

Here, at the crest of the High Seat of Aru'barrahk, Faron saw the sacred stone nestled up against the palace. It was pocked with strange aeolian holes and angled forward ever so slightly. Trapped in a cage of failing muscles, Faron stared up at the great cliffs with a feeling of impending dread. He had made it, but there were no crevices he might hide in, no outcroppings where he might climb without fear of arrows, at least, not for a long-distance upward.

Men threw themselves at the retaining wall, attempting to follow him. None made it over just yet, weighed down by weapons and armor, but they would sooner than later.

With a grimace, Faron stood to his full height. If it was a choice between being arrow-shot in the back or ran through with a scimitar, there was no choice at all.

As the cacophony of men rose from the lower terrace, Faron found footing in the large stone holes that marred the cliff for a hundred feet up and a thousand feet wide. He didn't know how they had been formed, and he didn't care. They could be climbed.

Automatically, and with an increased sense of desperation, Faron attacked the wall with all the fervor he still possessed. There was a crevice up above—a crevice he could hide himself in and finally escape this feverish mob that pursued him. He only had to reach it. Gripping the easy handholds, he rose hand over hand, climbing a ladder forged by cruel gods.

One man ascended the edge of the final terrace, then another, then four more. They seemed to have found something to climb. Faron sensed their eyes on him and tried to redouble his efforts but couldn't go any faster. He was spent—used up. He heard anxious voices decrying his blasphemy of touching their sacred mountain. He climbed, but the crevice was too far.

Stealing glances as his body shifted from one ledge to another, Faron saw the men below with shortbows, and his heart dropped. He had held out hope that they wouldn't dare shoot at the mountain, but he had been mistaken.

Grimacing so hard that his face pulled into a sneer, Faron threw himself higher. Panic shook him, but he couldn't be made to go any faster.

Desperate, he climbed, fighting for every inch of the nearly vertical surface, but he wasn't going to make it. In plain view of the near army below, he was going to be picked off like a fly. He heard the creaking of oiled wood and, gasping, lunged higher and missed his handhold.

Choking on his own scream, Faron clung to the cliff with one hand and spun about, back slamming into the wall. Consumed with panic, he flailed wildly as his fingers began to slip, then, somehow, managed to get something solid underfoot. Turned about and immobilized, Faron watched as a single archer flexed a bow, the nocked arrow trained straight at his heart.

"No!" he screamed, but it came out as a whimper. Blood pounded in his ears. It couldn't end like this, not after he'd come so far.

Despite his wild climb, he was close enough to the men to read the anxiety in their stances and hear the words from their lips.

"If you miss," one man warned, "it will be your blood to atone."

"I won't," the archer replied, pulling the string to its full draw.

A single second stretched into a thousand as Faron stared into the veiled gaze of his killer. He could see the red fabric shiver with each puff of breath—a quick breath in and a long breath out—the kind to stabilize a careful shot.

Faron closed his eyes.

"Stop!" a familiar voice yelled.

Surprised, all eyes turned on the newcomer. Faron's eyes fluttered open to see yet another man in the ubiquitous red of the palace guard, panting hard with hands on knees.

"A message… from the king," the man said between breaths. He held out a white scroll in one hand. "Let him go. Do not sully the mountain with his blood."

The archer lowered his bow, and breath filled Faron's lungs.

Twenty questioning voices tripped over each other, each

demanding answers, but they were silenced when the messenger removed his scarlet veil. Shocked, Faron recognized the man behind it: Harab'kun.

"Akwin favors the strong," he said with a crooked smile.

Smiling himself, Faron turned around and finished the climb. He felt a strange sense of spectation as the men below watched him defile their sacred mountain, unable to give chase without touching the stones themselves and unable to shoot without disobeying their king. They couldn't know that Harab was lying, just as they didn't know he'd slip away the moment he got his veil back on his face.

Thank you, Harab'kun, Faron thought as he climbed. *I'll come back someday. I promise. I'll repay you for this—somehow.* Renewed, Faron climbed and climbed until he rose out of bowshot and out of sight entirely. Finally, mounting a ridge, he pulled himself up between the crevice of two splintered peaks and crawled out into a narrow canyon.

He had done it. He had done what he set out to do. Jaru'tal was dead, and, in the end, he had led Faron to the Lost City.

Finally, he knew where Sadagon was hiding. Finally, he knew where Hadria was being kept. Finally, he had escaped the desert.

"I'm coming for you," he whispered to Hadria and Sadagon both.

A Cage of Frozen Metal

F aron's body had a difficult time adjusting from the shock of extreme heat to the frigid cold of the mountain passes. The cloth wrapped around him was intended to ward off the sun, despite being dyed black to meld with the shadows. In any case, it did a poor job of keeping him warm in the narrow passes of the silent mountain.

After long hours climbing through the razor cliffs and over sudden, seemingly endless, drops, Faron emerged at the other end of the mountains and into the vast, barren plains before the Winter Veil.

Fewer than fifty miles to the north, a stark line of white snow began, marking the end of the known world. Beyond that line—the Veil, it was called—no man in living memory had ever set foot and lived, except apparently Jaru'tal and an entire city lost to the ages.

His head rang to think about it. The idea of a city existing in the Frozen North among monsters shattered his previous understanding of the world. Snowbeasts were larger, stronger, meaner, and smarter than their non-white counterparts. It was said they were spawned by pure evil in the days before the Supernal Dusk. They were a manifestation of hatred and lust, evil and murderous rage. How was it possible for men to live among them? How did Jaru'tal traverse the White unknown and return alive? It made his head hurt.

Sitting under the stormy gray clouds, Faron tenderly opened the ancient map. A long tear had formed down the middle, no doubt from when he had shoved it in the bag the night before. Despite its age, the thing was detailed. The desert city bore a different name, but he found it all the same. Aru'barow, it was called in times of old, at least by those who made the map.

To the northeast lay the black point that resembled the Lost City. He peered out over the small hills of the plains and across the Winter Veil. Through snow and mountains and fields of ice, this path would take him—through the belly of hell, amid the very monsters who haunted his childhood dreams, who lusted to rip and tear his flesh.

Dread knotted his stomach. This path would take him to his death. His sling felt uncomfortably light on his shoulder. It held no food, water, tinderbox, clothing, or tools of any kind. In the narrow passes behind him, he had found trickles of water running down the stone and drank his fill, but was already thirsty again—and exhausted. All night he had run and jumped over the rooftops, and sleep called for him despite the cold, despite his dimly growing hunger, despite his exuberance at finally knowing where Hadria really was, despite everything.

He looked back at the map. If he went straight to the northeast, he estimated ten to fifteen days travel to Vam Aranath. Looking up, he sighed. There would be no use going straight north. He would die from starvation or the cold before the terrors above the Veil even had to lick their chops at him. Confirming what he already knew he had to do, he gauged roughly ten days to Anveil, maybe eleven. There he could find supplies and, with any luck, form a plan. He counted down the days. If he judged correctly, and if the Lost City was really there, that would put him ten days ahead of Hadria's nameday. He was going to make it.

Stowing the map and laying the pack under his head, Faron folded his arm and promptly fell asleep. He had run through the night, climbed through the morning, and was in desperate need of rest. An hour or two wouldn't be likely to make a difference anymore. None would follow from the mountain pass—he was almost certain—and it would take more than a week or two on horseback to reach him by traditional methods.

Open land before him, towering mountains behind, and tall, dark clouds above, Faron lay on the cold hard ground and fell into a deep sleep.

* * *

Everything was cold and gray. Deep shadow swallowed anything that wasn't near the one large fire that burned in the center of the room. The youngest children occupied cages in those spots, their fragile forms unable to withstand the biting cold farther out. Thin, mottled glass windows let in a stream of weak moonlight, falling through cold, rough iron onto the huddled form of a pathetic girl—*Hadria.*

She shivered in a gown that hardly covered her back and jumped whenever she leaned far enough to touch the icy bars of her cage. The pale light fell across long, deep scars that protruded from her back where she had been whipped, once flawless skin deeply mottled and bruised from beatings.

The others fared no better. A hundred feet across, the room contained hundreds of children—boys, girls, near infants, and teenagers. Some had iron shackles attached to their ankles, skin burning from the intense cold of the metal. Some cried openly. Always there was the persistent sound of weeping. Others sniffled from memories of a family, their impending doom, or simply from the cold—he didn't know—but it came from nearly every corner.

The loud, hateful sound of metal scraping against metal filled the dungeon, and weak orange light fell in through a door on unoiled hinges. The youngest children pushed themselves to the back of their cages, frozen bars stinging their bare skin, but barely noticed anymore as they pushed themselves away from the noise. The older youth almost seemed not to notice but stared harder at the ground, as if intent on not seeing the inevitable.

Iron shod boots crushed the cobbled stone floor as a dark, armored figure approached a cage and pointed with deadly authority. Smaller, weaker figures garbed in a white that somehow seemed to radiate blackness rushed forward and pulled a terrified boy from a cell. He hardly even resisted as he was torn from his prison, too weak to do anything but obey. Slowly he was half dragged, half led back into the open doorway, where he cast a long shadow.

He was pulled from view, and the rest of the children seemed to relax, guiltily. Even Hadria's shoulders dropped. Faron tried to reach out to her but was as mobile as a statue. He tried to call out to comfort her, to tell her he was coming, when a scream rang through the still-open door: a scream of terror, a scream of a dying child. Chills rushed down his spine. After a moment, the shadow-cloaked figure returned, a cup to his mouth, long red streaks leaving beaded lines down his otherwise indiscernible face. He emptied the silver goblet.

"Another," he demanded, deep voice shaking the room. His eyes fell on Hadria, and he pointed with a grin. He stepped forward into the moonlight that ensconced her cage. White hair fell upon large square shoulders, an aged jaw covered in blood under shock blue eyes—Sadagon.

"Bring me her."

The Winter Veil

Faron awoke, shivering, both in body and mind. His and Hadria's nameday was approaching—their eighteenth year. He tallied up the days again—a month and a week. That's all the time she had left. If it took ten days to reach Anveil and another fifteen to the Lost City, he would be cutting it very close, and that was assuming he could somehow pass the veil. There was the added problem of his complete lack of food, water, and warmth. He'd left his blacks, crossbow, and supplies with Harab, intending to retrieve them before he completely botched the job with Jaru'tal.

Shaking his head, Faron stood and peered to the north. It was growing dark. Half the day he had slept away, and, cold to the bone, he felt as if he had only just nodded off. Lightning ripped through the sky, carving light and noise through the air. Had that been what woke him? He shivered as a raindrop struck his cheek, just under one eye. He touched it softly and considered the sky. It was ominous—ominous and dark.

He would get no further travel done tonight, he decided. Stomach grumbling, he backtracked into the mountain and found an overhang that might offer a modicum of shelter from the rain. It began in the north, not as rain but as snow.

He could see the storms through the narrow, near-vertical pass that let out toward the Winter Veil. Thick heavy drifts, barely noticeable because of the distance, that blanketed the world in the venom of winter. Closer, the clouds shed rain, and they did it with an abandon.

Uncomfortable and cold under his slanted overhang, Faron closed his eyes and hoped for better dreams. At least he was dry.

Faron woke that morning with the sun as a ray of light broke from the dappled sky and struck his face. It's warming effect was enough to rouse him from an uncomfortable sleep with even less comforting dreams.

Counting his nap throughout half the day yesterday and the long night, Faron doubted he had slept so long in his life. He didn't begrudge himself the reprieve, though. The past day and night were long and full of exertion, and the night before that had been filled with hard mining in the dark. His limbs were sore from their long punishment and stillness in the cold. As his stomach grumbled, he realized he hadn't eaten in just as long, except a half loaf of bread Harab had given him before returning to Jaru'tal's residence.

In the excitement of his escape, Faron had been able to mostly forget about his tricep being skinned by an arrowhead, but it ached horribly now. He had managed to bandage it on his easy journey through the narrow pass. These wrapping desert clothes proved incredibly useful for creating makeshift bandages. He had simply unraveled the length of long cloth that served as his sleeve and wrapped it again, but far tighter on the wound. He could feel scabs separating as his arm moved, and blood seeping through the cracks, but the wound was relatively small, considering. He would manage.

He pushed himself into a sitting position and hopped down from his small, sloping shelter. The rain had created great floods that receded into small trickling rivers where his tiny footpath had been, and he didn't bother trying to avoid them. Water splashed on the pigskin boots and trickled through the laces, though, not much. The clouds overhead were still thick and gray but not nearly so threatening as before. It must have stopped raining sometime in the night.

Once again, he left the mouth of the thin mountain pass and watched as the miniature river sloped away to the left. Curious, he peered off in that direction and spotted a hint of green foliage. Stomach grumbling, he followed the small river and found, to his surprise, a hillside covered in a dense, low growing bush. They were laden with blueberries.

Faron laughed to himself and bent down, picking a large round berry coated with rain or morning dew. It nearly burst in his hand; it was so ripe. He popped it in his mouth and experienced sweetness like he hadn't in months. Sweet and tart together, the berry overwhelmed his senses, and his eyes widened in delight. Pulling on a finger, he tugged off his black gloves and set about feasting on the natural banquet laid out before him.

After he had nearly eaten himself sick, Faron emptied the casket into his bag and filled it to the brim with berries. He locked it to make sure none would fall out and ruin the ancient map.

Pleased with himself for the fortuitous find and a good start to his journey, Faron picked an oversized handful of even more berries, knowing he probably couldn't fit them, and snacked on them as he made his way west, sticking to the base of the great range of mountains. He was so content that he almost forgot about the Veil for a while—almost.

From his position at the base of the mountain, which wasn't nearly so tall from this side, he could spy where the land became white. Was it closer than yesterday? Towering mountains made small by the distance leaned out in rough, jagged peaks, white and deadly like a gate of teeth. As terrifying as it and the denizens who surely lay just beyond that line were, the beauty and danger of it held his attention and gaze.

As he walked in the growing sun, Faron's limbs loosened and gave up their protests, and the farther he descended from the peaks, the warmer it became. The land passed by in unbroken monotony, and so did the day.

With the setting of the sun came a chilled wind from the north, and with it, anxiety of what followed the cold. He slept only a few hours before finally giving up and walking through the night.

When morning came, he curled down on a flat rock and fell asleep, warming his aching bones in the sun. A few hours later, he was roused by the sound of his empty stomach. He continued on, eating a few berries from his small supply.

He found enough pools in rocks or streams to stay more or less hydrated, which was a blessing considering his lack of a waterskin, but hunger was still a very real problem. He could travel for a few days like this—he knew from unfortunate experience—but would need something more to sustain him soon.

That afternoon, in the dwindling light, he found the familiar tall and thin leaves of a carrot and tugged it out of the ground. Thin and wiry, it tasted more like a muddy root than a carrot, but he choked it down anyway. It wasn't enough. Frustrated that there had been only one carrot and not a patch, he ate a few more berries and walked until sunset. He was lucky enough to find a cave owned only by a family of red foxes who he scared out, claiming the shelter for himself before the clouds began to drench the earth again. Hunger clawed his belly through the night, growling worse than a cave bear, but he slept relatively well considering. The cave kept him dry and warmer than he had a right to expect while wearing nothing but thin black linen.

When morning came, the rain continued, showing no intention of breaking or letting up. Concerned, Faron peered from the cave. The small mounds that sloped toward the Veil ran with hundreds of tiny rivers—thousands even—all in the general direction of north.

He cast about, concerned. He had no way to protect himself from this weather and could catch cold sickness if he wasn't dry come night time, but at the same time, Hadria's nameday approached. He rammed a tongue to a cheek, pondering his predicament. He could continue on, risking hypothermia, or spend a day waiting out the storm. *I can't find Hadria if I'm dead*, he argued to himself. He decided to wait for a break in the storm. He needed to eat, though.

Freeing his arms from their wrappings, especially careful around his arrow wound, he removed his shirt and deposited it on a stone shelf. It would serve to keep it dry.

Bare-chested, he stepped from the small cave and into the rain. It wasn't as large of a downpour as the kind they had back in Alhalow, but the drops were cold—*very* cold. He shivered and hunted for more of the blueberry bushes. To his pleasure, he actually managed to find one, but it was alone and only provided a handful of berries. He also found a patch of wild onions which, to his disappointment, were long overripe and rotting inside their own paper skin.

Hungry and cold, he brought them back to his cave anyway. He would eat what he could. He turned to survey the small hills again for anything green he might have missed when he noticed something wrong about the expansive north before him. It seemed... bigger, somehow.

In a flash, it hit him. It *was* getting bigger. Rainstorms here were snowstorms there, and judging from how fast the line was moving, it would be snowing here soon too. Panic drove a stake into his heart as he rushed back to the cave, throwing the small onion bulbs into his bag.

Flicking the water off himself with numbed fingers, he didn't wait to dry properly, instead, wrapping himself quickly with his shirt. He would be soaked soon anyway. Dressed, he leaped from the cave and ran more than walked, heading west.

How could the North be expanding already? It would barely be late summer back home. He knew that Anveil's summer was short, but it couldn't possibly be *this* short. It wasn't even the month of Auger yet, and Anveil's spring didn't come until Maia—three months of spring and summer before winter came again? Being the farthest northern city, Anveil was the first to be swallowed by the Veil and the last to be freed from it, but even this far north, that kind of timeframe wasn't possible. Something was wrong. Somehow, winter was coming more than a month early, and soon it would swallow him.

He cursed himself as he ran, stomach growling. How could he have been so foolish, wasting a day in the shelter of a cave? Not only was Hadria's eighteenth year fast approaching, but the Veil was falling. He had to make it to Anveil before that happened, or they would both die.

Jaws of the Veil

The rain didn't let up. Well into the evening and night, it descended. The thick clouds blocked light from the moon and stars alike, and Faron stumbled in the dark. He cursed himself for not bringing along a lantern or at least a candle to see by. While he was wishing, he missed his leathers—and his horse for that matter. Blind, cold, and slow, Faron cursed the rain and the clouds that brought it, stubbing his toes against rock after rock in the endless night. He crawled through the dark, too wet and cold to sleep, too afraid to stop until finally, the rain turned to a drizzle as the sky grayed with the morning sun.

Rays broke the clouds on the third morning from Aru'bar-rahk, and Faron, shivering and depressed, crawled onto a flat patch of stone, waiting for the sun to warm him. The clouds departed, and he found rest for a few blissful hours as the sun dried his clothes, though he still shivered, even while warm.

As the danger of the storm passed, Faron eyed the snowline. It *was* approaching. His original estimate of fifty miles had been shortened to thirty, maybe twenty-five. He could identify patches of trees that only the day before had been untouched by the White, which now lay swallowed in its bowels. Snowbeasts were in there.

He shivered again and not from the cold. It was a race against time and not a fair one. Not for the first time, he thought of Onyx and how she had been senselessly slaughtered. It brought red to his cheeks to consider still. Through fire and adversity, she had carried him nobly and even helped keep him warm at times. He longed for her warmth and speed now.

The fourth day passed without rain and without food—so did the fifth. His supply of berries had long since depleted, and the Winter Veil crept closer, mile by mile. The cold was a constant reminder of its impending arrival. That, more than anything, gave Faron the energy he needed to continue his flight.

On the morning of the sixth day, Faron woke nearly at noon. The sun was high, and he knew he had long overslept, but his body was exhausted. He couldn't maintain this pace, he knew, but he rose anyway and continued on. Blessedly, only an hour later, he found another patch of blueberries like the ones by the mountain pass as well as a ring of black mushrooms he recognized from back home. He ate those all at once. For two hours, he gorged himself on mushrooms and berries, then loaded up his entire bag with the fruit, folding the map smaller and putting it in a pocket with the gems, cracks be damned.

Even after eating himself sick, it was difficult to feel like he'd gotten enough, especially after being so hungry for nearly a week straight, but he managed it eventually. Faron doubted one person had ever consumed so many blueberries at once before, and even though they caused his stomach to grumble, they sustained him.

They were all he had to eat until the eleventh day. They ran out on the ninth. After so many days and so many miles, Faron's soft leather shoes had finally worn through. A particularly sharp rock had split his left sole open the previous night, but now the soles were more hole than leather. It wasn't long before he left a trail of blood everywhere he stepped.

The rain picked up that morning with bigger, colder drops than before. They almost felt like hail balls, except they clung to his skin with stubborn tenacity. That wasn't the worst of it, though—not by far. The Veil was nearly upon him. By now, it was only ten miles off, maybe less. It chilled Faron to the bone, both figuratively and literally. He briefly considered veering to the left to avoid the snowline as long as possible but decided against it. The straightest line was the fastest one, and Anveil was straight ahead, according to the archaic map. He would race the snow. It was a race he was losing.

He found no food that day—again. He barely thought anymore. He didn't smile when he stumbled into a raspberry bush the day before, though it had proven empty. He didn't occupy the day with thought. His mind had room for only two things: *keep moving* and *winter.*

That night he found a great lonely pine. Massive both in height and diameter, it sheltered him from the worst of the rain. At the base of that tree, he found a cluster of furry looking mushrooms, pure white like the evil that raced him. He swallowed them greedily, then tried to get a few hours of sleep, though he was still hungry and miserable and starving; but, he heard an evil, hungry, howling. It pierced his very soul. A snow wolf, he had no doubt. He would find no sleep, so instead, he walked through the rain and night.

The next day the snow had nearly overcome him. He shoved down his panic and continued faster, finding the energy from sheer desperation. He resisted the urge to turn and flee south.

It would buy him very little time, and it would be time only to starve. Anveil was near. He just had to go a little faster.

As he walked, he spotted a white patch of fur dash from behind a bush, and nearly swallowed his heart. Fumbling, he tore at his knife in its sheath, brandishing it pathetically. It was a rabbit. It ran from one bush to another, fearing what he might be.

Cocking his arm back, Faron threw the knife. With a squeal, he heard the blade strike flesh, and the animal took one failing leap away from the bush, then fell over, kicking softly. Hardly sparing a thought in the way of thanks or disgust, Faron stooped and broke the rabbit's neck.

How was he to cook it, part of him wondered? He mocked himself. If he were capable of cooking, he wouldn't be so damn cold. The obvious answer was not to cook it. He ripped the pelt away and sliced off the portions of the whitish meat that looked edible.

Like an animal, he devoured it raw, cramming his mouth as quickly as he could. He sliced his finger in his rush, but it didn't matter. He was starving. He cut off as much of the pelt as possible, time being of the essence, and it came away surprisingly easily. He wrapped it fur side down around his neck and used a bone to pin it in place. Instantly he felt it ward off the cold, if only slightly. His fingers and toes felt frozen, and his nose was flaking skin where the cold burned him.

A howl split the air, and he rose a feral head in that direction. He had wasted too much time. Fist full of raw strips of meat, he took off to the west. Anveil had to be near—it *had* to be. The disgusting meal disappeared quickly, leaving him hungry again, though he did feel more human afterward and was slightly revolted by what he'd done.

Within the hour, the rain turned to snow. Faron watched as the first, then a thousand flakes fell from the sky, landing on the ground. He panicked. Unsheathing his knife, he saw visions of snow wolves and bears feasting on his corpse. He ran, sprinting toward what he hoped was salvation. Over every crest, he looked hopefully for city walls or towers, only to have those hopes dashed to pieces each time.

Anveil was nowhere to be seen.

For hours he ran—long past winded, long past exhausted. He ran anyway. He ran for his life and for Hadria's life, and in a way, for Sadagon's life so he might take it himself. Before long, the snow began to stick, and the world was white.

If Faron had been panicked before, he was feral now. With every step, he left a bleeding footprint, a trail that led hunters right to him. Over rocks and bushes and tundra, he fled, searching desperately for safety. The light was failing. Through storm clouds and sheets of white as deadly as any blade, he could see the pale sun cresting the horizon.

Mounting another of the endless hills, Faron searched the horizon. It was difficult to see through the dimness and the snow, but he thought he saw the vague outline of a lonely mountain ahead. Breathing hard, he pushed forward when he heard a deep-throated growl not three feet away. Still clutching his knife, Faron wheeled around and found himself face to face with a snow wolf.

Teeth exposed in a rictus growl, the beast rose to mid-chest, even, with its shoulders hunched, ready to pounce. Its mane was the purest white, with two lines of gray that started on either side of its jaw and streaked down until they faded back to white. Its muzzle was red with the blood of its dinner—a gray rabbit, half-consumed on the ground.

Faron's heart turned to ice. The red eyes of the monster pierced into his very soul and petrified him with fear. He had seen visions of this beast ripping and tearing at his sister every night for five years. It had been a lie, he knew now, but it didn't make the fear any less real. He trembled, not from the cold. With a single step that showed both litheness and grace, it turned its attention away from the rabbit. Faron was the larger meal.

Maybe if he backed up, it would decide he wasn't worth the fight? He took a slow step backward, and the wolf released an angry snarl. He stopped, breath catching in his throat. What was he supposed to do? Should he attack and maybe scare it away? Everyone said snow wolves didn't get scared. Should he wait for it to attack? Should he run? Heart skipping beats in his chest, he stood petrified with fear and indecision.

He didn't have to wait long.

With a snarl, it leaped, and instinct took over. Twirling to the side, Faron jumped out of the way and sunk his small knife into its side, hopefully hitting a lung. The blade was nearly ripped from his grip as the monster sailed past, but he held on. It whimpered furiously as it hit the ground. Now, it was time for Faron to act.

Screaming at the top of his lungs, he charged the beast, thrusting with his blade. It dodged out of the way. It was incredibly fast. Following through with his missed attack, he spun, seizing a fist-sized triangular rock from the ground and throwing it with all his might. Despite being only a few feet away, he missed his mark, but it still smashed into the wolf's side. He swung again, and the beast dodged away. It knew he could hurt it.

Panting, Faron whispered, "Yeah, I have teeth of my own."

A normal wolf might have run away, but this was no ordinary wolf. It sensed an opportunity and lunged forward, teeth snapping. Faron jumped backward, but the wolf followed through, and he fell flat on his back.

Merciless in its attack, it grabbed hold of Faron's boot in a powerful bite. He felt its teeth digging into his flesh. Screaming, he yanked hard, and his foot came out of the shoe, long streaks already dripping blood from where teeth had gouged out his skin. For a moment, the animal seemed confused about how his foot came off so easily and how he still had that foot. Faron, though, in that moment, felt he understood the creature.

In a way, it was much like him. Wolves fought and killed animals much stronger or larger than themselves, as he did, not because they were faster or smarter, but because they were cruel. Like the wolf, Faron fought and survived where others wouldn't because he took *every* opportunity, no matter how unfair or dishonorable. When Jakal was downed on hands and knees, Faron broke his bones. When Garad was weak and defenseless, Faron attacked. When Jaru'tal took him into his home, he poisoned him. The wolf was the same—merciless. In that moment, he knew that he and the wolf were very alike, and he knew how to kill it.

The snowbeast dropped the empty boot, eyeing him warily, more than a little angry. As Faron scrambled back to his feet, he reached into his sack and grabbed the wooden casket. There being nothing in it to protect, it had been left unlocked and open. He put his fist in the box and, making a show of dropping his guard, Faron sat.

The wolf lunged at him, jaws open wide, almost big enough

to close around his head completely. Blood pounding in his ears, Faron leaped forward to meet the wolf and, with a punch as powerful as he could muster, shoved the box into its jaws.

Deep into his mouth, he forced the box as the wolf plowed into him, knocking him back again onto his back. Tooth punctured metal and wood, but the box held.

Pinned under the monster with one hand stuck in its maw, Faron plunged the short knife into the dog's chest—once, twice, three times, five times. Boiling hot blood spurted from its wounds, and it tried to leap away, but its teeth were too deeply embedded. Faron wouldn't let him go. It shook its head, trying to get away, but Faron, like the wolf, took every advantage. With a thrust, he sunk the blade into its throat, then again, and again. Sickening gurgling noises escaped out of the slits in the monster's esophagus, along with blood so hot it physically burned as it touched his skin. He didn't care though. Pinning the snow wolf close, he got his arm around the beast's leg and stabbed into its side three times as it howled, shooting more blood through its destroyed neck.

Finally, Faron got the proper angle and stabbed the wolf through the eye. It fell limp on his lap, dead.

Soaked in steaming blood, Faron shoved the wolf off of himself. It must have weighed as much as he did, if not more. Through his elation and adrenaline, two things tried to make their way to the front of his mind: surely, more would be coming, and the pelt—it was familiar.

Puzzled, he studied the coat. He had seen snow wolves from a distance before, but something felt similar about the fur—something... else.

And then it hit him.

The cloak worn by Sadagon on the night of the fire and the

cloak in Jaru'tal's possession were the pelts of snow wolves. In a flash of understanding, Faron dropped the knife, and it all made sense. The way they traveled through the winter—the north, even—was the white fur they wore on their back.

Could it truly be so simple? Could such an unassuming thing be kept secret from the entire world? A snowbeast's fur was said to be riddled with disease, dangerous to any who touched it and highly contagious, yet Jaru'tal had owned a white cloak without harm. Studying the dead wolf, he became certain. The white cloak in Jaru'tal's possession was the pelt of a snowbeast. What had he called it? A snow cloak?

It had to be. Faron eyed the beast, dead at his feet. Merely handling the fur was supposed to be enough to infect him, but if there was a chance...

Rolling the giant wolf onto its side, Faron plunged his knife into its middle and slid it down. Working up the sides, he skinned the wolf in the last vestiges of the light. The body went from steaming hot to cold by the time he was finished. When it was free, he scraped the underside with his knife, removing all the flesh he could, but in the end, it stunk horribly anyway. He tried to use one of the wolf teeth stuck in Jaru'tal's casket to pin two ends together at his throat—as he had with the rabbit pelt—but the makeshift cloak was heavy and wouldn't stay pinned. Gripping a handful of long fur, Faron slung the heavy, still-wet pelt over his shoulders. He grasped two ends with one fist, clasping it himself. Snow spun around him all the while.

Sheathing his blade, he stumbled off into the night. It was completely dark now, with just enough of a nimbus in the clouds to find where the sun had set in the west. Over the hills, he limped toward the outline of the mountain he'd seen before, favoring his bitten leg. He realized that he had forgotten to retrieve his boot—too late now. He had to keep moving.

Both feet bleeding, he felt the snow and mud squish through his toes until he could no longer feel them. Over a mound twice the size of the others, he looked up and, to his astonishment, saw the yellow lights of a city. He gaped at it, tired eyes unbelieving.

The wet pelt was warm and fended off the wind excellently, but Faron could still feel his body failing. His vision swam—or what little he could see in the dark did, anyway—and his head spun relentlessly. He didn't stop though. To stop meant to die. The city was so far, but he could make it.

His left leg—the bitten one—had gone completely stiff. He could barely bend his knee to walk. Mounting another rise, Faron lost sight of the ground and fell, rolling down the snowy hill. He barely managed to keep hold of his disgusting cloak. At the bottom of the hill, he rose to his knees and vomited violently.

The raw meat he had eaten came up in waves. With stomach pains like he'd never had before, he choked on his bile until every last piece had been retched out of him. When he could stand again, he made for the city.

Red eyes emerged from the darkness. Swearing enough to make a sailor blush, Faron jerked for his knife and nearly stabbed himself once he had it. He held it wardingly as a wolf came close enough for him to see. Snow tousled the beautiful white fur of the majestic beast as it approached. Another appeared from the darkness to his right. Flipping the point of the blade between them, he yelled with wild eyes, "I've already killed one of you!"

They came closer, crouched low, and Faron pulled his sickly

cape tighter as if it offered a modicum of protection. Piercing him with red eyes, they slowly moved toward him. Knife-wielding hand quivering, Faron closed his eyes and dropped the blade. It couldn't save him. The wolves came closer.

Every instinct he possessed told him to run, but there was nowhere to go. Either he was wrong, and these wolves would kill him, or he was right. Shaking with cold and trembling with fear, Faron forced his face away and pushed his hand open, offering the wolves an open palm.

A wet snout pressed into his hand. Opening his eyes, Faron watched as the beasts that had filled his nights and winters with the purest terror sniffed his hands, licked the salt from his fingers, and stalked away into the night.

Relief and joy filled him, and he was overcome. Falling to his knees, Faron sobbed until tears froze on his cheeks and in his eyes. They hadn't killed him. Winter wolves had found him covered in blood and weak, prey easy for the taking, and they had let him be.

He was alive. More importantly, he knew how to survive the north. He knew where to find Hadria, and now he could do it.

Artur

A rtur, son Erdon, stood atop the Anveil wall—a hundred-foot-tall black stone structure—dressed all in black leather and fur. The five stripes of a wall commander adorned his left breast. Wind tossed his hair, mixing it with the first snow of a freakishly early winter. Fields would go unharvested. Stores would go unfilled. Merchants who had hauled their goods to Empyrion would be trapped there because of this disturbing change in weather. With stoic eyes, Artur stared into the storm that would spell famine for Anveil.

The Veil had been behaving strangely for the past several years, but never in living memory had there been a winter so early as Iulia. He tried not to think about it. The important thing was they had seen the storms coming and brought the farmers in from the fields before the wolves came.

Thinking of the wolves, Artur lit the mirrored brazier by his post, a giant swiveling torch that could illuminate the ground far below. They were freezing annoying to clean, but he was fortunate enough to have men to do that for him. Being captain afforded a few privileges.

Disastrously early winter or not, Artur searched for wolves like he did every time the Veil fell. Perhaps with luck, he could spot a snowbeast and be the first to make a kill. There was always a feast in honor of the first man to draw winter blood, though he doubted there would be this year. He wasn't a treasurer or inventory master, but he already knew that food was going to be a problem, especially after last year's long winter. Artur didn't care much for titles and feasting, but his men did, and it was a force of habit, so he swept the snowbound ground with his powerful lantern.

It didn't take long before it revealed a shape moving in the snow. Beside him, Coran son Yellet pointed a black-gloved finger.

"There!" he proclaimed. "Already, you found one!" He pulled a great crossbow off his back and loaded a bolt.

"Where?" Artur asked. His vision had not yet adjusted after lighting the flame.

"Only one hundred and twenty feet off, approaching the south gate." He raised the heavy weapon and aimed. Artur's eyes took a moment, but when they did, they widened in surprise.

"No!" he commanded, shoving the bow skyward. The quarrel spun into the night harmlessly.

"What's wrong with you?" Coran demanded sharply. "You want the honor of first winter blood so badly you deprive me of it?"

Artur ignored the comment, despite being more than five ranks above the younger man.

"No," he said again, pointing sharply and unbelieving. "Sound the alarm, Coran."

The inexperienced boy lifted his bow again. "Why? I can take care of this by myself."

"Sound the alarm!" Artur exclaimed, shoving the weapon

away. "And ready a rescue party. That is a man!"

The Mountain City

The white-haired man wore a cloak of shadow. Whenever he turned, darkness shook down his length, spilling onto the floor and wisping away, spreading darkness throughout the room. His face was obscured, except for dark red lines of blood that trickled down from the sides of his lips and eyes a pale blue.

With a finger gloved in an iron gauntlet, plates flexing as his finger moved, he pointed at Hadria's cage, the bars so cold they radiated a white fog. She shivered inside her prison, her worn and tattered shirt exposing her neck to mid-back. It was covered in long scars from whips, beatings, and lacerations.

"Bring me her," he demanded as two short, slouching white figures rose from the black mist pooling on the floor. They crept up on her, unsuspecting and cold, and wrapped too long fingers around her bars.

The cage leaped into orange flame, licking around their bonelike fingers harmlessly. Hadria screamed. It was the same familiar scream that played over and over in his mind, reminding him of the day where she had sacrificed herself for him, casting herself in Sadagon's way. In the end, he had escaped, and she had not.

He had never forgiven himself.

The once frozen bars of the cage were ringed in fire, and Hadria screamed as it threatened to close inward. The door to her cage opened, and two pale, wraithlike hands reached in from two unearthly demons, seizing her by either arm.

From her expression, Faron knew that their icy grip hurt far more than the flames ever could have, and her screams mixed with pitiful begging and crying.

Like a statue, he was only there to witness. Trapped in a cage of his own, Faron choked on his dread, fury, fear, and rage until the dream faded, and he became aware of a sense of self.

He wished he hadn't.

His foot hurt, his head hurt, his stomach hurt, his arm hurt, his toes and fingers hurt—*everything* hurt. In a rush, he remembered the events at the Anveil Gate. Before he'd even had a chance to pound on the massive barrier—not that he was sure he'd have had the strength—a group of four men wielding crossbows rushed out to intercept him.

When he learned the weapons were intended for snow-beasts and not for him, he nearly wept with joy. No one in this city wanted to kill him. It was an underappreciated relief.

When one of the many snow wolves and red-eyed lesser demons who were following him leaped from the darkness to attack, the men responded with arrows and poleaxes, hewing crimson onto the perfect white. Faron had never seen such a brave display as the men who risked everything to protect him.

When he could hardly stand, he was gripped under both arms and dragged behind the safety of the gates. Once inside, he fell to his knees and vomited again, losing contents from his stomach he didn't know he had. That was the last thing he remembered as his vision went dark.

Now, in addition to his aching body protesting his abuse, he felt a straw mattress and pillow beneath him. In an effort that felt monumental, he opened his eyes. Light, brighter than the noonday sun streamed through a crystal-clear window, the quality of which was exceptionally rare. His head pounded as the light assailed him. To his relief, a round object moved in front of the painfully bright light, blocking the window from his view.

He blinked away the fuzzy outlines that rimmed everything, and the round object became... a head?

"Synick!?" Faron yelped in surprise. Sure enough, his light-haired, slightly hook-nosed friend stood over him on the opposite end of the continent from where he should be. "What in Olsu's creation are you doing *here*!? Am I dead? If you're here, I've probably been damned."

Synick only laughed, wearing that stupid grin that meant he was going to say something irritating. "Oh, that's fresh coming from you—*literally* the laziest person I know. I mean, look at you. You're only now waking up after, what, three days? How long can one man nap, anyway?"

Shaken, Faron repeated, "By the dead god's, Synick, why are you not at the guild? How did you find me? Where am *I*, even?"

Pushing a finger to Faron's lips, Synick loosed a long, drawn-out, "Sshhhhhhhhhhh," that stupid smile plastered from ear to ear. "Don't injure your tiny brain, Faron. It's sleepy."

Finding his strength, Faron swatted Synick's hand away. "Will you not tell me what in the North is happening right now?"

At that moment, a tall, powerfully built man with black hair and a mustache, and wearing black leather and fur, strode into the room. His skin was almost as pale as Synick's and Faron's, or rather, what Faron's used to be. Despite the beautifully crafted and intimidating uniform he wore, the man's face was naturally pleasant, and he smiled when he saw Faron, bright green eyes shining.

"Look, Artur!" Synick chirped. "He's awake!"

Artur, his smile cracking slightly, turned a somewhat less pleased gaze upon Synick. "I can see that, Fayorian." His accent was thick, and he chopped words off too quickly but in a rather formal way. "How long have you been present?" he directed at Faron.

"A few minutes," Faron answered. "Where am I?"

"The infirmary of the Winter Wardens. Did this one not tell you?"

"He's told me nothing, actually." Faron shot him a glare.

"I am not surprised. He is an idiot, I am learning."

Confused, Faron responded, "Wait, you know each other?"

He nodded. "Synick came to us a little over a month ago, searching for someone—you, in fact, as I've come to understand. He has been pestering my sister ever since."

Surprised, Faron gave Synick a curious look. That was *not* the answer he expected. Well, on the other hand, what *had* he been expecting? Was the guild still after him? Faron's head hurt and not just from the constant hunger, dehydration, and fight with a creature from his nightmares.

Synick, in reply, shook his head as if to say, "Not true," but his sheepish look gave him the lie. What *was* he doing here? It must be serious, or he never would've left that cave. And who was the sister he was bothering? That much wasn't surprising, at least. Synick was a horrible flirt.

Thinking back to the last thing he could remember, Faron asked, "Why did you help me?"

"I am a Winter Warden," Artur replied. "It is my calling to defend the city and its inhabitants from the demons of ice and snow."

"I'm not one of your citizens," Faron said.

Artur drummed his gloved fingers against the windowsill. Faron noticed that at the tip of each finger was a small strip of illustrious metal, reflecting the light like silver. *Anveil steel,* he realized, impressed. If this man could afford to have that worked into his gloves, then he was an important person indeed.

Fingers clacking against the wood, he replied, "You are now." He sat in a wooden chair, carefully making sure his knife sheath didn't catch on the arm. "I originally thought you to be one of our merchants, trapped by this early winter, but either way, I am pleased to see you well. Our timing was fortunate. Even another moment and the beasts would have had you." He tapped his index finger on the arm of the chair. "Even so, you must be even more fortunate to have made it to our gates so long after the Veil fell. Tell me, though, traveler, from where did you come to us, to come so near to death outside my walls?"

Casting his gaze to Synick and back, Faron could see no reason to lie, though he still felt as if he was giving up something precious. "Aru'barrahk. I fled the men who enslaved me." Not the whole truth, but a piece.

He lifted an arched eyebrow. "You were a prisoner in the Jewel City?" Faron nodded. "I do not blame you for coming to us then. They are a savage people." Faron only nodded his agreement. "Enough evil talk," Artur declared. "I had come to give news to your friend concerning you, but seeing as you are awake, I shall deliver it to you instead." He shifted in the chair, aligning his view of Faron better. "Have you heard of our festival of Winter Blood?" he asked. Faron shook his head.

"It is a way our people break the drudgery of winter," he explained, "which we need now more than ever. The first of the Winter Wardens to slay a snowbeast is honored in our winter feast. The whole city knows his name. Women adore him. No baker will charge him for bread for many months. It is an extraordinary honor." When Faron didn't say anything, he continued. "Normally, the kill is made with a bow from the wall, but the first kill happened upon the ground where we found you, so that rule does not apply. Also, according to the diseased wolf skin we found you clutching around your neck, the first man to kill a snowbeast wasn't a Winter Warden at all, so *that* rule does not apply."

"Are you saying…" Faron began, not finishing the sentence.

"That if you will accept, the honor of First Winter Blood goes to you… Faron?" he asked, not positive if he had the correct name.

"Yes." He nodded. "Faron."

Artur nodded as well. "Then, the annoying one did not lie. A strong northern name. It suits you, slayer of wolves." He cleared his throat. "But that's beside the point. If you accept, you will be the champion of this feast."

Faron hesitated, taken aback. "I… The honor should go to your men, captain."

"I ag—" Artur started, but Synick cut him off.

"He accepts!" he yelled. There was the obnoxious friend Faron knew. He had been silent far too long and was likely about to burst. "Of course he accepts. He accepts the honor and whatever money, fame, or other carnal riches that may come with it. Don't listen to him now—he's obviously suffering from head trauma induced by a lack of proper bathing—but don't worry, I'll introduce him to the concept of a bath before the day is done."

Artur rolled his eyes, exasperated. "Very well. I will inform the tribunal of governors so they may have your name carved into stone." He rose to his feet. "A seat will be prepared for your friend as well, and if you allow it, the fame will be shared among those of my men who pulled you from the Veil."

"I insist that the honor should belong to your men," Faron asserted. "Wholly."

He scratched his head, hair slicked back away from his forehead. "I have known your persistent friend here long enough to know that doing so would mean several visits from him to change my mind." He shook his head. "No honor is worth that. It is enough that their names be carved beside yours."

Synick beamed at him, happy only to have his way.

"He won't bother you, captain. I would rather give the honor to your men completely, if I could, and share it with them at the very least."

Artur stopped at the door before opening it. "Very well." He nodded to himself, then spoke again. "I wish you to know, Faron Wolf Slayer, that any man who possesses the skill to singlehandedly slay a wolf of winter and survive will always have a place among my men. As long as you are here, you will have a bed, a meal, and a trade."

Further surprised and genuinely touched, Faron's eyebrows shot up as Artur left the dark-gray stone building. Wind-carried snow whipped inside in a drift before the door closed.

"What a lovely man," Synick said.

"Am I dreaming?" Faron asked.

"I could pinch you if you like, but I don't see why you would be dreaming. If anything, this is *my* nightmare. I came here *specifically* to get away from you, and from the belly of a freezing blizzard you appear like a cat I just can't get rid of; then, to top things off, the first freezing day you're awake, you have a job and a snowing feast in your honor! I literally can't think of a worse situation."

Faron smiled. "I have a pocket full of gems, so there's also that."

Synick cocked an eyebrow. "Actually..." he mumbled, lifting a black velvet bag, a wolfish grin on his face. Faron felt at his pockets. The pouches were gone.

"You little thief." Faron laughed, snatching the bag away. "I'm on my death bed and you go through my pockets." It wasn't a question.

"Look, I can't be held responsible. It was *you* who started clinking tantalizingly."

Faron laughed, but it hurt his sides. More seriously, he questioned, "What are you doing here, Synick?"

"I'm not the one who arrived in the middle of a freezing storm, Faron. How in the world did you avoid being torn to shreds?"

"It's a long story and one I'll tell you, but I have to know, what in *Atha's name* are you doing so far from Blackwood and the guild? Are they still after me?"

"I'll answer that by instead telling you what *you've* been up to," Synick said, evasive as ever. "First, you lit a snowing *mountain* on fire. Good work, but I don't see how it was necessary. Next, you made your way to Fayevew to check out that orphanage, where you brutally murdered Jakal and an idiot fat man, and *nearly* murdered a close friend of mine. After that, like an idiot, you went to Aru'barrahk to murder some more people. I'm guessing got yourself captured and only just managed to escape, and you've come here, I'm guessing again, to murder some more people? Just don't include Artur on that list. He's singularly amusing to bother." Taking in Faron's raised eyebrows, he went on. "Still haven't found your... cousin, was it?"

Faron let the jab wash over him. Synick knew perfectly well who Hadria was. "How do you know all that?" he asked, genuinely shocked, perhaps even more than at seeing Synick in the first place.

"Aerik told me," he answered. "Said you nearly put an arrow in his eye before deciding to let him go. Mentioned something about saving you too. Said you squealed like a tiny child, so he got roped into saving your sorry self."

"How do you know Aerik?" Faron queried. He didn't respond to the obvious insult. With Synick, it was simply faster not to refute things that he clearly made up. He enjoyed defending them.

"Actually..." He hesitated. "He kind of raised me."

Puzzled, Faron took a moment to understand that in its entirety.

"You're from Fayevew? And an orphan?"

He held up his hands. "You got me."

"How am I only learning this now, a thousand miles from that ice-cursed cave under Blackwood?"

"Oh, please, Faron, my name is Synick *of Faye*. How did you not pick that up? As for the last bit, it didn't matter in there." Synick shrugged. "It was the past. I had to focus on the future and all the gold and pleasures therein. Wouldn't have wanted to end up like you otherwise." He jabbed an elbow into Faron's shoulder, dragging the chair closer to his bed. "I mean, look at you now. You're a total basket case—lounging all week in someone else's bed, broken head, bandaged from head to foot, with an inability to bathe—the list goes on."

Faron laughed. He finally felt free enough to truly enjoy himself. "Well, what happened to your parents?" he pried.

Synick frowned. "You don't like talking about your parents," he muttered. Faron nodded, abashed, but he continued, "Never knew my mother, and the old man hanged himself for me to find." He left it at that.

In a flash, Faron realized why Synick had taken his attempted suicide so personally, and he reddened—both at the memory of how low he had been and for the pain he must have caused his only friend. It hadn't seemed so important then.

"I'm sorry," was all he said.

"That's beside the point." Synick waved him away. "In the end, I found Aerik, and he told me what you were up to. You just kept going north, so I figured that at some point, either after or before your excursion to the desert, assuming you survived, you'd come here. After I learned you'd killed Jakal, though—I figured nothing could stop you. I mean, I knew you could fight, but Atha's tits, Faron, I didn't think you had it in you."

"I didn't give him a chance to fight back," Faron whispered. "Couldn't afford to fight fair."

"Of course not," Synick scoffed. "How else are people like us supposed to make it? The world has us at a disadvantage.

We make up the difference where we can." Faron nodded.

"So, you were looking for me, then?" Faron asked, changing the subject.

Uncharacteristically quiet, Synick nodded. "Yeah. I was looking for you. Funny, because you basically found me. I thought I'd try some of the surrounding villages to the south, but this blizzard came rolling in in the middle of summer. Honestly, what a horrible place to live this is. Once it started snowing out of freezing *nowhere,* I'd given up hope of finding you. I didn't actually think you were suicidal enough to try walking—*through a storm.*"

Faron chuckled. "It was faster than I was. Besides, I lost track of time for a little while."

"What's the part that I'm missing?"

Summoning his quickly returning strength, Faron sat up in bed. "Synick," he said, "I know how to find her."

It was Synick's turn to look stupid-surprised this time. "You mean, Ulric was right? There is a crazy cult who drinks the blood of kids?!"

He nodded. "And that's not all. Synick, I know where they are."

"Well, why haven't you said anything? Where in the North is she?" He paused. "And why are you smiling like that?"

"Because," he laughed. "You don't know how right you are. In the North, Synick, I've found the Lost City."

He raised an eyebrow and punctuated his confusion with a pause. "Faron, if we knew where the Lost City was, we'd be the richest men in living memory."

His smile grew wider. "I *do* know where it is."

"Why didn't you snowing lead with that?" Synick yelled, jumping to his feet. "Is that where you got those gems? Oh, snow and ice, I'm going to be rich again!" After he elated, he asked, "Well, where is it? Can't be too far if it's north. We'll just wait for the snow to melt and go find it."

Faron nodded. "It is north, but not near. It's in *the* North, beyond the Winter Veil. My guess is maybe fifteen days northeast."

Synick sat back down. "And just like that, I'm back to being poor and boring again. Why even mention it if it's up that high? Might as well be at the bottom of the ocean."

"I can get there," Faron insisted.

"Yeah, but you can't, though," Synick argued. "I know that thick skull of yours thinks the world will move to your sheer force of will, but it won't, Faron. Set one foot past that snowline—past this wall, even—and you're dog food."

Despite his friend's pessimism, Faron smiled again. "Synick. I can." He waited until his friend looked him in the eye. "Synick"—he snapped his fingers—"I know how Sadagon and his men survive the winter. I know how they travel through the North."

Synick was on his feet again. "WHY DIDN'T YOU LEAD WITH THAT?!" he exclaimed. "By the dead gods, Faron, you can travel in snow, you claim to know where the Lost City is, City of Temples, City of Light, and you start this conversation asking how *I* got *here*? I rode a snowing horse. Honestly, this is world-changing stuff, Faron. What in Atha's snowing tits have you been up to?"

Faron laughed. His belly throbbed, but for the first time in half a decade, he roared with laughter, no bitterness or hatred to taint it. "It's all related to the man who stole Hadria and killed my father," he said. "You remember the night Ulric told me about my father? About who he really was? About

Sadagon and how he lives forever by the blood of children?"

"It's not the type of story I'm likely to forget."

"Well, I've been hunting them. I found slavers in Fayevew, and that led me to the desert where I found Sadagon's supplier of slaves."

"And?"

"Dead," Faron said.

"Well, I'll tell you what," Synick replied. "That man picked the wrong guy to mess with. He's going to rue the day he tried to drink your sister's blood—*rue* the *snowing* day!" Despite the morbidity of Synick's joke, Faron laughed. It felt good to laugh, even if it hurt his stomach—and lungs, and head. Ice, he was in bad form.

"I need to prepare," Faron said. "I'm not even close to being properly equipped to make the journey."

"Yeah, no kidding," Synick agreed. "You walk here through a blizzard, fighting snow wolves and wearing a giant, glorified bandage for warmth—and an *actual* snow wolf, half the size of a freezing horse. Yeah, you should take a breather."

Faron laughed again. It was *really* starting to hurt now. "Now tell me," he pushed. "How are you here? Why aren't you back in the guild?"

Synick's gaze fell to the floor. "Actually, that's not such a long story." He stood and lifted his shirt, showing his side to Faron. A long, pink scar stood off his skin, fiery and barely healed. It was the kind of wound that could kill a man.

"When Jakal didn't come back, Dageran put two and two together. He stabbed me and threw me into the chasms."

Faron's eyes widened. "You fell?"

"Oh, yeah," he confirmed. "But turns out, there's water below my quarters there and not too far down either." He shivered. "It's dark down there, Faron. You've never seen blackness like that."

"How did you survive?" Faron prodded, hands tightening into fists. He *would* go back one day and put Dageran's head on a pike.

"The current took me. At first, it was cold, and then the water got hot, then eventually it spat me out at the bottom of the Banshee Cliffs. It must have been hours."

"That's a long way," Faron confirmed, eyes wide.

"Did you know there are fish in the river under the chasms?" He shook his head. "I couldn't see them, but I could feel them. I thought I was dying—thought I was dead, in fact—every so often until one of those little ice-brained gits came up and nibbled at my side." He pointed at his scar, shivering, then put his head in his hands. "It was snowing disgusting; I won't lie."

Faron nodded his head and said nothing about the way the guild used the river as a sewer. They were both thinking it.

"In the end, I managed to swim onto a beach where I dried off. Some old lady found me after that. Had a little rowboat she used to get right up to the cliffs for fishing and found me there. Brave woman—the only one from her small village not superstitious about the cliffs or, at least, not afraid. I need to drop off a mountain or two of gold for her when I've got the time. She helped me heal up properly, and you know what? I was right! There really are people who enjoy hot beer and cheese. She's crazy but such a lovely woman. It was eye-opening, honestly. After that, I went the long way to Iron Shoals, then Fayevew, and then here. Without the guild, I don't know what I am, but here I am anyway, waiting for a friend who may or may not be alive, bored, and poor out of my mind."

"Poor?" Faron cut in.

Synick shuffled uncomfortably. "Well… yeah, actually—poor. I've, uh, rethought some things since Dageran."

"You've given up thieving?" Faron asked, incredulous.

"Keep your voice down, alright? Yes, I gave it up. Just didn't feel the same after you almost offed yourself down in those caves. Wasn't fun anymore." He shrugged. "Don't get me wrong, there were times where I stole food, or coin to buy food or a place to sleep, but it's not what it used to be."

Faron smiled and reached across the bed, gripping his friend's shoulder. "I'm proud of you." Synick buried his face in his hands and groaned. Trying not to laugh, Faron changed the subject. "How's Ulric?"

Synick shook his head again. "Dead."

"What? How?"

"One of Dageran's lackeys—don't know. When Jakal didn't come back, they realized what happened and came after us."

Faron slumped back against the headboard of the bed. "I'm… I'm so sorry," he said, more to himself than Synick.

"It is what it is," Synick replied. "Don't dwell on it. The old man chose to help you, and I did too." Faron appreciated his friendship in silence for a moment. "I mean, if *I'd* been killed, then yeah, I'd haunt you for time and all eternity, but seeing how things are now, I'm good."

Faron rolled his eyes and pushed past the ice forming in his gut. *Ulric? Dead?* That was not a weight he could so easily carry. He couldn't dwell on it. "Well, are you going to show me the city or what?"

Helping him rise, Synick led Faron into the city. His head throbbed powerfully, and he was so weak that he had to lean on Synick for support at all times. He noticed as he rose from the bed that his clothes had been changed. He felt the comforting tightness of bandages around his feet, ankle, arm, a few fingers, and his middle. He could still feel torn flesh from where the wolf had stood on his chest.

That reminded him, "Synick, what happened to the pelt I had when I entered the city?"

"You mean the snow wolf pelt? Faron, it was burned the moment you passed out. You wouldn't want the entire village falling to disease, would you?"

Faron frowned. He knew the fear circulating the winter pelts, but if that were true, how did Sadagon, Jaru'tal, and himself avoid disease from the white fur? He thought he knew the answer. There was no sickness or disease—only rumors purposefully spread to keep people from discovering how to travel through the Veil. He said nothing, but he suspected very much.

Outside the infirmary, the wind tossed snow into piles outside tall, dark-gray stone buildings, shingled in a tarred black wood. Log piles were stacked high in the small spaces between homes and in large sheds, already covered in snow. White puffs of smoke rose from every chimney. Iron fences decorated the tops of short, stone walls, topped with curved iron spikes. Every house stood mere feet from its neighbor—not unlike Blackwood—but every home here was both above and below another.

The city was built on a mountain, a solitary highland with the nearest other at least thirty miles off. The lowest part of the city was, in fact, the wall, despite being over a hundred feet tall, and the buildings had been built right up against it. From what he could see, it appeared to wrap around the entire mountain, shaping the city like a beehive. Anveil must have been ancient, though, because every spare foot was occupied by a stone brick home, plausibly quarried from the very earth it stood on.

Faron had never seen such well-aligned, beautiful homes before. In Fayevew, the Granite District had been laid out similarly, but it was where the rich lived, and the rest of the city was an unorganized shamble, not even including the vast portion of it built on a snowing lake.

Here, snow fell on steep roofs but melted—this early in the winter at least—and black-haired, blue and green-eyed people kept the streets swept and free of snow. It was all very orderly. From a stone patio, Faron surveyed the horizon.

Snow fell in soft drifts from a gray sky, and the world below was an unbroken sheet of the purest white. In the distance, Faron could see the mountains that bordered Aru'barrahk.

Watching Faron take in the considerable view, Synick said, "I know, right? Just awful, isn't it?" Faron turned to see if he was serious, but he was smiling—well, smiling more. "Come on," he beckoned. "This way." White puffs of mist escaped their mouths as Synick helped him up a staircase then began strafing around the mountain. Long, leveled walks wrapped about the mountain city at every level, as if Anveil had been entirely planned before it was built.

The wind picked up, and Faron began to shiver. His clothes had been changed from linen to wool, but he was still cold. He needed good leather.

"I'm not dressed for this," he confided in Synick.

"Yeah, probably," he agreed. "The infirmary warden said you shouldn't get out of bed today."

Faron grunted. "Did I really sleep for three whole days?"

Synick nodded, laboring as he half carried Faron up the

sloping path. "Yup, a whole day longer than the warden said you would."

"I'm starved," Faron said, only now realizing it.

"Yeah, there was broth waiting for you, but I drank it, so…" he trailed off.

"Git."

"What? You know I can't resist onion, and besides, I wasn't convinced you weren't dead." He gave a wry smile, which Faron returned. He *was* hungry though. "Oh, don't worry, you can have *my* dinner."

After passing seemingly hundreds of near-identical houses, Synick stopped outside of one that was particularly unique. To his surprise, a large portion of the gray building had no walls. Arches bore the weight of higher levels.

"This is where I work," Synick said.

"Wait," Faron said through clattering teeth. "You? Work? What on earth would *you* do for a trade?"

"I decided that if I was going to be a new man, I should start with something interesting." He led Faron inside. "This is the forge where I'm learning to blow glass."

"You have an apprenticeship blowing glass?" Faron repeated, incredulous.

"I'm actually pretty good at it." He grinned.

"I'll believe that when I see it—or when I'm dead. Whatever comes last, really."

"Let me show you!" Synick pulled him eagerly into the forge. It was cold for now. Intricate pieces of delicate glass hung from shelves and on tables. Bottles in all shapes and sizes lined shelving along the far wall, and even crystal roses could be seen glinting in decorated vases. "This is master Orothorn's work," he explained, leaning Faron up against an arch.

He rushed off to a table littered with broken glass. "He lets me make the round bottles, but when I'm not working, I make stuff of my own. I made this." He procured a small piece of glass that looked like an enclosed vial.

"It looks like garbage," Faron noted. "Expensive garbage."

"Oh, shut your mouth. It's snowing useful is what it is. I just haven't figured out why yet. Look." He prodded it, tapping one end. "This side is thick, and this side is thin. This small side would break if you flicked it with a fingernail, but this side is tough as iron." To prove a point, he smacked the fat end into the table. True enough, it didn't shatter.

Faron nodded. "That's actually impressive."

"I made this too," Synick chimed. It looked like a slightly oblong bubble, eternally frozen in time.

"It looks like it should be floating," Faron observed.

"Yeah, it doesn't, though," Synick said sheepishly. "I tried."

"Is that why there's so much glass in that corner?"

Synick turned to see what he was pointing at. "Oh, that? No, that's from something else. I've been trying to seal flash rocks in glass and get it to ignite. Thought it would look like fireworks in a jar and burn forever, you know? I'd sell a million of them."

That was the second time Faron had heard of these rocks. "What's a flash rock?"

"Orothorn calls it phosphorous. It's a rock powder that burns very easily."

"And you're trying to light it—in a sealed jar?"

"Right."

Faron shook his head. "I suppose that explains all the broken glass. You must know that'll never work."

"I know no such thing," he retorted. "It'll be useful one day, you'll see." Faron doubted it.

"Where's that dinner you owe me?"

Alone

Synick led Faron away from the forge and to a far larger building almost directly across the street. No less than four chimneys spouted woody smoke into the sky, giving the air a warm sort of smell despite the puncturing cold. Over the door hung a sign engraved with the head of a fox, although there was no name inscribed anywhere.

The inside was brighter than he had expected. Light streamed in from windows, and three fires burned that he could see. Mirrors reflected the firelight on several walls, lighting the place more thoroughly than most taverns Faron had seen before. Ornate iron lanterns hung from every corner, and a simple candelabra chandelier illuminated the middlemost section of the angular room. He suspected from the chimneys outside that there was another fire burning around the corner. Black haired men and women gathered around the tables, somewhat more sober than Faron would have expected. Taverns were generally either riotous or quiet, in his experience. This one fell somewhere in the middle. Men and women drank a clear, sweet-smelling liquid over laughs and conversation, but no one seemed to smile when they didn't think they were being watched. These people were covering up an anxiety; Faron could already tell.

At the counter, a green-eyed woman in a high collared black jacket layered over a white lapelled shirt polished the bar with a rough rag. The look was only slightly spoiled by a large tan apron. When she saw Synick, she smiled.

"There's my beautiful bastard. Have you been trying to make me lonely? Well, it's working. I'm on the verge of taking that man to my bed." She pointed at an elderly man alone at a table. "Or that one, just to forget about that damn smile for a day or two."

Faron gaped as Synick actually blushed. "And it's not just me," she went on. "Poor Orothorn has been eating all alone. He actually seems *happy* again. Honestly, where have you been, Synick?"

"Hi, Jesika," Synick stammered. "This is Faron." He motioned his way.

"Faron? The one you've been waiting around for? You're the man they found out in the storm just after the Veil fell."

Surprised, Faron nodded. "Do I know you?"

"Not yet, but you will." She gave him an up and down look that felt somehow emaciating. "My brother says you're to be crowned this year's champion of Winter Blood."

"Did we miss Artur?" Synick asked.

"No. He told me yesterday. And I could have told you, but you were nowhere to be found." Her look was placed somewhere between chastising and curious.

"Yeah, well, I was busy saving Faron's snowing life."

"Oh, how convenient," she said. "A handsome, mysterious man sweeps into town, seizing titles and glory and exciting all our young women, and you just happen to know him."

"Know him?" His cheeks reddened. "I taught the blistering idiot everything he knows! I practically changed his diapers, and that was just last week!"

Jesika threw a rag at him. "Now there's the sarcastic boy I know. You just take a little prodding, don't you?"

Unbelievably, Synick blushed again. "You do?" Faron asked, hardly making an effort to conceal his disbelief. Synick was rarely caught off guard, so in poor condition or not, Faron wasn't about to pass up the opportunity to capitalize on it. "Then why in all my years have I never managed to get you to stop talking? Only in your sleep, I'd have a reprieve, and sometimes not even then. You still jabber on, just less coherently."

Synick jabbed an elbow in his ribs, but Faron only smiled. Something about seeing Synick uncomfortable and awkward brought out his antagonistic side. Jesika laughed again.

"Hold on, Faron is a man, but I'm a *boy*? I'm nearly two years his senior!"

Pointedly ignoring the remark, she turned to Faron.

"You're really a foreigner? You look like a regular warden."

He shrugged again. "I've never been here before in my life." So long as he knew, anyway.

"You appear a man of the wall from your eyes to your chin," she elaborated.

"Yeah," Synick cut in. "But that doesn't necessarily make him attractive. I mean, he's been confused for a large potato before and will again, to be honest. I've personally made the mistake several times myself. He's got a scar, in fact, I—"

"A scar?" Jesika interrupted. "Where exactly?"

Faron blushed. This was certainly a new experience. "Oh, Jesika," Synick chastised. "You're an incorrigible tavern wench, do you know that?"

She dropped her smile and lifted a finger. "Don't think you

can teach me anything about propriety, you golden-haired beauty." She somehow managed to make that come across as an insult. "I see right through that innocent façade you've put up. You know a thing or two about wenches yourself, and I'll be as much or as little a smiling barmaid looking for easy tips as I like in my own tavern, thank you."

"I might've had some practice," Synick mumbled, but Faron could see his smile brimming. Had Synick actually met his match? Rare was the person who could meet him in banter. In a flash, Jesika's attention was back on Faron.

"I heard you approached the gates in the middle of a blizzard, naked, except a skinned snowbeast around your shoulders, and fighting a dozen winter wolves with your bare hands."

"That..." Faron's blush deepened. "That isn't entirely true."

"Entirely?" Synick was aghast. "It's not true at all! The snowbeasts didn't attack until you were nearly through the snowing gate, and it was hardly a blizzard!" he continued with zeal. "And honestly, wearing nothing at all? What a fantastic tale. I almost wish it were true, though. I can only imagine the effectiveness of such a well-placed bit of frostbite."

Jesika erupted into laughter, and Faron shot Synick a confused look. Had Jesika been *flirting* with him?

"Oh, Synick," she said, still bubbling with mirth. "I was wondering where that sharp tongue was hiding." She reached into an open window that connected the counter to the kitchen, pulling two large wooden bowls into her hands. Curling wisps of steam lifted from their contents.

"Your friend eats free here, Synick, because he is absolutely *diverting*." She flashed him a smile, which Faron had exactly zero idea how to return. "You, however, can thank Master

Orothorn for yours. I'd charge you double if I could." She slid the bowl over but gave him a little wink.

Sheepish grin on his face, he accepted the bowl and settled down at an open table. He sat with his back to the wall where he could see the door but also where he could peek at the girl behind the counter.

"You like her!" Faron exclaimed when they sat down. He expected a denial, but instead, Synick replied honestly.

"It's weird. I can't figure it out. She's not rich, particularly well endowed, or overly eager, if you get my meaning, but she's always messing about in my head. One moment she seems a breath away from taking me to bed, and the next she's buying drinks for every man but me."

It was Faron's turn to grin. "She seems as likely to put a knife in your ribs as kiss you."

"A dull knife," he quipped. "And she'd stab softly."

Faron laughed. "You're entirely hopeless!"

"Well, I already got stabbed once," he said. "Can't be any worse than that."

"Oh, eat your soup," Faron dismissed. He was ravenous.

The bowl contained a sweet kind of carrot soup but not for long. Faron inhaled it, nearly scalding his tongue in his haste. Before he knew it, another girl, also green-eyed with black hair, deposited a second helping for them both. He looked up to see Jesika giving him a small wave. Puzzled, he tilted his head.

The girl's voice was high and clear when she spoke. "Remember us after the festival when you're hungry." Her voice almost seemed to peal like a bell. "It'd be an honor to host you when you've been titled."

Jesika rolled her eyes when Synick mimed a "thank you,"

but he smiled anyway, and they happily helped themselves.

When both bowls were clean, they set them aside content-edly. Faron's stomach had shrunk considerably during his near-starvation trek from Aru'barrahk, but soup had a way of helping it expand, so when a third bowl made its way to him, he slurped it down as well, ignoring the stares from the bartender. Eventually, when they were both finished, Synick tilted his head back on his chair and closed his eyes. After a long, comfortable moment had passed, Faron began to speak.

"We need to talk," he said.

"About what?"

"I need to leave the city."

Synick's eyes opened, and he leaned forward. "Do you really have to be doing this right now?"

Puzzled, Faron furrowed his brow. "Doing what?"

"You only just woke up," Synick exclaimed, exasperated. "You're limping so hard I'm like your own personal cane, you hardly open your eyes outside because your head hurts so bad—don't lie, I know it does—and you only just came traipsing through all that remains of hell. Now you want to go back?"

"I have to, Synick. I can't stay here."

"Yes, you can!" he almost yelled. "For a few *days,* at least. Faron, these people—the entire snowing city—are throwing a feast in *your honor,* and you want to pick up again and go before you've even recovered your breath? Would it kill you to slow down for once in your life? Honestly, Faron, it's like you're not even happy to see me." He looked down after the outburst. That last bit wasn't meant to come out.

"Synick, I—"

"No. Don't. It's fine." He shook his head. "I know how hard

it is to talk you out of something once you've set your mind on it, but you have to at least stay for the feast."

"I don't have time for feasts," Faron argued.

"Yes. Yes, you do!" He was genuinely upset now. "That's the problem with you, Faron. You can't stop to see what's good for you. You're so snowing determined to burn yourself out."

"I have to find her," Faron said defensively. "I'm running out of time."

"She's *dead*, Faron!"

Screams.

Faron's expression turned to ice. All eyes in the tavern turned to them and grew silent. "You're going to kill yourself trying to accomplish something you can't. I encouraged you before because it was that or keep you around long enough to watch you eventually jump off a bridge, but now you're doing that anyway! I won't let you throw your life away for nothing! What must I do to keep you from doing everything you can to freeze to death or get eaten or worse?

"You've gotten farther than I thought you would, honestly, and I don't doubt that the white-haired man is real, or the Lost City, or any of it, but do you honestly believe that she is still alive?" He noticed everyone's gaze locked on him, and he sat down, lowering his tone to a whisper. "She's dead, Faron. I know it's not easy to hear, but you have to stop sacrificing your life for someone who's already lost hers."

Apoplectic and at a complete loss for words, Faron pulled himself to his feet and stormed out of the tavern. Jesika waved at him, but he paid her no mind, slamming the door behind him.

How dare he? How dare Synick tell him what to do or chastise him if what he did was dangerous, and how *dare* he even suggest that Hadria was dead.

Screams.

Visions of a time long passed swam before his eyes as he walked the stone pathways alone—memories of a time when Hadria would sing to the birds in the top of their secret treehouse and they would sing back. He saw the silver ring she had purchased and given to him, which he wore even now. Countless memories of flowers, hide and seek, and happier times came to him as he fumed in the falling snow, but most of all, he saw *him*. He saw the moment Hadria traded his fate for hers and flung him out of Sadagon's grasp. He saw flames rising all about them, licking the walls, the ceiling, even the floor with inexorable hunger.

He heard her scream—the scream of fury at being torn away from him by large, pale hands; the scream of terror as she saw their father, dead and burning, blackened skin pulled tight over a hairless skull; the scream of watching her brother die, pinned by a flaming timber, the ground beneath giving way to a fiery death.

The scars across his shoulders, chest, and hands, twinged in memory, and his palms echoed with pain in unison.

She was alive—she *had* to be. Not knowing where else to go, Faron stormed back toward the infirmary. It would be dark soon, and he wasn't dressed warmly enough to withstand another nighttime snowstorm. His limbs, joints, and head ached with a pain that demanded attention, but he ignored it. He stepped angrily along the cobbled path, covered in a dusting of snow when Synick grabbed his shoulder from behind.

"Stop, Faron. Stop."

"What?" he barked, whirling around. "What else do you

have to tell me, Synick? What other hopes do I have that you'd like to shatter for me?"

"Just listen!" Synick yelled, no pretense of keeping his temper. "You are killing yourself, Faron! You think that if you can just throw yourself at a problem hard enough, it will go away, but this one is too big." Faron brushed his hands away, but Synick persisted. *"Listen to me,"* he keened. "You can't bring her back by killing yourself."

Screams.

"And I can't bring her back by staying here!" Faron yelled in return, finally giving in to the argument. "She's alive, Synick—I know she is—and I can't stand by while Sadagon ages her, just waiting to slaughter her for her blood! She's all I have left, Synick!"

All anger and desperation bled away from Synick's face. "That's not true at all, Faron. I'd have thought you would know better now." His expression was pained. "You have me too."

Faron deflated as he realized the truth behind Synick's argument and why he was being so forward. "Synick... You know I have to find her, even if she is..." He couldn't say it. "I *have* to know."

Soberly, Synick nodded his head. "I know."

"You know I would do the same for you if it came to it." Synick didn't respond, except to meet his gaze. "I have to know, Synick."

"Well, I'm coming with you then."

Taken aback, Faron asked, "What?"

"I'm coming with you—to find your sister. Who else is going to keep you from offing yourself, if not me? I've got quite the track record by now."

"You can't come with me," Faron said. "It's too dangerous."

"That's exactly why I'm going with you. Otherwise, you're certain to meet something you can't overcome by sheer force of will and get yourself killed."

"I can take care of myself."

"Yeah, but you don't. I mean, did you see yourself when you showed up three days ago? You were on death's door. Iron Halls, Faron, you *still are*."

"You can't come with me, Synick."

"And I can't convince you to stay?"

"No."

"Then I'm going with you."

"You can't!" Faron yelled.

"Why, Faron? Why can't I go with you?"

"Because—" He hesitated.

"Because, why?"

"I... I don't."

"Why, Faron?"

"Because I can't live with myself if you die because of me!" His eyes stung as the truth escaped him.

Synick was silent for a moment, then shook his head. "You're an idiot, Faron. Don't you see it? You snowing fool. *That's* why I have to go. If I let you go alone and you die because of it, I will *never* forget it." Faron was silent. "You are willing to sacrifice everything for your family, but don't you get it, Faron? You're *my* family, and all I have left too."

Faron's rebuttal dropped dead before he could utter it. An unfamiliar sensation tightened his chest and pricked at his eyes. Tears of misery, fury, and even empathy had long been squeezed out of him, to the point that he had none left, but these were something else. He lashed out and pulled Synick into a firm embrace, squeezing the air from his lungs.

To his ever-growing surprise, Synick returned the embrace. After a silent moment, he pulled away. "You're seeing sense, then?"

Faron nodded before looking away. After the unexpected joy of finding Synick again, he was doubly afraid of losing him, but the relief he felt at the prospect of him coming along was stronger than he wanted to admit.

"Even if you really do know how to walk the White, if you leave in the condition you're in, you'll be dead before night's end, Faron," he said, drawing his gaze. Faron finished wiping his eyes and looked up. "We need to prepare. You look like a skeleton. A few days of feasting will go a long way for you." It took a moment, but Faron nodded.

"There's something that we need," Faron conceded. "But it won't be easy."

Synick rolled his eyes. "Honestly, Faron, when is anything *ever* easy?"

Faron only shrugged and allowed Synick to support him as he guided them back to his room above the forge, insisting that he sleep in his bed.

Coats of Snow

"You were right, this isn't snowing easy," Synick complained from below Faron on the rope. Two days had passed since their argument, and already Faron was feeling much better. His ankle still pained him greatly from where the snow wolf's tooth had dug away his skin, but it was a superficial pain. His headache had cleared up that morning, as well as any chest pain he'd had. His limp had lifted, and an uneasy energy drove him to move.

He was grateful for that as he lowered himself down the far side of the Anveil snow wall.

"Remind me why we're doing this again?"

"Because your aim is terrible," Faron replied with a smirk.

"Alright, that's fair, but what if we get these pelts and you're wrong? What if the wolves you saw just weren't hungry or, even more likely, you were only hallucinating and saw what you wanted to see? Or maybe the things just have standards and won't eat something as rank as you."

"They were there the whole time, Synick," Faron said through puffs of cold breath, lowering himself down the wall. "They followed me all the way here and only attacked once the Anveil guards rushed through the gate. They didn't even attack me then, only the Winter Wardens."

"Well, what about the diseases then?" he prodded. "You don't touch a snowbeast pelt. You'll start foaming at the mouth and go crazy, attack people, or just drop dead."

"What about me?" Faron offered. "I've touched them on three different occasions, wore one once, and I'm fine."

"I wouldn't call you fine," Synick argued. "Maybe ice-brained, or a git, or an ice-brained git for the sake of brevity, but definitely not fine." He grunted as he walked backward down the wall.

"And what about Jaru'tal? He owned one, and made it clear he used it, *and* that it was a gift from Sadagon. He hasn't started foaming at the mouth."

"No, but look at him now. He's dead. Wouldn't exactly call him the model of good health." Faron shook his head but heard Synick chuckle.

"It's just a bit farther."

"You realize how insane this seems, right? We're climbing down a snow wall, at night, in freezing temperatures, in the middle of an early winter so we can kill a snowbeast. Why? So we can take its fur and wear it, which could also kill us."

"Stop talking," Faron commanded. "We're getting near. We don't want anything to hear us."

Despite all those years provoking Faron for his fear of snowbeasts, Synick stopped talking immediately, not even communicating his acceptance. The wind seemed loud in the sudden silence. Before they dismounted, they turned around and inspected the empty night. Wind howled through the darkness, and the stone wall they scaled radiated cold in a constant, almost menacing way.

They relinquished their grips quietly. Synick immediately set about unslinging three heavy metal traps from his shoulder and setting them in the snow. Faron, however, drew a dagger and peered as well as he could into the night. Nothing stirred in the oppressive darkness—nothing he could see, anyway. He strained both eyes and ears but, thankfully, heard nothing. The Veil was long past. There would be monsters everywhere—hungry monsters.

With a satisfying click, Synick's traps were armed. He reached into his pack and placed a bloody slab of meat into the center snare. Before they scrambled up the rope, Synick bent and looped the rope through the trap, tying a quick knot. Like phantoms, they scaled the wall quickly at first, then more slowly as they tired.

At the top, Faron fell to his knees, and Synick leaned against the wall, both panting heavily. It was going well so far. If someone had happened by and seen the rope, they would have cut and tossed it at least. More likely, they would have raised the alarm. When it came to snowbeasts, people took things very seriously, especially so in Anveil.

That was why they had spent the previous day scouting for a spot on the wall where they wouldn't be disturbed by anyone, Winter Warden or otherwise, and why Faron had traded his entire pouch of large, Kaor gold coins to rent a small warehouse just on the inside of the wall, directly underneath them.

Atop the wall, they waited, nestled in a corner between two towers where no sentinels would pass by. They stared out upon their traps, hoping something would come to inspect them. Drifts of snow carried on folds of wind shifted in the darkness. Despite the moon passing in and out of clouds, it was difficult to make out any real movement from the constant ethereal shifting of the air. Even with the aid of the mirrored brazier, it was hard to see the ground below.

Only a few minutes after they returned to the top, Synick picked out a solid form on the ground—several solid forms, as it turned out. A leash of white foxes, almost imperceptible from the snow, skulked from the darkness and into the dimly lit spotlight, smelling at the meat.

"Does it have to be a wolf?" Synick asked. Faron shrugged his shoulders in the universal symbol of, "I don't know." Scraping together some of the dusting that adorned the top of the wall, Synick threw a snowball down below. "Shoo, you giant rats," he hissed. The hungry foxes watched the ball impact, then turned their attention from the meat to the two boys in the light.

For a moment, they only stared, then as one, they darted toward the wall and tried to scramble up it. Of course, they didn't make it more than a few feet.

Confident from his vantage, Synick crooned, "Oh, it's cute. Look how stupid they are." They shrieked back at him in response, a blood-curdling sound that fell somewhere between a howl and suffering scream. Before Synick could reply with an equally intelligent quip, the foxes fell silent all at the same time.

The oversized white canids flipped around, focusing their attention on a single point. From the dark strode a far larger, more powerful figure—a snow wolf. It was smaller than the one he'd fought in the plains outside the city but still far larger than any normal dog. It hardly paid any attention to the weaker beasts as it strode up, claiming the meat for itself. This time, Synick said nothing. It approached the snare, sniffing.

"Come on," Synick whispered. "Just a little to the left." Faron waited in focused silence. With a loud snap, clearly audible even from atop the wall, the iron claw slammed shut. The wolf barked suddenly, an angry noise somewhere between a whine and a howl.

"It's got his leg," Synick trumped. "We got him." The wolf snarled and barked furiously, making an awful racket. "Come on, quick. Let's pull him up." Tied to the far column of the adjacent tower, the rope was pulled taught. Already it quivered with the frantic, furious movements of the beast below. Together they pulled, lifting the muscled mass into the air. If it had been angry before, it was absolutely rancorous now. It thrashed in a seething mass of hurling white as it struggled to bite off its own leg to free itself from the trap.

Faron knew that feeling well. "Shoot it," he said, leaning back. It was maybe only twenty feet closer now. Not wasting the time or breath on agreeing, Synick released the rope to Faron's control and lowered the small crossbow. Taking a moment to sight down, he fired a bolt. With a clang, it shattered on stone. Faron's arms were beginning to strain. His triceps and ankle hadn't healed completely, and this wolf must have weighed at least a hundred and fifty pounds. It wasn't fully grown.

"Snowing fool," Synick whispered as he put his foot in the step and heaved, rearming the bow. The wolf snarled louder than ever now, barking, teeth flashing in a rage.

"Just shut him up!" Faron hissed. The bow sprang again, and this time the wolf went quiet. Setting the crossbow aside, Synick took up the rope and pulled, dragging the carcass up the wall.

"It's gonna leave a bloody trail all the way up," Synick noted. Faron only grunted. He doubted anyone had ever done so much work to get a snowbeast *into* a city before.

When they hauled it over the battlement, the carcass was still steaming, hot blood spilling from the bolt in its neck.

"Good shot," Faron murmured.

Synick shrugged. "It was all I could see, to be honest." He kicked the corpse. "That's for all the bad dreams." He kicked it again. "And that's just in case your nasty fur gets me sick."

"It won't," Faron argued. "Now come on. We need another one."

Synick groaned. "Why can't we just arm the trap and toss it down?"

"Because they'll all end up triggered, face down, or completely exposed like the first one you threw. And then we'll have to climb down, find, and reset them, which will take longer, and I don't know about you, but I don't want to spend any more time in the snow than I have to."

They peered over the wall. Nothing stirred in the swirling mists.

"Come on," Faron continued. "Let's get this over with."

"You know you're a persistent little git, right?"

"Hurry up. We don't want anything catching the scent of all that blood before we get down there." They untied the rope from the trap and tossed it back over. Holding it in both hands, they slowly backed over the edge of the wall and began the arduous process.

Neither boy spoke this time. Except for the wind, it was eerily silent. Faron's nose began to itch, but he didn't dare release the rope.

At the bottom, they turned and surveyed the fog, dimly lit by the spotlight up above. Flecks of snow stung Faron's cheek as he quietly studied the shifting wind. Somewhere in the distance, there was a wolf's howl. It went unanswered.

Last time he had been nervous, but now Faron felt true fear. He almost insisted on returning to the safety of the wall, but he balled his fists and planted his feet in the snow. He tried not to let his voice quiver.

"Set the traps," he instructed. Synick was apparently nervous, too, as he didn't respond with a joke or complaint. He knelt and set about tying the rope to another spiked metal snare. Blood speckled the ground all around them, pooled especially where the other trap had been. Faron kicked snow over the deep scrapes their prey had made. Snow wolves were reputedly the most intelligent of winter beasts, and they might sense an obvious trap.

Synick, on hands and knees, scooped snow and piled it over the circular snare, enshrouding the metal teeth. In his eagerness to not have to enter the hellish snows a third time, Faron focused on concealing the tracks left by the last attempt. The wind fell silent.

"Faron," Synick whispered.

"What?" he asked, tossing snow on the last bit of track.

"Faron," he said again, only slightly firmer.

He looked up, and his blood froze. Every hair on the back of his neck stood on end as three pairs of red eyes gleamed from the swirling mists. The wolves stepped forward, crouched low with hackles raised high.

Synick stayed frozen on his knees, watching the beasts with the same intensity as they watched him. The first among them let out a low growl, and he leaped to his feet. Blood pounded in Faron's ears, and he felt nearly deaf.

Almost choking on his heart, Faron turned his head and whispered, "Throw the meat."

Slowly, Synick reached for the pocket on his pack. Suddenly

more alert, the wolves began barking and growling fiercely. It sent shivers up Faron's spine. Synick tossed the slab of red meat at their feet. They stepped over it without a glance, crouching low with teeth bared in a fierce snarl.

"Run."

Synick didn't need telling twice. In a flash, he was on his feet and pulling himself up the rope, feet slipping in the frozen gore trailing up the wall. The snow wolves snarled and barked as he ran but didn't give chase. Faron remained planted, and they closed in around him. Slowly, he reached for his belt knife. It was bigger than the small thing he had been carrying when the Veil fell.

The barking grew louder, and Faron switched his attention and blade point from one beast to the next. Slowly, they closed the circle, tight like a noose. Blood pounded in his ears. Fear filled him so completely he could hardly think. Synick was high enough up the rope now that he could use it himself, but the wolves had closed in, teeth bared and hackles raised. He wouldn't make it ten feet. The trap Synick armed was behind him and roughly to the left. If he could dodge just past it, maybe he could catch one of the predators with it and fight off the other two. It was a narrow chance, but he didn't see any other way.

The smallest one of the three, nearly on Faron's left, snarled suddenly and leaped into the air. Even it was almost half again as large as a normal wolf. Wind snapped at its shock-white fur, and snow flew in and out of its gaping jaws as it sailed through the air, intent on ripping out his throat.

Faron leaped back, knife raised, but the wolf never made it to him. A black mass slammed the snow wolf to the ground in mid-leap, a horrid crack splitting the night as bones shattered, and a thin stiletto of a dagger was rammed into its skull. With a sharp whine, it was still. Synick rolled to untangle himself with the beast.

The two other wolves snapped their heads around at the sudden impact, surprised. Even regular wolves didn't fear predators from the sky.

Seizing the opportunity, Faron lunged forward and thrust with his blade. The white beast leaped out of the way, but he had expected that. Rushing forward, he followed through with the attack and rammed the dagger into the wolf's side. It howled an angry, hateful scream and leaped back again, lacerating its shoulder further as the blade tore away, but Faron managed to hold on. It howled into the night sky once it was away, an unexpectedly loud, pealing scream in animal form. It seemed to last forever. The hair on his arms rose off his skin.

The injured wolf retreated several feet. It wouldn't run away, but it wouldn't be quite so aggressive now either—hopefully. Faron's attention turned to the last wolf who was dodging away from Synick's thrusts with the bloody stiletto. Faron threw his knife with full force, and it sunk into the animal's chest just under the foreleg. It dropped, legs writhing in furious agony. He had been aiming for its neck but couldn't argue with the results. Together they turned to the only remaining beast. Synick raised his knife and shouted. It didn't flinch, only waiting.

While Synick kept the wounded dog busy, Faron jumped behind the thrashing wolf and yanked fiercely on his knife. Boiling hot blood evaporated the ice as it gushed from the deep wound. With a quick motion, he sank it again into its neck, and it was still. Spinning, he grabbed the rope and sliced it a few inches above the trap.

"What are you doing?" Synick asked. "There's still this one to deal with. Help me with it."

"We need to go," Faron said. He looped the rope around the first of the fallen wolves, careful not to step on a trap. He heaved and lifted the corpse off the ground, high enough to fit the rope underneath its neck.

A new howl split the night. "Oh no," Synick said. Faron didn't look up. He knew what was out there. First one, then two, then three howls raised from the darkness. They were close. Again and again, the howls came, erupting from the swirls of snow. Faron's nightmares had come true.

"We have to go!" Synick yelled over the din of wolves. A pair of red eyes emerged, glowing faintly in the dim light.

Faron looped the rope around in a knot, tying it just below the skull. He wasn't leaving without what they came for.

"We really have to go!" Synick yelled. More pairs of eyes reflected the spotlight from above—five, six, more. "What are you doing?" he yelled at Faron.

He synched the knot as tight as he could.

"Run!" Faron yelled, and he did. He bolted again for the rope, and this time Faron was right behind him. He took two running steps up the wall before seizing the literal lifeline in both hands. In such a terror, Faron thought he could have managed three or even four but grabbed just below Synick as he scrambled to get higher.

The wolves were after them now. Some howled, some barked, and some growled or snarled as they closed the distance between them and their prey. They were too low. Synick flew up the wall but not fast enough. A wolf leaped from the ground, and Faron only just managed to push off the wall enough to avoid its teeth sinking into his calf. Even so, he slipped on a patch of frozen blood and lost his footing. His side slammed into the wall, and another wolf jumped for him.

Hanging from the rope, he kicked fiercely, smashing the dog's nose. Its jaws snapped shut but closed a hair's breadth from his thigh. He pulled and managed to get his feet back on the wall. Synick was above, turned around, and watching. He appeared to have been fumbling with a knife, preparing to throw it if necessary.

"Just snowing climb!" Faron yelled.

He did. Stepping and pulling in unison, they pulled themselves away from the mass of hungry winter beasts. Faron's heart pounded intensely, and rising up the wall suddenly seemed like no challenge at all.

Less than halfway up the snow wall, the beasts began to cry into the sky. Howls rose up at them—angry, mournful, and hungry. The beasts wanted to rip the flesh from their bones. So loud was the clamor and so many were the wolves, that it sounded as if every demon of ice in all the frozen world had come to keen their fury at them.

They rolled over the top of the wall and, with no break for their arms, began heaving in unison on the rope, lifting their prize off the ground. From the left, Faron could see a bobbing torch running in their direction. He heaved faster. They didn't have much time. The wolves continued to howl below, spiking his heart with panic from even this distance.

"Bloody, snowing wolves," Synick muttered.

Gasping for air, they pulled the white fiend over the wall, and Synick, holding the rope taught, tossed the beast over the other side. The rope whistled and fizzed as it spooled through his gloved fingers, singeing the cloth as it generated heat. After a moment, it thumped to a stop. With only a look, Synick leaped over as well and slid down the rope at speed. The gloves would likely be worn through after that.

While he descended, Faron scooped at the pooled blood on the wall. It had frozen and came away in chunks. He tossed it over the side and kicked snow on what he couldn't scrape in the few seconds he could afford. The rope went limp, and the torches were getting closer.

Frantic, he hauled the rope up, the empty end whipping as he reeled it in. Trying not to think about the absurdity of what he was doing, he lashed it around the first wolf's limp neck and heaved it over the side. The weight of it slammed him into the battlements, but he didn't let go. The rope singed his cloth gloves, which Synick had purchased only that morning, and his fingers started to feel hot. The lights were almost upon him now. He could make out the face of a man. It was Artur. More lights followed behind. At the last second, Faron sliced the rope, releasing the carcass. Hopefully it didn't have too far to fall. As he sheathed the knife, the rope snaked down into the darkness of the city. Faron spun and peered down at the roiling, still seething pack just as Artur came rushing toward the tower. He jumped as he saw Faron. "What in the North is happening here?" he asked, peering over the wall with Faron. "And what are you doing up here, Wolf Slayer?"

"I heard the noise," Faron lied. "Had to see."

Artur seemed to accept that. "What are they hunting down there?"

"What do you mean?"

"They don't gather like this unless hunting something large," Artur explained. "Or dangerous—like a bear. Ice demons are gluttonous things. If one thinks he can kill and eat you by himself, he will. They only summon others of their kind if the prey requires a pack to bring down." He scanned the snow. "So the question is, what were they hunting, and where is it now?"

Another man reached the small area between two towers, dressed in the same all-black of the Winter Wardens. "What is the cause?" he asked. "Should I raise the alarm?"

"No." Artur waved. "They are dispersing. Fire a few flaming bolts, though, and see them dispersed faster." He was right. The pack began dissolving from the edges, ceasing their long, hateful cries and padding away, vanishing into the dark of night.

"What stirred their summons?" the second man asked, unslinging a large crossbow from his back. He dipped a few bolts in oil and lit them in the flaming spotlight.

"Our friend here," Artur patted Faron on the shoulder, and his gut knotted. If he were discovered smuggling snowbeast fur into the city, he would be imprisoned at best. The belief that they were diseased, and the superstition around the creatures in general, was taken very seriously. Did Artur know? Was he going to try and arrest him?

"They sensed the presence of the Wolf Slayer—he who walks the White and fears no living beast—and they howled their remorse for their fallen brethren." Artur and his man laughed in unison. Faron only stared over the edge. Could they see the blood trail that scraped up the wall?

Artur patted his shoulder. "Ah, I should not jest so. Only a few days ago, you were pulled from the jaws of slaughter. You must forgive my poor taste." He leaned his back to the wall, turning away from the howling.

The second man fired the flaming bolt into the darkness, missing the wolves over such a distance, though, only narrowly. He swore under his breath, but the last of the wolves disappeared all the same. Faron admired the weapon with a hungry expression. Something like that would be unmeasurably helpful above the Veil, but he wouldn't have a way to reliably light the arrows.

"You are safe here," Artur comforted. "No beast has ever made it past these walls—not even when the snow piles higher than the stones."

Faron blinked, unsure of what he was talking about. Then he remembered—the wall. He was talking about wolves.

"I appreciate your kind words," Faron said. "I need to go now, though."

"Hearth keep you," Artur nodded a lazy bow from his slouched position against the wall.

"And warmth go with you," Faron said, reciting the northern greeting and turning from the light. He had picked up the greeting on his second day awake when Jesika taught it to him. He was fairly certain she only talked to him to make Synick jealous.

He strode away toward the nearest stairs and left the two men in the light of the mirrored brazier. Hopefully neither of them thought to ask who started it.

"Nearly dropped a snowing wolf on my head," Synick complained when Faron made it to the small warehouse they had rented. "I never would have gone to all the trouble of rigging traps and climbing walls if I knew the damn things were going to just fall from the sky."

Faron wasn't in the mood to smile. "Where are they now?"

"Come on. In here."

Inside the warehouse, the wolves lay on the ground, red eyes still staring daggers. Faron groaned internally. This was going to be messy.

"Come on. Let's get to work."

A short while later, when a fire was built and after numerous complaints and disgusted gags from Synick, they managed to skin both animals and left the pelts soaking in a barrel of lye soap. Faron had tanned a few skins as a child, and that knowledge translated over well. Synick, on the other hand, was almost no help at all. Eventually, Faron sent him away to work on something else while he focused on the pelts.

It was bloody work, but the one good thing about winter was how wonderfully accessible water was. Buckets of melting snow lined the fireplace, and Faron cycled them through whenever they turned too brown with blood. Before long, the undersides began to resemble something close to leather, though they weren't nearly done. The skins would take several days to cure and finish tanning. When the moon had set and the lamp burned low, Faron wiped the sweat from his brow—earned, despite the cold—and finally left for bed. The feast of First Winter Blood was tomorrow, and he was their supposed champion. His gut clenched as he anticipated being the center of attention, but he was so tired he managed to sleep anyway.

Champion of Firstblood

aron stared in the mirror in the washroom above the forge. Synick shared the space with him, and it was more luxurious than he would have expected. Mirrors were a rare thing for Faron—and for nearly everyone, in fact—but for a master glass smith, they were common. The bed was large and secured by thick wooden posts, and every seat was well padded.

Faron touched a piece of peeling skin on his nose, burned by the cold from his excursion in the snow. It was ugly, but Faron was just glad to be free of frostbite. There were similar spots of flaking skin on his fingers and toes, though not nearly so bad. His arm throbbed from where the arrow had split his skin in Aru'barrahk, and his ankle hurt a little more keenly from the wolf's teeth that punctured his boot, especially after his misadventure outside the wall, but all considered, he was healing quickly. The pain was annoying, but only that.

He ran a hand through his dark, lengthy hair. It had long ago passed unruly and was now downright out of control. The white silk under his buttoned black coat felt bunched, so he tugged at it. Silk was something he had never felt before, and he wasn't sure he liked it. It felt like cold water was continually being poured over his back and front, and he pulled at it uncomfortably.

Faron felt odd admitting to nervousness after what had happened with the snow wolves outside the wall, but he would rather face them again than this. The feast was today, and he, by chance, was to be their champion. What did that entail? What did it mean? Was there something expected of him? Clearly, there was, or they wouldn't have provided him with these ostentatious clothes. Black and white—why was everyone in this city dressed in the same black and white? Didn't anyone own anything colorful?

Normally the lack of color would have suited Faron just fine, but being forced into their finery had put him in a raw mood. His twisting gut didn't help either.

Synick walked into the room. He wore his livery far better than Faron while simultaneously managing to slouch and appear nonchalant. "About ready then?" Faron only groaned in response. "Oh, come on. It'll be fun."

"That's not the word I'd use," Faron replied. When was the last time he had even been to a feast?"

"To be honest, I'd prefer if you didn't use any words at all."

Faron tried unsuccessfully to ignore the knotting stone inside him. Hadria would have loved events like this, and she invariably would have convinced him to come along or dragged him along anyway.

Combing through his hair with his fingers, trying to push it back into some semblance of a kempt appearance, Faron shoved the anxiety down and exited the home. Outside the forge, there was a group of four men dressed in black tasseled with blue. He was surprised by the display of color, no matter how minute, until he realized it was intended to draw attention and set them apart. This was his honor guard.

Faron shook his head, face burning at the ridiculousness of being escorted, but resigned himself to the embarrassment. With swords in white gilt sheathes, they escorted him and Synick up to the very top of the mountain.

A massive pavilion joined by hundreds of giant tents spread atop the peak of the conical mountain, and unlike everything he had seen of the city before, it burst with color. Streamers of red, yellow, purple, and green arched across the open building, spanning hundreds of feet at a time. The huge pillars that supported the roof in place of walls were decorated with hanging wreaths, baskets of fruit, and colorful ornaments and baubles. Around the base of the pillars were pillows thrown on carved stone benches, much like the style in Aru'barrahk. Long wooden tables spread through the massive building and adjacent tents, and at them sat hundreds or thousands of people.

The din of the gathering rose high into the stone rafters despite everyone speaking in a low voice. The people of the city seemed strangely respectful to Faron. Never before had he seen so many people in one place. He swallowed hard. His head spun from the prospect of sitting among them. He wanted to run. If not for Synick's grip on his arm, he might have.

Fires roared at intervals inside long rectangular hearths that spanned between tables. Faron hoped that anyone who noticed the sweat on his brow would attribute it to those. As he watched, an older woman in a deep red shirt and white trousers stood from a seat at the far end of the room. A glittering crystal goblet sat in one hand, raised into the air, a clear shimmering liquid contained inside. From this distance, Faron could see the contents of the cup steaming slightly.

As if on cue, the rest of the room raised their cups. "To the slayer of wolves!" she said in an aged voice.

All eyes turned on Faron as he was shoved into the banquet hall. Men, women, and children took up the call, shouting or pounding fists on tables as they drained their cups. The roaring didn't die down, though. It only grew louder.

Faron was ushered to a seat—throne would have been a better word—beside the woman. Face burning from embarrassment, Faron sat in the carved wooden chair. At its head, engraved in stone of all things, was his name. His seat was slightly raised over the rest of the gathering. He wished he could shrink through the back of it as the eyes fell upon him again, though there were far more talking and laughing than before.

Synick sat down beside him, and if he felt even the slightest bit self-conscious, it didn't show. He beamed as he sat at Faron's left in a far less ostentatious throne, waving at anyone who peered his way, face bright and smiling. On his right sat four men garbed in the all-black of the wardens—the men who pulled him from the white, he realized. Their chairs were less opulent than his, but still large and decorated, unlike Synick's.

The elderly woman, who seemed to be running the affair, remained standing by her chair just below and in front of his own. She stood firm despite her apparent age. Beside her sat a man, young with dark hair and a goatee, and another man even older than her. He wore a kindly smile and looked warm inside his heavy furs. The woman raised her goblet again, which was already refilled, and the clamor died away.

"Every winter," she began, in a voice that carried farther than one might expect, "the Veil falls, and with it comes the terrors of night and snow." It became utterly silent, except for the crying of a few babes, as all ears strained to hear what she said. "It is to the Wardens of the Wall that we owe our gratitude and safety," she proclaimed. "Every year, when the snows climb our walls and the wolves come hunting, it is the wardens who repel them. It is the wardens who, at their own peril, push away the mountains of snow when they come too high and defend Anveil when the walls cannot." She stopped to breathe. "It is the wardens who sacrifice a life of comfort for the mantle of courage. It is the wardens we honor this day."

The crowd cheered their agreement, but Faron sensed the same reservation he had felt in Jesika's tavern.

"There are those who opposed my organizing this celebration," she went on. "This unexpected winter will prove a challenge to our city. Supplies will be short. Stores will be rationed. There is no way to deny this. A winter as early as this is a terrible calamity, but hear me now, citizens. We will weather this storm."

The sea of men and women seemed to sit a little straighter, listening more intently. It only just occurred to Faron what an early winter could do to a population.

"We have warehouses with grain, aquifers with fish, and a people as hardy as can be hoped for. We need not fear for food this winter."

Faron couldn't help but notice the two men behind her who seemed to hold back their disagreements.

"The greater threat will be with the wardens. The snow will climb high this year. The white wolves and bears will rise to our walls, and it will be the duty of our wardens to keep them at bay. If ever there were a year to feast in their honor, it is now!"

"Hear!" the crowd called in agreement, raising their cups, stamping their feet, or pounding gloved fists on tables. They seemed to be overcoming their silent anxiety.

As the tension seemed to melt away, Faron's mind wandered. The Anveil snow wall must have been over a hundred feet tall. Could the snow really pile so high? Even with this shockingly early winter, it didn't seem possible.

The din died down again as she raised her goblet. "It is for all wardens that we owe our gratitude, but it is he who drew first blood that we are here to praise tonight—one among many, whose bravery and valor must not go unrewarded." Clapping took up the hall until she silenced it again with her goblet in hand. "This year, for the first time in twelve, the honor of First Winter Blood falls to a man outside the wardens." The crowd remained silent as she paused.

"The first man to slay a snowbeast this season did so, not with a bow or with pitch, stones, or the safety of a wall, but with a dagger and the heart of a wolf." She turned, back nearly to the crowd, and pointed a knobby finger directly at Faron, almost accusatory in its aggression. "I name thee, Faron Wolfslayer—Walker of the Veil, Wolfbane, and Wolfheart. Your courage and your skill have set you apart as the Champion of Firstblood, and I declare it so."

Faron burned with self-consciousness under the gaze of the thousands who sat before him, even as they stood and began clapping and calling out the titles the woman had named him. None, though, were as fast upon their feet as Synick, who managed to clap several times before anyone else had even risen.

Through the scrutinizing fear came a small pinprick

Faron had rarely felt before and never in such a scenario—pride—slight at first, then more significant by the
moment until all desire to shrink had been pushed out of him.
He beamed a smile of radiant joy. What was that feeling in
his chest? It welled up and filled him from head to toe. He
was happy, he realized, to be among people who understood
and applauded him. Never had he received such a level of
praise or even any praise at all, except manipulative sparks
from Dageran. The cheers and accolades reminded him of
when he and Hadria were younger, and she had taught him
something new.

That dampened his spirits a bit, but he smiled on. Not only
did no one in this city want to kill him, but they actually *liked*
him.

"Praise also the men who pulled him from the Veil and
repelled the beasts that pursued him. I name thee, Nara,
who intercepted the jaws of winter from our champion; thee,
Caron, who carried him to safety; thee, Ranara, whose bow
never fails; and thee, Harfor, who was the first to face the
White. We honor your courage and valor!"

Faron thought the crowd roared for him but was corrected.
The applause he received was nothing compared to the
booming adoration for the four wardens.

"And finally," the old woman continued. "We toast to our
brave wardens—Watchers of the White, Protectors of Anveil.
Praise!"

Thousands of voices rose up in demonstration for their
black-garbed protectors.

"Praise!" she said again.

The applause he received seemed pathetic now, but Faron
was only glad to be out of the spotlight. He clapped and

whooped alongside the thousands of men and women who called out for their wardens.

"Drink now, for the health of the Winter Wardens. Drink to their strength, drink to their fortitude, and drink to their service!" Raising her crystal glass high, she brought it to her lips and drained it. Everyone else followed suit. Faron only just noticed the glass placed in front of him and reached for it, but everyone was already putting theirs down by the time he reached it, so he left it alone.

"Let the feast begin!" the short-haired woman said.

On cue, the five doors to Faron's left on the one actual wall of the building slammed open, and teams of men and women garbed in black and white lifted massive, gleaming trays with monstrously sized boars upon them, fruits, vegetables, and greenery piled high about the sides. Ten pigs, each larger than Faron, filed through the doors and were placed at intervals at the empty tables closest to the hearths. All of them were massive creatures, but the last one put them all to shame. Through a pair of double-wide doors came a team of six men guided by black-haired women carrying the largest boar Faron had ever seen.

Almost as tall as a horse and longer than Faron was tall, the beast must have weighed over four hundred pounds. The great wooden slab that carried the thing was so comically large it was more of a stretcher than dinnerware. The women guiding the cooks stood sentinel by their beasts now, slicing into them with pronged forks and blades of razor edges. Servants rotated between their kitchen mistresses, bearing plates or goblets or bowls aloft, filling them each respectively. In moments, stacks of plates were filled and distributed throughout the pavilion, served to those seated in the back first and quickly progressing up the hall until Faron himself had been served.

His plate was piled high with meat, carrots, potatoes, eggs, snow peas, and a few white vegetables he didn't recognize. At a command from the Mistress of Winter Blood, the feast began, and everyone was apparently every bit as eager as Faron. The meat was delicious, hot, and flavorful, spiced with a kind of white pepper. There were more types of carrots than Faron knew existed—steamed carrots, stewed carrots, red, orange, and blue carrots, even a soft, sweet, white carrot cooked and drizzled in golden honey.

So tall was the plate that he doubted he could have finished it all in three days. Attention turned from him as people began feasting with gusto, and he did the same. Never before had he seen such an elaborate meal, even when stealing inside the white marbled manors of the rich. In his crystal and iron chalice steamed a heated white liquid which was sweet and spiced, effectively keeping the cold at bay. If this was how Anveil feasted during times of hardship, he wanted to see them during the months of plenty.

As Faron devoured his meal, he felt a sense of pleasure overcome him. Synick was gorging on nothing but pork beside him, and he spied Artur and Jesika seated together only a single table away from his own. Synick—shocking enough that he was in Anveil at all—had fallen into an apprenticeship and given up thieving, and Faron himself had been offered a position among the Winter Wardens. Only a week in the city, and he had been nursed to health and even honored for his escape from Aru'barrahk and his race against winter.

A sudden longing pulled at his heart, and it took him a moment to identify what it was.

He was happy here. He put his chalice down mid-drink as the realization stung him. He wanted to stay. For the first time since the fire, he had found a place where he felt he belonged. That was why, even under the stares of so many people, he had sensed himself brimming with happiness. That was why, even now, he felt a guilty pull on his conscience.

He could have a trade here, honest and earned, and camaraderie where there had never been a chance for it. He belonged here. It made his heart sting.

Cutting his thoughts short, the woman stood again and raised her goblet in the air. Attention turned to her, but no one stopped feasting. "May those who have brought gifts for the Champions of Firstblood bring them forward now."

Gifts? Faron felt an annoyed panic rising again. His eyes widened almost as much as Synick's, though not with the same reaction. They wanted to give him gifts? Faron didn't know how much more attention he could endure. Hopefully, they would be only for the actual wardens. He was never sure how to behave or react during gift-giving and hadn't had much practice since the night of the fire.

All the experience he did have came from shared namedays with Hadria, where sometimes boys and their fathers would come from the village and leave her a gift of flowers or some new toy. They usually brought him something as well, though it always felt like an afterthought.

That was nothing compared to the hundred or so people lining up to present gifts to the five champions at the raised table. Apprehension knotted his gut as the first few people approached. For a moment, he thought he would rather be outside the wall.

The first two people through the line went straight past him and presented wrapped parcels to Ranara and Harfor at the end of the long table. He breathed a small sigh of relief until he noticed the third person staring directly at him. He was a broad-shouldered man, maybe a blacksmith or carpenter, well shaved, and hair neatly trimmed short to his head. He gave a nervous smile as the man simply stared at him as if sizing him up.

"It's been a long time since we've named a champion, Wolfheart," he said gruffly. "You're young," he huffed, but continued, "but you've the look of a man in your eyes. Here." He hefted a wrapped bundle onto the table. "Only a desperate man fights a snowbeast, and only a fool would fight one with a knife. With this, you'll fare far better." He nodded at the wrapped bundle indicating Faron should open it, so, nervously, he did.

His mouth gaped as he revealed a small, slender crossbow on the table, painted black and red. It was deceptively heavy for its size. As he unwrapped it fully, he thought his jaw might hit the floor. Except for the stock, the weapon was forged of Anveil steel. It was likely worth half the bag of Jaru'tal's gems he kept in his pocket.

"This is far too fine a gift," Faron managed to stutter as he turned it over. "I cannot accept something so princely."

"It's rude to decline a gift, Wolfheart. It is yours by right. Artur says he offered you a position on his wall, which makes you our protector, so take it, and use it to kill snowbeasts."

He nodded slowly. "Thank you."

Studying it, Faron saw that it was far more complex than any flatbow he'd ever seen before. The limbs were shaped more like an egg than a bow, and there were painted springs inside. On the top of the hollow frame was a sort of lever.

The giver must have interpreted his expression because he went on to explain.

"It's my own design. I call it a lever bow. It'll shoot faster and farther than any other and is sturdier than anything that fool, Barkhan, might make."

"Who?" Faron asked.

"Never you mind," the gruff man said. "Just know that it's the finest weapon you'll ever lay eyes on. It'll kill anything within nearly a hundred yards with a draw weight of four hundred pounds."

Faron's eyes bulged. "Four hundred pounds? I'd need a windlass to load that."

"That"—the man nodded—"or you could use the goat's foot."

"The... what?"

"That's what I call it. The lever arm attached to the frame. Give it a pull."

Hesitantly, but infinitely intrigued, Faron lifted the exotic weapon to his chest.

"Now, put the stock to your shoulder and pull that lever."

Curiosity peaked, Faron reached out for the handle of the metal lever. As he pulled, he noticed two thick pins that leveraged it downward. He tugged on it and, to his delight, found that it hardly felt like more than fifty pounds. The farther he pulled, the easier it became until the string clicked into place. The springs inside the bow arms were stretched and tense.

Faron's eyes went wide. "That's four hundred pounds?" he asked, surprise playing across his face.

"Yes, it is." The man appeared smug.

"I can never repay you for a gift like this."

"Nonsense," he replied. "Just remember when people ask

you about it, you got it from Bowyer Jorgen. With enough happy customers, I'll win that warden contract from Barkhan within the year.

Faron committed the name to memory and understood why he was being given such a kingly gift. Seeing the Champion of Firstblood with your weapons or in your establishment was effectively free advertising. He fingered the paint on the lever bow. He was alright with it.

"Thank you," Faron said again, releasing the catch and carefully replacing the string with the lever.

The man snorted happily, pleased to see him disarm the weapon with care, then, without another word, ducked his head and retook his seat, resuming the feast. Faron ran his fingers on the bow in shock, feeling the smooth lines of the steel under the black paint. It was almost half the size of the bulky thing he had purchased with Synick the day before, but he suspected it would outperform its wooden counterpart in every regard. It was a princely gift.

Others came and passed him, most of the gifts intended for the true wardens, but several other people stopped by him as well, offering him delicacies, candles, perfumes, packaged bread, and even a cloak made of green wool. A few people gave him rings, studded with glass or polished smooth, and one woman gave him a map of the city.

His heart filled with joy as he felt the welcome of the people of Anveil, but for every modicum of joy, he was equally burdened by the knowledge that Hadria was out there, waiting for him to come and find her. It felt immoral to enjoy himself while she was waiting at the edge of a knife.

The boar lost its flavor, and his appetite faded away as he thought of the certain contrast between Hadria's situation and his own. At best, it was a mountain of difference; at worst? He couldn't bring himself to think about what the worst might be.

Synick grabbed his shoulder, and he snapped out of his reverie. He was clutching a bottle of pale liquid. Leave it to Synick to find something strong. "Have you tried the pickles yet? They're unbelievable. Go on, try one with one of your turkey eggs."

He didn't even peer down at his plate.

Synick sighed. "It would be rude to leave, Faron. At least wait until everyone's done eating."

"I should be tanning those skins," he said absently.

"There will be time for that," Synick insisted.

"I'm not staying here," Faron cut in defensively.

Synick recognized that look in his eye and said lightly, "Look. You're going to be a long time past the Veil. There won't be much—or anything—out there to eat, and you won't be doing your sister any good if you drop dead of hunger." He paused, sensing how well Faron was taking his words. "You owe it to her to fatten up as much as you can while you can. It'll give her the best chance."

To his great surprise, Synick's words lifted his spirits, and Faron nodded in agreement. He ate like a wolf after that, shoving eggs, pickles, pork, carrots, potatoes, turnips, parsnips, giant mushrooms, onions, radishes, beets, and so many others he couldn't identify down his mouth; he nearly made himself sick. No matter how much he ate, though, a serving girl would stop by and load more of whatever was missing onto his plate.

In the space of an hour, he had consumed more than he ever had in his life. He could hardly move and was certain that he'd vomit if he tried. He sat, pleasantly enjoying the spirit of welcome Anveil had extended to him, but silently he planned. The wolf pelts had been soaking in barrels of saltwater for an entire day now and would be swelling. He would have to go and thin the skin before tanning them, to reduce both the weight and smell—tomorrow. He could wait until tomorrow.

Long after the sun went down, Faron remained in the feast hall until he was eventually helped to his feet and given a bag to carry all of his new prizes, except the crossbow. He wore that on his back. Slowly, he made the long walk home with Synick, and before he knew it, his head was on the pillow. He slept long through the night.

Bolts of Flame

When the sun had risen, Faron became aware of a slight buzzing sound. Slowly, he cracked open his eyes. It was his head. That annoying buzzing was a hangover. He groaned as he pulled himself up off the spare bed that had been dragged into the room. Realizing that he was alone, he spun his head about the loft. Where was Synick?

Perhaps he had left to begin working on the wolf skins, Faron thought, and tottered out the door. All the way across the town, right up to the base of the wall, he walked, until he found the locked warehouse space he had rented. He tried the door, but it was locked. Pulling out the small brass key, he let himself in.

Synick wasn't inside, but Faron only grunted to himself and locked the door behind him. The space was filled with barrels, tanning racks, strange knives attached to a table, and tall stools. That was partly why they had chosen this location.

Heaving, Faron lifted one of the skins from the saline barrel. Sodden, it was heavy, but he wrung it out and lay it on a rack. The flesh on the underside was soft and bloated with water from soaking the past forty-eight hours. Pulling on different corners, he attached the pelt to clamps with a large grip until the skin was tight from being stretched in twelve different directions.

From what he remembered, it would need to dry like that for a few hours before he began thinning the hide, so he did the same to Synick's pelt and let himself outside. The wind from yesterday had let up, but the snow was not relenting. It fell in large, fat flakes, lazily floating down to land on a frozen stone.

He peered into the sky. What day was it? He mentally recounted the date and frowned. Hadria's nameday was only a few weeks away—the day Ulric predicted would be her last. He had to leave. He marched off to the market.

The markets in this city were like none he had ever seen before. Merchants stood in stalls or storefronts under awnings, occasionally sweeping away or brushing off snow from their wares. Carved signs hung over lamp posts, the heat from the torches keeping them clear of snow and ice. While they couldn't exactly be described as quiet, they were certainly not as aggressive as the merchants anywhere else he had been. They talked and laughed with their neighbors, but otherwise didn't harass anyone passing by. Shoppers occasionally stopped at certain buildings or stalls where they exchanged set prices for goods and went about their way. No one hawked their wares; no one haggled with tired customers. It was strangely polite and respectful. Faron found himself liking this city even more.

The smell of baked bread competed with the sound of an instrument merchant stringing a lute and the sight of gleaming steel and silver. Compared to Blackwood or Fayevew, it was quiet.

A group of girls giggled as they approached, staring at him

openly. His brow furrowed as they passed him by. What had that been about? Spending so much of his youth in the caves below Blackwood had left Faron with no idea how to converse with girls who were not slaves. This, though—this was something far beyond his understanding. He decided not to waste time on it and continued on. He fingered the black velvet pouch in his pocket, thinking of the gleaming gems within. They were not particularly large, but they couldn't be easily traded for what he needed. He had to find a money lender or banker to sell them to.

New crossbow on his back, Faron wandered the streets a little aimlessly, searching for someone to trade with until he caught sight of a sign piled high with coins. Certainly, that was what he needed.

Sure enough, inside was a thin, white-haired man who weighed the gems and studied them under a small magnifying glass, then announced his offering price. There were no asked questions about how he came to possess such treasures. Perhaps he recognized Faron from the feast, or perhaps he was simply accustomed to back-alley dealings. Faron didn't stay around to find out, leaving only a few gems in reserve and attaching a large pouch of kingpence to his belt.

Money in hand, he made his way to a tavern where he purchased a small tub of animal lard to tan the wolf hide. He carried it under his arm as he walked back to the warehouse but noticed a leatherwork shop on the way. He eyed the goods through the window but decided against going inside. The pelts were plenty dry by now and needed to be worked. If he left them too long, they would need to soak again. He would come back later.

When he returned to the warehouse, Synick was there

waiting for him.

"So that's what you've been eating," Synick exclaimed, eyeing the lard. "I thought I had narrowed it down to straight cream, but this makes more sense as it explains the smell as well."

"You know," Faron cut in, "if you had come earlier and actually helped me with these, I'd be nearly done with the tanning by now."

"Well, just what do you think I've been doing?" Synick complained. "Something unproductive?"

"Wasting your energies on Jesika, no doubt."

"I wouldn't classify it as wasting, so much as attempting to fill an emptying well using nothing but spoons and a lake a mile away, but no, I've been on to something else. I couldn't sleep last night. I had this idea running through my head after we talked and couldn't get it out, so I gave it a shot." He lifted a glass vial-shaped object.

Faron admired the clear tube. It was vaguely pointed at one end and filled with a grayish powder flecked with white at the tip. A thin, concave layer of glass separated the dry substance from a yellowish-clear liquid. Lamp oil, Faron thought it was.

"What is this?" he asked skeptically. "Is this why you haven't been helping me with the pelts?"

"Yes, in fact," Synick said pointedly. "But let's be honest. It's not like I was ever going to touch those anyway."

"How is this helpful? The vial isn't stoppered; it's completely sealed."

"Look," Synick pointed out. "This, in the top bubble, is flash stone." Faron raised an eyebrow. "And the other, larger section, holds oil."

Faron's brow furrowed. "So, it's a way to make fire without

a tinder box or flint?"

"Well, yeah, but no. Here." He gestured at Faron's crossbow until he unslung it from his back. "Probably easier just to show you."

"You mean to shoot it?" Faron asked.

"In a way, yeah." He loaded the vial into the bow and took aim at a large, empty stone wall and fired. The brief sound of shattering glass was drowned by the roaring fire that exploded from the broken vial, oil spilling across the wall and onto the ground, igniting in an instant inferno. Faron jumped.

"What in the freezing North is that?" Faron exclaimed.

"I made fire!" Synick said. The flames spread to a certain point but didn't rise any higher. There was only stone for it to consume.

"Synick, that's brilliant!"

Betraying how proud he was of himself, he blushed slightly and smiled. "Took me quite a bit of attempts to make that; I'll be honest. I might need to compensate Master Orothorn for all the wasted glass and whatnot."

"How many of those have you made, Synick?"

"Well, two. One I tested earlier, and that one there. Feels like a bit of a waste of my effort now, though."

"Do you think you could make more?"

Faron's earnestness seemed to encourage him. "Without a doubt!" He leaped to his feet. "I'll have to drop by the market, though. I've run out of oil, or at least, Master Orothorn has. I'll need more rawhide gloves as well. The last three were in a state of perpetual fire from all the oil spilling over the glass when I shaped it, and I'll need to replace them."

Faron reached into his belt pouch and tossed Synick a few kingpence. "Buy whatever you need, Synick. Any cost is worth more of those… things."

Synick bolted out the door, and Faron chuckled to himself. A fire weapon? Now that was something he could use.

He turned his attention to the stretched pelts, pulling a knife down them to shed the excess skin, but his mind never left the idea of Synick's exploding tubes.

When the pelts had shed enough weight, Faron greased them with lard, getting his hands and arms disgustingly slick in the process. He'd let them sit for another day, and then they'd be ready to cut into shape.

He intended to be gone the same day.

A few hours later, Faron found himself in the leather-worker's shop, being fitted by an aging man and his son.

"You have made a wise choice, Faron Wolfheart. These will fit you well and will turn out the snow and wind."

"How long will it take?"

"For you? I can mold something new in a week's time."

"A week?" Faron asked. "Could I pay you to expedite your process?"

The man rubbed a smooth-shaven chin. "If you required it, Wolfheart, I could modify an existing piece. Your form is a little difficult to fit, but I think I could find something to suit you."

"Please," Faron insisted. "The sooner, the better."

"I can make it sooner. Give me until the day after tomorrow. It shall be as comfortable as a queen's pillow."

"No," Faron interjected. "Not comfortable. I want it rugged. I need thick, strong leather."

"The two are not mutually exclusive, Wolfslayer."

"Just so long as it's durable," Faron conceded. "I would like epaulettes on the shoulders, and if you can manage it, woven strips of metal on the forearm to stay a wolf's bite."

The man raised his eyebrows. "You're taking the Wall Captain's offer seriously, I see. Still, that is a strange request."

"I mean to travel come spring," Faron said, not really knowing if it was a lie or not. "A lonely traveler could be assailed by any kind of hungry beast."

"You could stay, you know," the man said, measuring around his chest with a supple strip of leather. "The captain is fair to all men—especially those of valor." Faron didn't respond, and the leatherworker took it as an answer. "But I suppose every man has his own journey. Perhaps you'll return to us one day."

"I need to go my own way," Faron confirmed. "But I'd like that very much. Perhaps one day."

"You know," the man said, changing the subject. "If I could convince you to wait another day, I could stain your leathers a good, healthy black—not unlike the wardens."

"That isn't necessary," Faron said.

"Are you sure?" the man asked, seeming squeamish. "Every man and wife will see my goods on your shoulders, and I would not have them find my work lacking."

Faron understood after that. That was why the man had made no bother haggling and was so insistent. Like the bowyer, Jorgen, he intended to use Faron as a showcase for his goods. His smile slipped slightly. The amenable old man was happy to work at a discount because Faron would essentially advertise his store for him. When Faron disappeared in the middle of the night, though? He would quickly come to regret the exchange. Faron determined to pay in full, regardless of the price offered. He couldn't use the coin in the North anyway.

"Do whatever you have to, but I value utility far higher than fashion."

"Well, I believe I can find a common ground then. I'll get started right away, Wolfheart. Is there anything else you'd like me to add?"

"Pockets," Faron said after thinking a moment. "Lots of pockets. And don't forget the metal and epaulettes."

The aged man nodded. "It seems to me you want something more akin to armor. I know the like. I think you'll be satisfied when you see it."

"In two days?"

"Two days—if I can't convince you to allow me to stain them properly."

"Two days then," Faron confirmed, counting down the days to Hadria's nameday for the hundredth time. "And I'd like to purchase a pack as well."

"I have a selection you can choose from, and so does Master Bartan across the square."

Faron readied himself to leave. "Would you like me to pay now?"

The man frowned but replied, "I don't see why not. Three hundred and eighteen pence, if it pleases you, Champion." It was expensive, but he had only raised the price by three tenpence for the pack. Fishing out four thick golden coins, Faron deposited them on the desk on the way out, leaving a few extra silvers on top just in case the discount offered was steep. Faron had no use for the coins anyway.

He left in search of a tailor. The air was cold and crisp, plumes of mist rising from the breathing masses that crowded the market square. The sun was at its zenith, but it always felt like it was just about to get dark. From a fragrant brick building came two nearly identical girls close to his own age. One looked to be a year or two younger and the other perhaps a year older. He nearly stepped on his own foot trying to get out of their way, and practically tripped when they stopped in front of him.

The older girl concealed a smile, but the younger made no attempts at all to hide a beaming grin. "Compliments of the Kneading Board," she said, pushing a hot parcel into his hands. Faron supposed that was the name of the bakery they had come running from.

"Oh," he stammered. "Uh, I suppose…"

They both giggled at his lame attempts to find his tongue and turned tail, running back into the bakery. "Thank you," he said into the air, watching their blue and red hair ribbons bounce away playfully. He blushed. What had *that* been? He supposed they were pretty and realized, with some embarrassment, that after years spent as a form of slave in a massive cave, he truly didn't know how to determine if a girl was pretty or not. He had met only a handful in his life except for Hadria, and most of them had hated him, either because they were newly joined to the guild and hated everything to do with it or because they were among Dageran's favored and he was not.

His skin shivered when he thought of the black-haired man, and his blood boiled from the memories. He forced them down. One day he would have Dageran's head, but now was not the time. He directed his attention to the warm parcel in his hands and discovered that it was a form of bread, cooked with small cloves of baked garlic and thyme.

Glancing once more at the door that had concealed the two sisters, Faron turned away and sought out a tailor—both for ideas on how to cut a cloak and for warm liners to go under traveling leathers. Before he was done, he purchased the warmest underclothes that money could buy.

The sun was nearly set by the time he returned to check on Synick, and his eyes bulged when he did. Synick stood in the largest pile of broken glass Faron had ever seen, focusing intently on a red hot, molten tube, gloves and tongs flaming like coals.

"What in Atha's name?" Faron exclaimed. Synick's gloves were on fire, yet he stared intently at the closing glass vial, twisting and rotating it until it was completely sealed.

Master Orothorn, a white-haired, long-bearded man of subaverage height, tapped his foot impatiently, whirling on Faron when he approached.

"He's used more glass than he could pay for in a year!" he roared, unstoppered by the presence of someone who could hear him. "He's gone through over half my supply of flash stone and claims only that *you*"—he jabbed into Faron's chest—"told him to do it! I don't care how many ice demons you killed. Someone has to pay for it!"

Gaining his composure, Faron interrupted. "I will. I did ask him to do this, though I had no idea it would be so... messy."

The short man was calming down a bit now. "He's brilliant with the torch, but if he's anything, he's messy."

Faron fished two gems from his pocket—an emerald and a ruby. "Will this cover your expenses?"

Orothorn's eyebrow raised. "A fair bit more, I'd say, but I'll take it." He scraped the stones off Faron's hand. He had only one left now. "It's about more than just expenses. If I run out of flash powder before winter is out, I'll have no way to replace it. The only source in the world is an alchemist in the Kaor, and even in the peak of summer, he's snowing impossible to reach."

The cylinder Synick held extinguished, and he let out a shout. "I did it! The last two broke from the heat, and now I need new shoes, but look how well this one turned out!"

Synick lifted it for Faron to receive, but he made no move to take it. "Your gloves are still burning, Synick."

"Ah, only for a moment. Besides, it keeps Orothorn from trying to take them from me. Grab that scrap of leather and take it."

Faron accepted the hot glass into his hands gingerly, admiring it. The tip was pointed like an arrow, with excess glass on the side of the front pocket that contained flash stone, shaped almost like a barb.

"You've gotten better," he remarked.

"He's incredible," Orothorn said. "He has more natural talent in one little finger than my last apprentice did in his whole body. He's completely incorrigible at the same time. I never know if I should be praising him or spanking him."

"Coming from someone else," Synick cut in, "they could be done at the same time."

Faron reddened slightly at the racy joke, unsure how Orothorn would react, but he burst into laughter, head turned to the sky. He very nearly caught a snowflake drifting in on a breeze.

"It's that ridiculous tongue that convinced me to grant you an apprenticeship and let you touch the forge half a year before I should have. And I'm glad of it." He patted Synick sharply on the back. "Perhaps now you'll tell me what the purpose of these is?"

"They're for crossbows," Faron said.

"I'll sell a million of them," Synick claimed. Faron let him lead with the lie. "I'll be rich overnight, I tell you."

"You'll be imprisoned is what you'll be, responsible for burning down the entire town!"

"Oh, relax," Synick said. "We won't fire them in the walls. They're for wolves."

"Well, if you're going to be a pack of snowing fools, at least do it right." He pulled the smoldering gloves off Synick's hands. "Give me these. What you're trying to make is called an ampoule, and you're doing it wrong. I'll show you how it's done without burning my forge to the ground, you freezing idiot, but you're going to have to reimburse me for the materials."

"Wait," Faron cut in. "You want to help us?"

"I didn't become the wealthiest glass smith in the city by passing up ideas everyone called crazy. Here, let me show you a better way."

Into the White North

The pale sun kissed the shrouded horizon, sagging deeper into the dark embrace of night. Only the glowing orange spot of the sun was visible, the sky covered in a deep, uniform gray. Snowflakes, small and sharp, landed on the exposed faces of Faron and Synick, melting as they were warmed. They stood on the wall, silently watching the sun set as they overlooked what was by all accounts a certain death.

White shrouded the world. Blankets and heaps of snow piled against the wall, stacking high, freezing, and stacking higher. Trees appeared shorter, their bases ensconced in ice. Both of them were garbed in leather—Faron in the light brown apparel he had received that morning, Synick in his thief's blacks, newly reinforced with wool. Both wore large, heavy white fur cloaks on their backs, two long gray stripes running from neck to ankles, and packs as well.

On Synick's pack, there was strapped a small hatchet, a flint, a lantern, his crossbow, and a bedroll. Faron's pack was thinner and sat on his left shoulder, crossbow sitting comfortably with a strap on his right. Together they surveyed the landscape, waiting for dark.

"You don't have to come," Faron said.

"I know." Synick's mood was serious.

"It could mean the death of us, Synick—if not by wolves, then by cold, and if not that, Sadagon will surely have designs for us."

"You don't have to go," Synick said morosely. "No one is blaming you, Faron." He turned his gaze away. "You've come so far," he continued. "No one would have expected you to make it here, but it's not too late to turn back."

"Synick…"

"I know," he said, picking up the pause. "I know. You have to go. You're like a force of nature."

"You don't have to come," Faron repeated.

"I will though. I've invested too much time keeping you alive to give up now."

Faron offered no further protestations, only nodding his ascent. The silence stood between them for a long moment.

"Come on." Synick clapped him on the back. "Let's go get eaten by some wolves."

In the dark, Synick tossed a rope over the edge and was the first one off the wall. The soft snow crunched underfoot when they touched down, and the wind whistled ominously, almost in a way that made the night quieter.

They turned their backs on the wall and left the rope behind. Someone would find it soon, and the people of Anveil would likely piece together what had happened, but it would be too late. It was already too late. They stepped carefully into the night. Darkness shrouded the tree line beyond the wall, curls of snow shifting just within sight. Shadows moved barely beyond their vision behind the snow-covered pines and naked aspens that scattered sparsely through the landscape. Somewhere a wolf howled.

Despite his cool demeanor, Faron could hear Synick's ragged, fearful breathing. It caught in his throat unevenly, and he could hear his friend swallowing hard. Men had died doing things far less stupid. Faron's confidence waned. Could he be wrong? What if the wolves he saw were simply normal wolves? He shook the notion from himself. He couldn't forget those red, hungry eyes. He wasn't crazy. The snow wolves had approached that night and let him be. They would do the same here. They had to.

They approached the tree line, tendrils of snow undulating past them, and both stopped wordlessly. They could be ripped to shreds if he was wrong. He tried to keep it from his face, but Faron could see the fear in Synick's eyes. He felt it in his own. He set his jaw and stepped into the trees.

In the failing light, the wall had been easily visible, but it quickly fell away from view, and Anveil was gone. Ahead lay only darkness in the thin trees.

"Why did we do this at night?" Synick whispered almost under his breath.

"We can't afford to have anyone try to follow. They'd try to rescue us from our misadventure but would be in far more danger than we."

"You think," Synick said. It wasn't a question.

"Now is not the right time to start doubting."

Synick remained silent for a few moments. "No sense wasting time here."

They continued moving, stepping through the thick snow. The sharp wind and their footsteps were the only sound for several minutes, and then came the wolves.

A pair of glowing red eyes reflected from before them, springing open at the sound of their shuffling through the

217

snow. Synick jumped, and Faron froze. Images of the beast that had attacked him when the Veil fell sprung into his mind—memories of the feral teeth and the almost sentient, angry eyes.

Synick whipped his hand up to his back and pulled at his crossbow with all the dexterity of a long-practiced thief.

"Synick, wait," he hissed, but it was too late. As soon as the bow was in his hands, he fired at the glowing eyes. A pure white wolf exploded into flame as glass shattered, and oil spread down the length of its back, its chest, and tail. Even the pads of its feet were on fire. Its stance went from cautiously curious to furious in a single heartbeat. Whipping around, it tried to find the source of the pain it felt, spinning and yelping in a confused fury.

Synick was reloading the bow. "Synick, wait!" Faron said again, louder, and caught his arm.

The wolf ran into the night, yelping and barking as it died. The low hanging branches of a few pines caught the oil from its pelt and burned feebly, but lasted only a few moments before extinguishing.

On the ground where the wolf had been, a white light flickered ominously, casting long shadows around the forest. Caught in the light of the fizzling flash stone stood another three wolves looking directly at them.

Synick's muscles clenched visibly when he noticed them, and Faron had to jerk his arm down to keep him from firing again. He cast a hot-eyed gaze his way in reply.

"Wait," Faron seethed. "We have to know."

"If they'll attack us?!" he said incredulously.

"Just wait," Faron said. The wolves were small for snow wolves but still far larger than any dog or wolf in the normal world. They pinned the two boys with their gaze for a moment until the largest of the three directed his attention to the strange white light and then back. The other two seemed to take it as a cue.

Padding slowly and seeming to stay on top of the snow with massive paws, the wolves approached, crouched low and hackles raised. Faron felt the hair on his neck and arms stand up in return. Had the wolves that followed him to Anveil done that? He couldn't remember. Of course, he had been nearly delusional from exhaustion, starvation, and hypothermia at the time, but he wished now that he could.

The largest of the three came within ten feet, eyes boring holes into his own, then five feet. His teeth were not bared, and Faron took it as a good sign, extending his hand to the feral animal the way he would to a dog of uncertain demeanor. Synick raised the bow, and Faron let him. His finger hovered on the trigger.

Heart pounding blood into his ears, the monsters came within stabbing distance—or biting. On a whim, he pulled his hand from its glove and stretched his quivering fingers outward, slowly at first and then all the way, leaving only a few inches between himself and the predator. The she-wolf closed the gap and sniffed his trembling fingers. Faron closed his eyes.

A cold tongue wet his knuckles and then his hand. He looked to see the monstrous wolf licking his palm. Faron was struck so hard with relief that he had to suppress a full-bellied laugh but still let out a breath of air from his nostrils. Terror ebbing away, he stood there and allowed the white wolf to lick his hand until she decided to stop. A few moments later, it ended, and the wolves turned away, diverting their attention back to the glowing flash stone.

Faron could hear Synick's shuddering breath loose from his lungs as he lowered the bow. "Atha's grave," he cursed. "You were right. By the dead gods, Faron, you were actually right." He let out a nervous laugh and struggled to keep his voice low.

Euphoria flooded Faron as well, and he let out a small chuckle. "You didn't believe me?"

Synick crouched forward, supporting himself on his knees. "I thought we were dog food," he said through fits of morbid laughter. An actual tear escaped an eye and slid down his face; whether from mirth or relief, Faron couldn't tell. "I thought we were both dead," he said again.

The white wolves turned their heads to see Synick's laughter but spread out around the glowing light, inspecting it from behind fallen logs or shrubs.

"Your firebolts work," Faron said, examining the pale light.

Synick only nodded. "Hopefully, we won't need the others." He exhaled sharply from his nose. "This is unbelievable. Faron, you've done it." He gestured with his crossbow. "You've discovered the secret of winter. You can go *anywhere*."

"We go north," Faron agreed.

"Well, let's not waste time gawking," Synick said in a reprimanding tone. "Your sister isn't going to save herself."

The words struck like a hammer on hot iron. *Hadria.* His thoughts turned to her, and impatience welled in his heart, impatience and something else he couldn't immediately identify—perhaps longing, or a sense of finally having the end in sight. Tears almost escaped him.

I'm coming.

The wolves followed them through the forest, quickly

growing bored of the dimming, sparking light. Eventually, they came into a clearing. More wolves found them there and followed along until they seemed to lose interest, padding away into the darkness. Synick laughed as every snowbeast joined or left their unlikely group, relieved, almost to madness, to still be alive and in one piece. Through alternating patches of forest and clearing, they walked, long into the night until the sun began to rise.

When the sun finally crested in the east, Faron was shocked by the change of landscape. The trees had become shorter and shorter, the snow burying them ever deeper. A few of the pines still bore needles, but most had turned to dead trunks. Snowflakes whipped around what was left of the bone-like limbs, twisting through the air in a dance. Mountains could be seen in the distance, but the landscape here was wide and open, the remaining trees obscuring very little from their tired eyes.

Faron rubbed fists into his lids and checked his map. It wasn't very detailed, and this part of the world was wide and open, but the mountains in the distance were portrayed on the ancient canvas, if perhaps not with the utmost accuracy.

He turned to see the mountain city, Anveil, rising into the sky like a single jagged dagger. A black ribbon spun along the bottom of the giant knife of a city, ensconcing it safely away from the rest of the frozen world. They would likely notice his absence in a few hours if they had not already. Faron turned to see Synick staring back at the mountain as well, a strange expression on his face.

"What is it?"

"Nothing," he answered. "I'm just tired."

"It's been a long night."

"I'm not entirely sure I didn't hallucinate half of it. I'm still alive, though, and that's honestly more than I expected." He poked his ribs with a black-gloved finger. "I think I am, anyway. This could be some sort of purgatory, though. I mean, you're here, after all."

Faron changed the subject. Letting Synick get too far with his jokes was unwise. "We should rest."

"And eat." Faron nodded his agreement. "Hopefully, our food will last." Faron laughed, causing Synick to raise an eyebrow. "What?"

"Oh, it's just funny you think our food will last."

"Well, I suppose we can hunt for some deer or elk to help with that."

"And carry it all with us?"

"Oh, stop your laughing. You look like a weasel in heat." He poked Faron in the side when he doubled over, laughing harder. "What do you suggest we do then?"

Faron wiped tears from his eyes and grew serious. "I don't know, to be honest. We could carry enough supplies with horses, but we've been over that. They'd likely be attacked by the snowbeasts just as we would without cloaks, and we can't get them out of the city anyway. Honestly, Synick, I'll be surprised if we're not eating wolf before this week is out."

"That?" Synick said incredulously. "You're laughing about *that*?" He jabbed a finger through the air. "Well, the joke's on you, my privileged friend. I was raised in a freezing orphanage. I ate dog more times than I can count, and that's only the times I knew it."

Faron chuckled slightly. "I ate a raw rabbit outside of Anveil," he said.

"It's like I always say: you are what you eat."

"And what's that?" Faron asked skeptically.

"Harebrained."

Faron groaned as Synick cackled, but inside, he smiled, and that felt good to do. After a few minutes had passed, Synick unslung his pack and crossbow, sitting on a frozen rock or log, and Faron said, "I'm glad you're here, Synick."

Synick hesitated, pulling a broken stick from the ground and tracing white lines in the snow before responding. "You know, funnily enough, so am I." When Faron didn't prod, he continued, "Before the guild, I had nothing. People don't go out of their way to help a little street rat. They only kick at you if you don't get out of the path fast enough.

"I starved in that cold, stone orphan hall. I eventually ran away, only to get scooped up by Aerik. Things were better then, but not really." Faron didn't interrupt. "No one cares about starving children, Faron—not until they become an annoying problem and not a moment after." He drew more lines in the snow. "I hated them. I learned to hate them, and honestly, I still do. They kicked at me, called the guard when I begged for a coin or a piece of bread, so eventually, I stopped asking."

Faron knew what he meant. He stopped asking and started taking. "I really got a taste for it then—the stealing. For the first time, I was the one in control, and everyone else was the one to be pitied." He let out a long sigh. "I ended up in the guild after getting into more trouble than I could handle. Thought I was lucky at first, but it all got away from me."

"What do you mean?"

"It wasn't just thieving anymore. Well, you know what we did. We had no choice. I had to convince myself that I liked it because what else could I do? I had to make the most of things."

Faron's eyes lit up. "That's why you were so eager to help me escape? You were considering it yourself." Shock rushed through him as he realized the truth of it. Synick had always put up a false face, but he had never really known why. It suddenly made sense.

"I was, and I wasn't," Synick obfuscated. "I loved parts of it, you know? Stealing from the rich, destroying their grasping for power—I mean, how many jobs afford you the opportunity to kick a noble prick in the balls? It wasn't just that, though. We stole from everyone. We hurt everyone. Besides, I wasn't sure how to go about it. I knew I couldn't outrun Jakal, and they would've known I'd go straight back to Fayevew." He threw the stick. "I'm a snowing coward."

"Look at you now," Faron objected. "Out in the middle of freezing winter, no walls, and wolves everywhere, yet here you are." Synick waved a hand dismissively. Faron continued, not eager to bring up the memories. "And all those times in the guild where I couldn't finish a job and you stepped in to help me? Ice, Synick, I had no idea they were as hard on you as they were on me. I leaned on you more than was fair all those years, and you never said a thing." He paused a moment, letting it sink in. Synick's eyes had fallen to the snow, shrouded behind his fur-lined hood. "Then, in the end, you sent me off without you when it was the one thing you wanted and, instead, stayed behind to face the consequences... You're the bravest person I know, Synick."

His eyes stayed on the ground, but Faron noticed a single tear sliding down his friend's cheek. After a shared moment of silence, he leveled his gaze with Faron, eyes misty. "I don't know how this misguided adventure will play out, Faron, but

I'm glad to be here with you."

A white wolf chose that moment to prowl into their view. The wolves from the night before had long since departed, going their separate way, but this one was different. He was angry, and he was enormous. Faron and Synick leaped to their feet, Synick yanking at the crossbow on the fallen pack. It was stuck under the snow.

The wolf barked angrily—a savage, feral sound that sent shivers down Faron's back. Synick gave up tugging on the crossbow, rolling the pack over and pulling on his shock white cloak. It was still attached. What was wrong?

Synick yanked a long, thin knife from a belt with five others at his waist and sent it flying end over end. It struck the wolf in the chest but hardly seemed to hurt it beyond inciting its rage. The beast gave up crouching and sprinted their direction. It was fast.

Nearly as fast as thought, it closed the gap between them, running directly toward Synick. "No!" Faron yelled, lifting the small, almost egg-shaped metal crossbow from his back. Synick dove out of the way, rolling into a crouch. He came up with his stiletto dagger in his hands.

Unlike Synick, Faron didn't keep his weapon loaded upon his back. He shoved the stock into his shoulder, heaving on the lever to draw the bow. It clicked into place. Fumbling at his belt, he drew one of the vials of oil and loaded it into the weapon.

The wolf had come around by now and pounced again, teeth gnashing in the air where Synick's throat had been. Again, he rolled away. Faron lifted the crossbow, aiming at the wolf, but Synick's back got in the way.

"Move!" he yelled. Synick backed up a few paces and then

dove to his right, fumbling in the snow. Panic filled Faron as the wolf saw an opportunity and leaped again, this time landing square on Synick, who managed to get flat on his back.

"No!" Faron yelled again, but it wasn't Synick's end. In Synick's hands was a short, thick stick, sodden with snow and ice, that he placed in front of himself, just as the wolf bit down. It gnawed on the wood, trying to snap it. They were so close that Faron couldn't ignite one without burning the other.

Putting the bow aside, he drew his knife and rushed the snowbeast. He sank the blade into its back. In a flash of white and red, the snow wolf turned and snapped at Faron but returned to Synick in a whir. The knife ripped from Faron's hands, sticking between the wolf's shoulder blades. If it was angry before, it was blind with rage now. Feral snarls and grunts filled the air as the snow wolf struggled to get past Synick's wooden shield and rip at his throat.

Before long, the beast would stop trying for the throat and change aim for his stomach instead. Synick wouldn't survive that. Leaping back, Faron made a snap decision, picking up the crossbow and taking aim. At the last second, he adjusted the aim slightly to the wolf's hind legs—nearer himself—and shot.

Fire poured across the wolf's hind legs and back, and it leaped from Synick, yelping and snarling, spinning to try to catch the flames in its fur the way a dog chased his tail. Faron would have laughed, But Synick was covered in the flaming oil too.

Across his legs and on one foot, the flames lapped at him, eager to consume. Synick's eyes widened as he fell from one danger to another. In a flash, Faron was there, bailing snow onto Synick's legs, but it wasn't needed. Synick smacked at the flames for a moment and then started rolling in the snow. Oil transferred from leather to the ground as he rolled, and the flames extinguished. In a few spots, the fire still burned on top of the snow, but Faron tamped it out.

The wolf screamed—an enraged, almost pitiful sound—as the fire rippled through its fur like a spark in a tinderbox. It fell still and then was silent. As hot-blooded creatures, snowbeasts couldn't survive without snow and ice, and fire killed them faster than it would a regular animal. The brilliant spot of flash stone fizzled in the snow, emitting a large cloud of acrid smoke and burning brighter than the shrouded sun.

"You caught me on fire! I had things well in hand, and you dumped oil on me and lit me up like a torch!"

"Oh, calm down," Faron panted. "I know this isn't your first time being on fire or even the most unusual."

"Hey"—panting on his knees, Synick lifted a finger in the air—"that brothel was on the cutting edge of intrigue, and I won't tolerate you slandering it."

Shaking his head, Faron laughed. The edge of the clearing smelled putrid with burned fur and flesh. It brought unwelcome memories. "Let's move. I'd rather not attract anything unwanted our way."

"Unwanted like a horse-sized murder dog who doesn't care about my magic cloak?"

"Yeah."

"What in Olsu's freezing creation happened?" Synick asked.

They stood and retrieved their fallen daggers—Synick's from the snow and Faron's from the wolf's back. It was stained black with oil-smoke, but the metal retained its temper.

Faron felt at his cloak. "I don't know. These have worked well so far—until now."

"Does it have to stop working the moment a big one shows up? It couldn't have—you know—chosen a more convenient time, like when the fox came sniffing our way?"

Faron shook his head. "Only thing we can do is hope they keep protecting us and move forward."

They hiked north and steadily downhill until the snow was so deep they were walking among the treetops. None here still bore their needles. They had died centuries ago, the constant cold not allowing them to decompose. The air was so cold here that the snow was frozen solid. Except for a few inches of the freshest flakes, they were walking on ice. It was then that Faron realized they had passed the Winter Veil.

They had made it to the White North, land of eternal winter.

Cold

C old—cold, cold, *cold*. Synick jammed his gloved hands into his armpits, his annoyingly lady-like cape wrapped tight around his frame. A small fire flickered between him and Faron, lit with the aid of a tinder box and a hundred-year-old frozen tree, the top of which had snapped easily, but it did little good. Wind whipped at them from all sides it seemed, and the warmth of the flames was carried away into the night.

Curse this freezing place, he thought. *And curse him!* He looked across the weak fire at Faron, who hardly looked cold at all. *Probably warmed by the fires of his willpower*, Synick thought glumly. Despite every inch of his body being wrapped in lamb's fleece, soft leather on top of that, and a giant, lady-like snowing cloak, he was still chilled to the bone.

Faron rose from the fire. "Where are you going?" Synick asked.

"We need something more to burn."

He wasn't about to argue with that. Faron disappeared behind him in the darkness. It had been a glum three days since they'd left the comfort of Anveil—three days since he'd not said goodbye to Jesika.

You didn't have to come, he berated himself. *You made a choice.*

And truth be told, it wasn't a very difficult choice. He could be happy and warm in Jesika's tavern, badgering her with his advances—he was fairly sure they weren't unwanted—but he would have had to abandon Faron. He shook his head. He wasn't going to do that twice. He regretted letting him go alone the moment he had sent him off the first time. How desperately he had wanted to go with him.

He hadn't though—because of Jakal, Dageran, and his damn selfishness. He had feared them too much to go with Faron that night and, instead, stayed behind to line his own pockets and whore without end. He had gotten stabbed and tossed into the cave for it. He didn't blame Faron for that, though. It had been his idea, after all, and not a random one. It was a thought he had nurtured for many years, deep in the belly of Blackwood.

Synick was a natural thief, but Dageran always wanted more. Before he knew it, Dageran was forcing him to burn down struggling businesses, frame innocents, extort small-time urchin organizations, blackmail, anything he could imagine, and so many other things he didn't care to name. He had even killed a few people—people who certainly didn't deserve it. He still saw their faces sometimes when he slept. That was usually a sign he hadn't been drinking enough.

Despite Synick's natural thirst for revenge on the mundane masses for a singularly terrible childhood, his hatred was quickly outpaced by Dageran's cruelty and unending creativity. It wasn't long before he dreamed of finding a way out. However, Synick was, above all things, pragmatic. Too many people had been murdered trying to flee for him to openly dissent. Instead, he played the part, taking the dirty jobs and kissing Dageran's ass to stay above suspicion. He almost came to believe the act from time to time, getting so wrapped up in his own self-fulfillment that it didn't matter who he hurt. Faron had ruined that for him.

When he had washed up outside the cave beneath the Banshee Cliffs those few months ago and learned that he wasn't going to die, he decided he would never abandon Faron again. He had to remind himself of that at the start of this journey—climbing beyond the wall on some fool's errand—but he had done it. He had needed to vomit from the fear, but he had done it.

The wind whipped his brownish-blond hair over his head, tugging at his hood. He secured it more tightly around his face and stared into the flickering light.

Faron was an interesting person. He could be infuriatingly single-minded at times and never knew how to respond to a proper pun, but he was the opposite face of the same coin as Synick himself. At least, that's how Synick saw things. Neither of them had what you would call a happy background, and both had ended up in the same place, trading their souls away for another month's rent on life. Synick was the outcome of that hateful crucible that Dageran desired, or at least, he pretended to be. He had abandoned his morals and glutted himself on the pleasures of man with no regard for consequence. Faron, however, was the more broken outcome. He had stuck to his principles with zeal, even when it bent him so far out of shape he no longer wished to live.

Synick understood that, though. It's what he wished he had done. Faron had had the courage not to betray himself when *he* had hidden behind false pretenses the very moment he was prompted. He had an undying respect for Faron because of that—a respect he could never stomach mentioning—but there all the same. Faron was brave, selfless, and determined, but that wasn't why Synick loved him. Faron was a version of himself—a better version that had made better choices. He was the closest thing Synick had to an actual family. As far as he was concerned, Faron *was* his family.

Synick would protect him because of that and wouldn't make the mistake of sending him off by himself again. Next time Faron faced peril, Synick would be there, right by his side. He wouldn't back down from the face of fear, or danger, or hunger, or cold like he knew he was inclined. He would be like Faron. He would be better.

Faron returned with an armful of branches from the few trees that weren't buried in snow, freeing Synick from his dreadful reverie. Their shelter on the side of a small, steep hill was pathetic, but at least there was wood to burn.

"There you are," he said. "I was beginning to worry you'd gone off and met the she-wolf of your dreams."

Faron gave the little smirk he did that meant he thought the joke was funny but didn't want to encourage him. "Let's see if we can get this a bit warmer," Faron muttered. "I'm freezing."

"Freezing ugly, you mean, but now is hardly the time for a confession." Faron rolled his eyes, but Synick chuckled to himself and helped set the branches.

Glass Lake and Frozen Peak

Faron's white cloak flipped in the wind, snowflakes brushing his cheek and twisting away. From a high place, he overlooked the frozen valley in front of him, illuminated by a pale sun wreathed in thin clouds. It was impressive. Sharp, jagged mountains, stones like a thousand swords, pierced the sky, snow and ice covering everything that was not vertical or steeper. Entire hills made of ice gouged clear paths down the sides of those mountains—glaciers, the like of which Faron had never imagined.

Beneath it all lay a deep blue—a frozen sheet of clear ice. It had at one point been a lake, but it would never unfreeze. It probably had been this way for centuries—maybe millennia. Down below, prowling on the ice were several snow wolves, staying in a pack.

They were loath to put themselves in the path of any such beast, white cloak or not. The past ten days, they had been attacked by individual wolves almost every other day. They had seen nearly ten times that amount of snow wolves who seemed to seek them out to lick a palm, some of the smaller ones even depositing a dead white rabbit or fowl at their feet and padding away. They couldn't puzzle out why some of the wolves attacked them—never in a pack and only ever the largest of the already monstrous beasts—while others offered them tribute. Synick attributed it to his bad luck, but Faron suspected there was something else behind it. He just didn't know what. Whatever it was, it was dangerous to approach a pack.

On the other hand, their food supplies had run out the day before, even with the supplemented gifts of hare or fowl from the smallest of the wolves. They had to choose between avoiding the snowbeasts for fear of attacks or actively hunting them themselves. Wolf meat was tough, greasy, and difficult to chew, but it was nourishing, and they were hungry.

Synick stood beside him, a long puff of white mist escaping from his mouth. His nose was red, but he hadn't complained about the cold in several hours. "It's so vast," Synick said, awestruck. The mountains, glaciers, and valleys they stood before indeed seemed endless. Somewhere in those jagged peaks hid the ancient city, Vam Aranath—City of Temples, City of Light. Faron thought he could see all the way to the end of the world.

Beneath him fell steep cliffs of bluish ice, merging at the bottom with the long-frozen lake. "We have to get down there." Faron pointed.

"You don't intend to climb, do you?"

"If I have to, but I don't think it'll come to that. There looks to be a sluff to the west."

"We've already gone too far west," Synick argued.

"We'll have to make up for it. I don't see a better way down, and we're nearly out of rope. I don't think we could get down anything this shear besides. I wouldn't unless we were desperate."

"Well, we're nearly there," Synick said. "My stomach feels

like it's trying to claw its way out of me."

Faron nodded his agreement. "Let's get down."

A few miles to the west, they found an area where the cliffs had crumbled, offering a possible, if treacherous, path. They half-slid, half-climbed down the precariously balanced slide of stone and ice, each boy losing his footing more than once.

At the bottom, wind assailed them. A constant gust of freezing air picked the ice clean of drifts and flakes, gathering and hurling them against the base of the great white cliffs. The surface of the ice was so smooth and compacted that they gasped to look at it.

Like strings of pearls strung from the bottom of the world, small bubbles of air rose from below, now frozen eternally in the ice. Faron's breath caught in his throat when he peered down through the strings of trapped air, realizing just how clear the ice was. He felt as if he could see hundreds of feet before it became too cluttered to see any farther.

"It's like glass!" Synick gasped. "An ocean of pure glass." He lay prostrated on the ice field, hood pressed against the surface. "You can see so far!"

Faron felt much the same amazement, but he didn't tarry. It was time to move on. His heart thumped with anticipation. He could practically hear Hadria calling out to him. He was close. He could feel it.

"Where are you going?" Synick called. "Come see this!"

Faron's heart pounded in his chest. He couldn't stop. "I'm coming, Hadria," he said under his breath.

"Faron? Faron, stop." It wasn't until Synick caught up to him and tugged on his shoulder that he stopped. "Look," he gestured.

Faron followed his finger and saw the pack of snow wolves

running their way. They looked angry. The wolves that had approached them before and had been friendly were only ever in packs of three or four. These were seven, and none of them were small.

Synick tugged at his arm. "Come on!" He pointed at an island of rock on the glass lake. Stumbling on the slick surface, Faron allowed himself to be pulled.

"You don't know that they aren't friendly," Faron panted as he ran, doubting it even as he said it.

"And you don't know that they are. Come on!" They were almost to the outcropping of stone, but the wolves were closing in. Faron could hear them barking and growling now, and not just one but all.

"Why is this happening?" Faron yelled.

"Just snowing run!"

Synick reached the rock first, but he slid to a stop and laced his fingers together, bending to one knee. Faron knew the prompt. Slowing, he put one boot in Synick's gloved hands and allowed himself to be launched into the air. The wolves were close, barking and snarling ferociously.

Slamming into the side of the great stone, Faron got one foot on a decent hold and wrapped one hand around the top. Not waiting to make sure his hold was secure, he lowered his other foot as far as he could. The wolves were nearly upon them. Synick jumped, grabbing onto Faron's boot, and he heaved. Scrambling against the wall, Synick pulled himself up just as the wolves closed the gap. He came level with Faron, and they pulled themselves over the edge onto the small, nearly flat space atop the boulder.

The wind was fierce upon their faces. Barking, a wolf bounded up the side of the boulder, scrambling wildly before it fell back to the ground. He erupted in flame when he did. Faron shot a glance at Synick, who was already reloading.

Faron followed suit, lifting the bow from its leather harness over his cloak and pulling the oval metal lever to load the string. The wolves yelped below, the fire spilling from the hide of one to the feet of another.

Another wolf tried jumping, but hot oil erupted on its head and down its body as Faron shot it, not waiting for it to fall.

The wolves stopped jumping.

"That's snowing right!" Synick yelled, reloading the bow. "I'll cook you all right here, and when I'm done, I'll eat every one of you!"

The wolves split up, running around both sides of the rock. For the first time, Faron noticed the shape of their stone fortress. Behind them, it sloped downward until it nearly touched the ground. The wolves could leap right up and overwhelm them.

Thinking quickly, Faron grabbed Synick's loaded bow and pointed it at the ground. Synick didn't resist and released his weapon. Aiming just far enough away not to include themselves, Faron fired the bolt at the ground. Flames leaped up between them, forming a temporary barrier. He pushed the weapon back to Synick, who began reloading.

The wolves congregated beyond the flames, acrid smoke pouring into the sky, bright white light sparking in the middle of the fire.

"That bought us a few seconds," Synick remarked. He loaded a regular bolt into his bow and loosed it through the fire. He was rewarded with a high-pitched yelp.

"Why are they attacking us?" Faron questioned in the frenzy.

"Maybe if you ask nicely, they'll explain," Synick said. "Just lay on down and offer your throat for them to rip apart."

A wolf, braver than the others, leaped through the greasy flames, brilliant light from the flash stone casting odd shadows under the pale creature. Synick promptly lit it ablaze, arm extended, finger already on his rough trigger.

The white wolf writhed on the ground, spreading the oil in its death throes, and the flame stretched closer. It yelped and managed to jump off the rock. Faron loaded another firebolt into his lithe bow.

"We can't keep this up long," he cried.

"We've got more bolts than they have bodies," Synick argued.

Faron eyed the prowling wolves through the black-tipped fire. They met his gaze with a hungry intensity. A second wolf braved the fire. They were hungry. This one bore the bolt that Synick had planted in it before, but it fell to flames as well, this time from Faron's crossbow. The oil caught in the perfect fur, igniting eagerly, but also dripped onto the stone, closer and closer to their feet.

"We're running out of room," Faron said. "And we can't use all our fire here."

"That's tomorrow Synick's problem," he replied. "And he'll have a real hard time of it if he's eaten by a wolf instead of eating a wolf."

The first fire was flickering out now, the oil burning up and the flames finding nothing to consume. The wolves fell back into view. There were three left: two—small for snowbeasts—and one nearly the size of a horse.

It was this one, the largest of the group, that locked red eyes with Faron. Even here, days above the Veil, it was the largest wolf he had ever seen. His heart froze, and his blood turned to ice. Despite the necessity of recent events, Faron was no warrior.

Sensing his weakness, the white wolf pounced. Flying over the flame, it landed squarely upon him. Unloaded, his crossbow fell from his hands. Nowhere to dodge out of the way, the wolf crashed down, jaws snapping. Faron managed to push himself away from the great white beast but only barely. The force sent both Faron and wolf flying off the edge of the boulder.

He landed hard. Pain assailed him as his lungs constricted, forcing air out and not allowing any to return. He was vaguely aware of Synick calling his name, but it hardly seemed important.

Chips of ice flew away as the wolf's sharp claws shattered the clear sheet, a piece even stinging Faron's cheek. Saliva dripped from the open maw of the great creature, and Faron dared open his eyes. It stood over him, growling, toying with its kill. It didn't even bother to pin him with a paw.

Amused cruelty turned to hatred in the wolf's red eyes as it reared in anger. Synick had jumped on its head. Blood so hot it melted small patches of the icy lake fell around and on Faron, sizzling as it struck. A sharp barking and low growl escaped the snow wolf as it snapped its head upward, trying to bite at Synick, but he was firmly in place.

In a flash of unbelief at seeing Synick mounted on the snow wolf's back, he noticed the glint of silvery glass falling through the air. His eyes widened as he saw Synick's firebolt falling toward him. If it cracked, he would be smothered in flame before he could even attempt to save himself.

Like a coiled viper, he struck out and caught the revolving

incendiary. Seeing him move, the wolf turned its monstrous jaws back toward him and growled. Acting on an unformulated instinct, Faron threw the vial with all his might. It lodged in the wolf's maw and cracked on a tooth.

Faron watched as the oil escaped, coating the back of the wolf's mouth and throat, and like a rippling wave, the blue flame ignited.

The snowbeast screamed—an unholy, ear-piercing sound that made him want to claw his ears off. Leaping and spinning, the giant creature continued to loose the horrifying shriek, smoke puffing from its mouth and nose. Its lungs were on fire. Faron covered his head and rolled forward, narrowly avoiding being stepped on by a clawed paw.

Synick slid to the ground, the wolf spinning, howling, and clawing in terror as it burned from the inside. He clutched two handfuls of the long white fur.

The two remaining wolves rounded the corner, snarling and ready for a fight when they stopped dead in their tracks. They saw their pack leader fall to the ground, whimpering now as smoke escaped from the raging inferno inside, and the surviving wolves eyed him warily.

It wasn't fear Faron saw in their animal eyes but something else—something far more complex. They almost seemed to be reevaluating their odds.

The yelps and whimpers came to a stop as the giant wolf died, its head falling to the glassy, frozen lake. The two smaller wolves turned their head to Faron and Synick once and then fell on their fallen brother, ripping and tearing at its still-hot flesh with a fervor.

"Should we run?" Synick asked, approaching and grimacing at the ghastly display.

"Wait," Faron said, still lightheaded with adrenaline. He watched as the hackles on their backs fell, and they ripped and tore at the thick fur. "They have what they want."

Sure enough, they seemed to be so occupied with their meal that they'd given up on the fight completely.

Synick shook his head. "That's disgusting."

"Come on. Let's dress one of these."

Faron knelt by the black and white carcass of a smoking wolf and unsheathed the smaller of his two daggers.

"Not until I fetch and load our crossbows," Synick said, eyeing the feasting wolves. "I don't think, for one second, that ugly thing tastes better than I do."

Adrenaline still pumping through Faron's system, he didn't laugh, but he thought it was funny. More accurately, Synick likely just didn't want to watch as Faron skinned the dead creature. He had no stomach for that kind of thing, so Faron didn't stop him.

When Synick returned from the top of the smoking, stinking slope, white flash stone still casting harsh shadows, the sound of the wolves' ripping came to a stop. Faron and Synick flicked their eyes up, Synick ready with the bow.

Padding their way over, the smaller of the two wolves—although only slightly—approached them calmly. A bleeding red mass dripped in her jaws. She deposited the gift at Faron's feet. It was a large, uneven slab of meat, white ligaments still attached at one end. It steamed.

Faron raised an eyebrow, flicking his eyes between the wolf and the bloody muscle.

"Um... thank you?"

Synick spoke up suddenly. "Oh no, you don't! You think you can just go from rage-fueled murder wolf to obedient little doggy and I'll forget about it? I don't think so. I'm still going to eat you—every bit except those nasty red eyes. I'll truss you up over a spit and laugh until the gods are reborn, claiming my soul for darkness." The wolf turned around, ignoring him. "And you know what?" he yelled after it. "I'm going to enjoy every bite! Even if I have to make a tent out of your fur and camp here for a month! Both of you!"

Faron chuckled at his tirade but not so loud that Synick would hear. The wolves returned to their dead companion and resumed gorging. Synick came and plopped down onto the ice, careful to put his back to the partially skinned animal.

"That smells positively cantankerous."

"It'll probably taste that way too," Faron confirmed.

Synick groaned and slid down onto his stomach, staring into the strange depths of the pearl-like pockets of trapped air. "Let me know if anything else wants to eat me," he said, pulling the hood over his head. "That way, I'll be prepared and just let it."

"You rode a wolf," Faron offered. "Thanks for that."

"Don't mention it."

Faron laughed. "You looked so bizarre, hanging on for dear life."

"I looked bizarre saving your skin again, you mean."

"I'll repay the favor, likely before this week is out."

Synick only groaned in response. "I'm hungry," he complained after a pause.

"Go start a fire. I'll bring the meat in a few minutes."

"I'm tired." Faron threw a small giblet at him. "All right!" Synick practically shrieked, brushing at the red piece of intestine. "You're an animal. Just give me a moment."

Faron smiled as his friend stalked off to the north side of

the lake, where a few small bushes tried to grow against the shelter of a small outcropping. He hadn't started shaking yet as he did after every encounter with wolves, but he was still warm from the adrenaline pumping through him. At least there was that silver lining, however small compared to the constant attacks. What did it say about his state of mind that his first reaction after being attacked by a pack of red-eyed monsters was to sit down and cook one of them?

Why were they being attacked, anyway? Why were most wolves leaving them alone and others not? Faron didn't understand, but either way, he hoped they would stop. They had been lucky with each fight and had avoided taking any serious injuries, but they were bound to run out of luck.

They did—but not in the way Faron expected. After Synick lit a fire and Faron cut all they could eat and reasonably carry from the dead wolf, they were never attacked again. After a few days, Faron wished they were.

The wolf meat ran out quickly. Three days after they left the glass lake behind, their stores of food ran out completely, and the wolves that saw them kept their distance. They saw a herd of pure white deer bounding away from them between openings in sharp stone crags, but Synick missed the shot, and they escaped.

Besides hunger, the only constant was the cold and ripping wind. Always, it howled, tearing at their cloaks and hoods, trying to cut them away.

Neither of them spoke much after a few days without eating. They couldn't spare the energy. Synick walked head down, belt tight, only following Faron's footprints, light and shallow in the dusting that lay upon a solid sheet of ice. Their lips cracked and grew bloody, burned by the wind and cold. To make matters worse, they were thirsty. Though they were completely surrounded by water, it was always frozen and seemed to leave them thirstier the more of it they packed in their mouths.

Through the hunger and pain, Faron set his jaw. He had experienced it all before. It was for Synick that he grew irritated. His friend didn't say anything by way of complaint, but Faron knew he was thinking it. Where was this city? Was it even a reality, or had he led them both to their deaths, searching for something that wasn't there? Despite his conviction, the doubt ate away at him.

His impatience seemed to grow with every crest, with every view over every jagged peak. Night fell sometime over half a month from their departure from Anveil. Near the top of a windy, broken ridge, Faron and Synick huddled together, stubble thick on the older boy's gaunt face. They shivered uncontrollably. The inexorable cold was ever-present and inescapable. Even with fine fleece and leather, they were going to freeze. Without food, their weak bodies couldn't produce enough heat to survive, and they were nearing the ends of their limits.

No fire flickered on the top of that mountain, as none had for several days. There was simply nothing to burn this far into the White North. They hadn't eaten a thing in four days, and both looked as gaunt as a man already dead. They certainly felt that way. Backs pushed into the overhang of a stone peak, Faron felt more sure every moment that he had led them to their deaths.

"Synick?"

No response.

"Synick?" Faron asked again. This time Synick started.

"What?" he shivered through chattering teeth.

"I... I'm sorry."

Again, there was no response.

"I don't know where we are. We should have found the city three days ago, at least."

Silence.

Faron hesitated himself, but fear and guilt prodded him. "If we die here... I'm sorry."

"That's it," Synick said, pushing himself to his feet. Faron hadn't thought he could get any colder, but Synick's absence proved him wrong. "Get up."

"What? We're exhausted."

His teeth chattered uncontrollably, and his speech was slow and slurred, but Synick replied, "If you've got the energy to waste on fripperies like this, we've got time to find that bloody, freezing city."

"Synick, I mean it. I don't know where we are."

"You never really did, though. Come on." He pulled Faron to his feet, pushing gloved fingers to a temple as he did so. Faron was ashamed of how much of his weight Synick actually had to lift to get him up. "Let's get moving. You won't want to talk in stupid poetic verse after a few more hours up and about."

For almost the first time since Anveil, the clouds parted, revealing a bright moon and the brightest stars in existence, but it was still dark.

"We can hardly see where we're going. We're more liable to fall off a crevice—"

"Nonsense, these stars are so bright you can hardly even see any black in the sky at all." He was joking, but there was some truth to it. Olsu's rift cut a bright white path through

245

the massive sky, its luminescence nearly rivaling the moon. Formed by innumerable stars, it almost appeared a solid milky white ribbon in the sky.

Mind turning slowly, Faron overcame his exhaustion and walked with Synick. They had climbed the mountain before sunset to see the lay of the land but had been forced to make camp when a blizzard hit. It had passed now, though, and the clouds with it.

Supporting each other, they shared cloaks and slowly stepped down the mountain.

Trying to hide how tired he was, Synick struck up a conversation. "What's the first thing you'll eat when we find the tavern there?"

"Tavern? In the Lost City?" The cold seemed to assail him from everywhere. He felt its bitterness in his very bones.

"Well, why not? If there's a city, there's a tavern. It's just common sense."

"I think the ice has got to your brain." His vision flickered and wobbled, nearly forcing him off his feet.

"No, it's you who got to my brain—made it all soft and mushy—and now I'm following you to the coldest freezing place on this earth. I'll rephrase, though, for your tiny wit. If you were in any tavern in the world, what would you eat?"

Faron's vision flickered black. Ice, it was *cold*. "What would I...?" He breathed hard. His sight wasn't coming back. "Eat?" Stopping, he shook his head. Something was wrong. "What... I... I can't think." He tripped, landing face-first in the snow.

Faron slid twenty, thirty, forty feet down the steep incline.

"Faron!" Synick called, sprinting through the thick snow toward him.

Faron tried to reach out with an arm to stop himself, but

his head swam—both from the rolling through the snow and from a complete inability to process what was happening in his dying mind.

"Faron!" Synick called again. Finally, he slid to a stop, and Synick caught up. He was vaguely aware of the older boy shaking him. He even thought he felt a dull slap across the face, but he wasn't sure. Under the ocean of stars, losing his life force to the cold, Faron didn't know if his eyes were open or closed. He thought he saw Synick—or rather, Synick's back—and had the sensation of moving, but it may have just been imagined.

If We Die Here

S tupid boy. Stupid, freezing, idiot boy. Why hadn't he said something? He'd been freezing to death or starving—Synick didn't know which but figured they weren't mutually exclusive—and said absolutely nothing. He'd started all that mopey, "if we die here" talk, and Synick had been forced to distract him. If Faron was at that point, he was truly low.

He'd only been snowing wasting his energy by trying to distract his friend when he fell flat on his face and tumbled halfway down the hellscape of a mountain. He tried not to think about how close he'd gotten to that long, dark crevice before he'd finally come to a stop. He hadn't woken up even then, even after a good slap, so Synick was left with little recourse.

Wasting no time on the decisions, Synick wrapped Faron in both white cloaks as tightly as he could manage, and feeling like he'd stepped from an ice bath to the bottom of a frozen river, he pulled Faron along down the sheer mountain by his boots. *The wolves*, he thought. *They'll come for you. How will you fend them off if he has your cloak?* He ignored the ever-growing piece of himself that produced such thoughts, pulling harder.

He wasn't sure where he found the strength, but he dragged his friend like a sled over the snow, and they moved quickly. The stars were lit well enough that he could avoid the more obvious cliffs, if not entirely plot a course down.

He heard a howling in the night. His hairs stood up on the back of his neck like they did every time he heard or saw one of the ugly abominations, but he didn't stop to think.

They know you're here. He shook his head. *They can hear you. They smell you.*

He was running now. Another howl rose toward the waxing moon. "No," he whispered as he ran.

Leave him. Take the cloak and leave him!

"No!"

The howls turned to barks as the distance closed between them. The wolves were coming. They had never left, really, only watched him starve from the shadows.

RUN! his inner voice panicked, and he did, but not without Faron. Down the mountain, they flew, throwing his head over his shoulder to see the wolves behind him.

Suddenly, the mountain fell away, and only open air was beneath him. Screaming the pent-up terror from his lungs, he flipped and tumbled down a nearly vertical, rocky surface. He never let go of Faron, though. He knew that he was Faron's lifeline and Faron the one unconscious, but it felt the other way around. He wouldn't have let go if a wolf had its jaws around his head. In the dark, they rolled to a stop, Faron still not waking up. Massive walls of ice and stone blotted out the light from the heavens like tall bastions of evil on either side. Only directly above did any light filter in.

Coughing out what surely must have been at least half a lung, Synick stumbled to his knees. He spat blood, hopefully not too near Faron's head, and looked up. He made out the dim silhouettes of four wolves, hungry red eyes glaring down at him. He reached back for his crossbow—and it wasn't there.

The wolves turned, barking, undoubtedly going around for a more sure path. He had a few seconds, no more.

Take the cloak! his conscience screamed.

"No," he croaked through painful lungs, arguing with himself out loud as he never allowed himself to do. The wolves might or might not attack him with a snow cloak on, but he had no doubts whether or not they would attack Faron, unconscious and defenseless on the frozen floor. It would be a fight either way.

You're no warrior, you freezing idiot!

Synick ignored the screaming voice, tossing his hands about in the darkness for his crossbow. He couldn't find it, and then he remembered—Faron's bow. Frantically, he felt at Faron's back, and there it was, mounted in its half-back sling, far more beautiful than such a weapon had any right to be. He tugged it off Faron's back and flipped around, facing the only way in or out of the sharp ravine.

He saw tall vertical slats of darkness, somehow deeper than the rest of the world behind it—trees? He stepped forward and heard a branch snap underfoot. It wasn't his foot.

YOU SHOULD HAVE RUN! You'll be eaten, snowing fool.

Sharp sting of terror stabbing his heart, a tear rolled down his eye.

"I'll eat you first!" he screamed, firing the barely loaded bow into the perfect darkness. Four wolves were swallowed in blind white and yellow light, crouched only yards away, shoulders low as they hunted him through the white-frosted pines. They recoiled from the sudden brilliance—but not

Synick. Eyes blurry with terror, he fell on them. The firebolt had missed them all, but he could see them now.

Throwing the bow, he hit the second closest wolf on the skull, forcing it a step back, then plunged his stiletto blade deep into the nearest wolf's black heart. Blood hissed, steaming on the ground as he yanked the knife out, but he didn't stop to think. There was no time.

Whirling to gain leverage, he yanked a firebolt from its protective pocket and sent it spinning with a left-handed throw. It shattered on the trunk of a massive pine, but the flaming oil flew from the collision and caught in the third wolf's fur. It screamed and gnashed with powerful jaws, but they couldn't save it. The flames consumed it with an unrivaled hunger.

Already tugging at another pocket, he whipped another vial at the closest living wolf, it too erupting in a gout of hellish light. Screaming, he turned on the fourth, final wolf, who, despite her fallen brothers, still wanted to rip him apart.

"Come on!" he shouted, voice clawing at his throat. He dove at the monster with his blade, but it dodged out of the way. He swung again, this time leaving a false opening so she might attack, but again, the wolf dodged. Warily, it cast its eyes from him to Faron.

"No! You die here," he hissed. The wolf turned and closed the short distance to the easier prey. Fast as lighting, Synick threw his favorite dagger. He didn't consider for a second the possibility that he might miss and that if he did, he might hit Faron or that the blade wasn't balanced for throwing. He trusted his arm. Only once, the knife revolved before it sank nearly hilt-deep into the beast's hamstrings. Synick wasn't far behind. The wolf snarled as the knife struck, but it stopped, and with the space of a second, Synick was there, fists flying before him, second knife lost in the fall.

Angrily, the red-eyed beast bit his left arm. He let it. Its teeth punctured keenly through his leather blacks, but he repaid the wolf tenfold. With his right, he punched its skull, eyes, and neck until it let go, but he wasn't nearly finished. Left hand now free, he grabbed at its neck and slammed it to the ground. It kicked its legs wildly, sharp paws clawing him, but he gave no notice. Hind legs now in reach, he seized his dagger from its flesh, lacerating the leg with a wicked twist as he pulled it free.

The snow wolf actually had the audacity to whimper, sensing its fate, but there was no mercy in Synick's heart. Dagger rising, he plunged it into the wolf's back as it scrambled to get away, then its side. It yelped and whined with every puncture. He stabbed its shoulder, belly, then side again—once, twice, three times, more. He stabbed and stabbed the wolf. Even after he was sure it was dead, he sundered its flesh with his blade until the entire pelt was soaking and red.

A cough interrupted his panicked breaths, and he spat up blood as he finally released the thing and freed his knife one last time.

"Ice take you." He bloodied his boot with a kick.

He heaved over and sat in the snow between Faron and the dead wolf. Covered in steaming blood, he was warmer than he'd been in weeks. For several minutes, he sat that way, staring at the two bright points of light in the forest. Eventually, his mind caught back up with him.

Trees! They hadn't seen trees in nearly a week and, consequently, hadn't had fires either. Struggling back to his feet, he pulled dead branches off the pines and piled them all next to Faron. In this light, he almost appeared blue, but he was breathing. Scooping up one of the now dim remnants of flash stone, he set it in his pile and blew. It winked out. He thought to try the other one—maybe hold some dead needles to it for a torch—but it died too, swallowing them in complete darkness.

Sighing, he fingered the pocketed pouch at his side. He found a firebolt in its sheath and pulled it out. It was the last one. He flung it at the ground on the far side of his woodpile. Light washed over the clearing, and the oil happily consumed the gathered wood. Warmth poured over him as sap popped and crackled under the pines. He had no idea how they survived this far north or how they hadn't seen them before, but he didn't care. They were here, and they were burning.

"No need to protect you from this," he said, unwrapping Faron the rest of the way—the fall had mostly done that on its own. He left a cloak at his back and underneath him, positioning his friend to curl up toward the flames, and gathered more wood to burn. They would need it.

Into the Light

From darkness, Faron gained a sense of self and was aware of a powerful, flickering light and warmth washing over him. For a few long moments, his mind stayed in the world of dreams until he tried to remember where he was. Confusion sparked through his thoughts. There had been the mountain where he was so dizzy he could hardly maintain a conscious thought. What had happened after that?

His eyes fluttered open to see the biggest fire he'd seen since the feast of Firstblood. Trunks of frost covered white pines, spread through a narrow canyon he didn't recognize, and Synick sat on a dead white wolf.

"Really?" Synick asked, incredulous. "That's what wakes you up? Not the fire, not the snowing wolves, the slapping, or even the three-mile slide you took down the mountain, but the first hint of fermented cat piss smelling wolf meat and you're wide awake?"

Faron cast his eyes around the forested ravine. There were three other dead wolves he could see, two of them scorched and one so bloody it must have been eviscerated. Strips of tough meat dripped small amounts of fat onto the flames, spreading the smell of cooking meat into the air. His head throbbed and felt five times heavier than it was.

Taking a moment to think through the last thing he could remember, he guessed, "I fell."

"Like a sled. Was pretty funny, actually." Synick shoved a thin scrap of meat into his hands, fresh off the fire. He received it, trembling violently. His stomach turned, hunger clawing his insides. With weak jaws, he tore at the tough meat. He could barely choke down a single bite. He reached out for a fistful of snow, but Synick stopped him, handing him something else.

"No need. Take this." It was a water skin that had remained mostly empty in the North but had since been packed and placed by the roaring fire. Sap popped and threw a piece of orange ember near his hand. Gratefully, Faron drank from the water skin, still half laying on one side. It was blessedly hot. How long had he been unconscious?

"The wolves," Faron croaked, wiping a stream of water from his chin. "What happened?" He took another bite, and suddenly the meat seemed full of flavor and wonderfully revitalizing. His stomach growled, eager to accept it.

"Oh, these? They're not much." Synick slapped the one underneath him. "This one is my seat—chose him for his plumpness." He pointed to the two charred dogs. "That's Ash and Dash, and this red one here is Ted."

Faron took a slow bite of the meat, then with a smile said, "Ted is delicious."

Synick snorted, coughing into the fire. "Oh, by Atha's tits, you choose *now* to crack wise?"

Faron chuckled lightly and pushed himself to a sitting position. A migraine exploded across his vision, but he ignored it. The night air was freezing, but the fire was warm.

"What happened, Synick?"

"Not much to tell," he lied. "You fell a ways, and I dragged your sorry blue corpse down the hill a ways more. There were some wolves. They're tasty."

Faron sighed. Getting a straight answer out of Synick was never easy, especially when he didn't want to give one.

"Thank you." Synick waved his thanks away as if it had been nothing, but Faron knew better. "I go to sleep cold and hungry and wake up warm with food and water. I ought to pass out more often."

"It'd certainly be easier on my ears," Synick agreed. Faron shook his head, shivering. He scooted close to the fire and undid the buckles on his gloves, yanking them off. Despite the flames nearly singeing his skin, he felt as if he couldn't get close enough.

After a few hours, they had consumed as much as they could, and more strips were left to dry out over the flames to be packed and eaten later.

Mid-conversation, an unearthly green light filtered through the frost-covered pines, cutting them off instantly.

"What in Olsu's creation?" Faron cursed, looking up through the trees. The hair on the back of his neck stood on end. Synick appeared similarly stricken.

"What is that?"

In answer, Faron stood and rose to his feet. His head pounded, and every muscle seemed ready to rebel, but he forced himself up and through the trees. Synick followed, bearing a flaming stick for a poor torch.

The trees only got thicker as he walked among them, so he changed course for the slope at his right. Light paw prints had been pressed into the snow. They were old, and Faron thought he knew where those particular wolves could be found.

As he rose higher up the incline, the wind picked up, and his cloak wrapped around him on both sides, hugging his frame until he turned to see the sky.

Blazing ribbons of green fire and light streamed across the sky in an impossible display. Like a ream of silk, the color and brightness were staggering. Faron's mouth fell open as he failed to comprehend the vastness of what he saw. Defying all reason, the shimmering sky fire bent and broadened out, like a banner in the wind.

Air escaped his lungs in large white puffs. "Gods," was all he managed to whisper.

"No one is going to believe this," Synick agreed.

As they watched, the tips of the strange green bands of light shimmered at the tops and became red for a few moments, then broadened into a deep violet. Faron felt mesmerized.

The mountain slope they stood on blocked half the sky, and Faron tugged Synick along to skirt it. It wasn't long before they had a magnificent view. The shifting bands of light now covered the entire night sky, filling the air above them with shocking hues that didn't exist in the natural world. Blues and yellows joined in the celestial storm—and reds, oranges, and hues of purple he had never seen before.

While he stood above the treed valley, staring at the lights in the sky, Synick pulled on his shoulder.

"Faron," he whispered. His voice was heavy and strange. Faron followed his extended finger to see another multitude of lights—only these were on the ground. They were windows.

His eyes widened further, and his breath caught in his throat. Below them, nestled between enormous, glacial peaks, lay hundreds of buildings the size of temples, all joined together in the same white stone, glowing green in the light of the sky fire.

"You found it," Synick said, half-whisper, half-laugh. "The God City, City of Temples, City of Light. Faron... we did it."

Chills rushed down Faron's back in an avalanche of shock. His heart tried to leap from his chest as he stood in awe and disbelief. "I found it," he whispered.

Visions of Hadria filled his mind's eye. He was coming.

Wind whistled past his ears, and he realized he was running. After all this time—from Blackwood to Iron Shoals, to Fayevew, to Aru'barrahk, to Anveil, and finally to Vam Aranath—The God City, City of Temples, City of Light lay before him on the valley floor. No wall surrounded the flying buttresses, massive stained-glass windows, or steeples.

Slipping and stumbling, Faron ran down the mountain and into the tree line. Wind tore at him as he rushed through the pines, Synick close behind, not bothering to shout. Faron would not have heard him.

Blood pounded in his ears, drowning out everything but one single thought—*Hadria.* He had come so many thousands of miles to reach this place, and after all the doubt, all the tribulation, it was *real.* Everything seemed easier to bear with that. Tears threatened to brim, but he ran past them. He was so close. Finally, he was here. All that remained to do was find her and bring her home.

He imagined the state he might find her in. Would she be pale and emaciated or fattened like a calf before slaughter? He forced the thoughts away. There was only to find out now.

At full speed, Faron exploded from the tree line, and all of a sudden, the wind stopped. The constant, piercing wind had been a never-ending source of noise and chill for him, and now it was gone. With its sudden departure, he felt oddly deafened and almost warm.

A wide, level, open field stood before him, the massive, towering, interconnected structures barring his entry, except for a few expansive archways. Synick grabbed a shoulder.

"Stop! You don't know what's in there. We should be careful about this."

But Faron was already gone. Hadria was here. Growling, Synick dropped his torch and gave chase as best he could. While he was no lumbering thing, it was difficult to match Faron's speed.

As Faron ran through the empty space, the ground underneath him changed. Frozen tundra gave way to cultivated fields. In the blazing green light, Faron saw figures bobbing up and down. One of them stood, rising to two feet. It was a person, he realized. He carried what looked to be a large basket.

Casting his eyes about, he saw that there was more than just the one. Closer now, he could see hundreds of bent figures, working the soil with hands and tools in the dark. Were they tending rows of flowers? One nearby form stood, staring his way. He froze.

After a few long moments passed, Faron dared speak. "Who are you?"

The shivering form didn't answer, except to flinch as Synick caught up.

"Who are you?" Synick asked, repeating Faron's question but with more danger in his voice. "Why are you working frozen dirt—and at night, no less?"

A small voice finally answered. "The soul of Olsu bends the

light. We must work when the Lord Creator bends daylight into night." It was a girl, and her voice was soft, timid, and held a questioning tone. She obviously thought her answer was apparent.

"Lord Creator?" Synick said, echoing Faron's thoughts. Did Vam Aranath still follow the ancient path—at least those who didn't know the true nature of the 'gods,' anyway?

"From where do you come that you don't hail the Twinborn Gods, and how did you come here?"

"The gods are dead," Faron replied. "Please, what day is it?" He had lost the exact count of the days between here and Anveil, but he knew he was close.

The small girl turned back to the ground. "I cannot speak with you anymore."

"You worship the dead gods?" Synick asked.

"They will be reborn," she whispered. "Please... leave."

"Please," Faron said. "What day is it?"

"Auger twenty-two," her small voice answered. "Please go."

The date hit like a wall of water—twenty-two. Hadria's nameday was on twenty-six. He had made it.

"Four days," Synick said.

"We made it," Faron replied.

Tentatively, they stepped away, further through the fields. More people noticed them now and stopped their efforts to stare. They *were* tending flowers, Faron realized, row after row of them. In the eerie green light, Faron noticed that not one of them wore a cape like his. Instead, their clothing seemed to be made from the long white fur, not one of them bothering with a cloak.

The hooded figures started whispering.

Surprisingly, Synick was the one to break the silence. "We

are looking for a girl," he said aloud, so all the dark figures could hear. "Light hair, nearly eighteen years of age, Hadria by name. Do you know where we can find her?"

"Who are you?" one of the voices responded.

"That doesn't matter," Faron cut in. "We've traveled a long way to find her. Please."

"Did you steal that?" Faron realized they were pointing at his cloak.

"I made it," he replied. "Please, where is Hadria?"

"That is forbidden," another voice interjected. "To kill a dire wolf is death for any but the archons."

"Are you from beyond the Veil?" another girl asked.

Something felt wrong to Faron, circled by these small, cold forms, and suddenly, he realized why. Every one of them was his own age or younger. He couldn't see a single person who looked to be above the age of eighteen.

"You're slaves," he said aloud as he realized. They shifted uncomfortably.

Noticing their behavior, Synick chimed in. "Yes. We're from beyond the Veil, and I'd wager a guess that most of you are too."

Their discomfort grew. "We are not to speak of our lives before our service to the gods."

"Why?" Faron asked.

Suddenly, a voice cut over the small gathering. "What's going on here?" All heads ducked as the children scattered. An older woman appeared from the mass of bending bodies, walking with self-important authority. She appeared to be in her forties.

Faron's first instinct was to hide, to crouch down in the field with the others and become invisible, but instead, he stood erect and faced the person approaching. He could see in Synick's stance that he had the same thought process.

The woman carried a thin baton.

"Why aren't you working?" she asked before she recognized the cloak on his back. And where did you get that? Been thieving from the Appointed, have we?" Faron recognized her accent as coming from Fay Lake.

"You run these fields?" he said, changing tact. "You're the taskmaster here?"

"Aye, and I won't be spoken to that way by a little pair of thieves." She whipped the baton at him, but he dodged aside.

"I wouldn't do that if I were you," Synick cut in, forcing her hand toward the ground. "He has a tendency to kill people who swing things at him."

A flicker of fear appeared in the woman's eyes. She was clearly not used to those younger than her standing up for themselves.

"I-It's my job to keep the fields running smooth," she stammered. "I'm no monster. I only take instruction from my betters."

"That's us," Synick instructed. "And we're looking for someone—a girl—light hair, nearing her nameday, bears a passing resemblance to him." He pointed at Faron, whose eyes bore holes into the woman. He wanted to kill her. Already, the drive to free these enslaved souls bubbled within him.

"I don't know any girl like that. Don't know if I'd know anyway. If it's her eighteenth year, though, she'll be prepared for judgement at the temple."

"Judgement for what?" Faron asked, afraid he knew the answer.

"All slaves receive judgement on their nameday," she answered, nervous. Synick still gripped her baton, pulling her close. It was Faron who held her gaze, though. "Some are recruited into the World Steward's army, some to manage the fields or tables, but most are taken into the Steward's Priesthood."

An army? The World Steward?

"You speak of Sadagon?" Suddenly, the woman's eyes became angry, and she pulled the stick from Synick's grasp, swinging again at Faron, though he dodged her easily enough.

"You do not name him, lowly thief!" she shrieked. "You are not worthy to even think of the Prince of Dusk, let alone name him!" She stopped her screeching when Synick flashed his long, thin blade to her throat. It was caked in blood.

"Swing that thing one more time, and you'll never breathe again."

"I-I only seek to defend the purity of the World Steward—may he join the world with light."

"You can defend him to your death if you want," Faron said, stepping closer. "Or you can take me to where the slaves await judgement."

"Take you to the temple?" She gulped, the blade pressed to her throat. "The likes of I aren't allowed anywhere near it."

"Well," Synick suggested. "How about you take us to someone less useless?" She swallowed. "Or I could always stick you."

Her eyes flashed between the two of them until she finally gave a small nod. "I can take you." She nodded more. "This way."

When Synick lowered the knife, the woman whirled around and tromped through the fields. Bowed heads pretended not to notice as they passed. Synick and Faron fell in line behind her.

"I forgot how effective you are at coercion," Faron muttered to Synick.

"What can I say? People love not being stabbed."

Faron was too panicked to chuckle. Hadria was *here*. Their guide was infuriatingly slow, and Faron thought he might kill her himself out of impatience. "Have you ever actually stabbed someone?" Dageran had offered assassination jobs to the upper echelon of his slaves, but that was one area Faron had never gone.

"Thought about stabbing you a few times. That count?"

Over long fields, they followed the woman to a small stone structure—not of alabaster but something more common—that stood alone, still beyond the apparent border of the temple city. A small light flickered from the shack's only window. She threw the door open and strode right in.

Three men, in a whitish-gold armor made of scales and plates, jumped as the door flung open, tossing down cards and reaching for swords.

"Ice, Gretha," one man said. "What is it?"

"Arrest them!" she shrieked, pointing at Faron. "They have stolen from the Appointed, threatened my life, and slandered the name of the High Prince!"

Swords sang as they drew from scabbards, and the men filed out. Faron took a few steps back but stopped. In the middle of these fields, there was nowhere to run. They would have to fight. Nervously, he regained his footing, and Synick sensed his intentions. His heart pounded with anticipation. Never before had he fought three men at once. He hadn't even fought one man at a time without an extreme advantage. It wasn't like fighting beasts, which were predictable in their rage. Men were cautious, wary, and unpredictable.

"Take them to the dungeons!" the woman shrieked again.

Impulsively, Faron flicked his eyes between the woman and her guards, then drew his lever bow. Synick must have used it because it was loaded.

"Put that down!" one man shouted, all three raising their swords at him. Faron trained the tip on the one in the middle and held it steady.

"You're not taking us anywhere," he said, eyes narrowed to slits. He had been captured and enslaved too many times to allow it again. He would slaughter every last one of them before they took him.

"Put that thing down before I have to hurt you, boy."

"Take one step toward me, and I'll put a bolt in his chest," Faron promised. He meant it. Every inch of his body hurt with abuse and exhaustion, but he had come too far to let three men stop him.

"Blood and snow, Gretha, where did he get that?"

"Are you men of Olsu's fist or not?" she said impetuously. "Arrest him!"

"Where did he get that?" the taller man said again.

"Drop your swords," Faron demanded, cutting off the taskmaster. Beside him, Synick held his own long dagger.

The man bearing the full weight of Faron's withering glare looked to consider the request, but no one moved.

"You're in no position to make threats," the big man said. In only a few minutes, a patrol will come around that corner." Faron didn't turn to see where he was pointing. "It'll be the pyre for you then."

"Not if we kill you first," Faron said, finger brushing the trigger. "I've come too far to let you stand in my way, so either surrender your weapons to me or die."

"It doesn't have to be like that," the man on the right said. "Return to your labor, and we'll pretend this never happened."

"I'm not one of your slaves!" Faron spat, hysteria edging his voice. "I'm not some soulless husk to be ordered about. I'm an assassin of slavers, a killer of killers, and if you don't get out of my way, I'm going to cut you all down." Faron thought of firing right then, just to catch them off guard and capitalize on his advantage, but he wasn't so eager to kill as that.

"Rathan," the man in the center said, slowly as to not agitate Faron. "Look at their cloaks and the state of that leather."

The big man shuffled but didn't answer.

"They're not archons' cloaks," he went on. "Gods, Rathan, they're not slaves. They crossed the Veil!"

The man on the left furrowed his brow. "Impossible," he said.

"He's right," Synick said. "We came from Anveil. We're not your slaves, and you have no right to command us."

"They're lying," Gretha cut in. "They stole those cloaks and intend to run."

The man who shrunk beneath Faron's crossbow spoke again. "Have you ever seen an archon's cloak with so poor a cut as these? And why else would they be covered in mud and dirt?" He turned his eyes back to Faron before dropping his sword to the ground. "Let's be calm about this," he said.

"What do we do with them?" the left man asked Rathan.

"It's not possible," he said. "No one has ever crossed the Veil before."

"It's possible," Synick said again. "Just a pain in the ass. Now, are you going to get out of our way, or are we going to kill you and gallivant about in your armor?"

"What do we do with them, Rathan?"

It was a long minute before he answered. "The priestess will know. They aren't workers, and they aren't guests. We take them to the priestess."

Faron straightened his crossbow again. "We're not going anywhere," he reiterated.

"Why did you come here?" Rathan asked. "If I can't believe how you got here, at least tell me why."

"My sister," Faron said. "Hadria. She turns eighteen in only four days. I came to find her."

"Olsu's balls," the man on the left said. "You really did come from across the Winter Veil."

Gretha shrieked. "Don't take his name in vain!" she said. "Do you want to be stripped of rank and thrown to the wolves?"

"Calm yourself, Gretha," Rathan said. "We've never seen this before." He turned to Faron and Synick. "I can't take you prisoner, and I can't let you wander free, but I might be able to help you."

Faron's arm was starting to shake from the weight of the lever bow, so he pulled it to his chest.

"Help by getting out of my way," he said.

"I can't do that," the leader of the trio replied. His sword was still pointed toward Faron but had lowered significantly. "But I can take you to someone who'll know what to do with you, and above that, she might be able to help you."

"And what's to stop me from putting a hole in your friend, killing you, and taking your armor? I'll go see this priestess myself without your swords at my back."

Rathan opened his mouth to reply, but Synick cut him off. "No, Faron. He's right." Faron shot him a harsh look, but

Synick carried on. "We're strangers here, Faron. We don't know the city, the customs—anything. Even with a disguise, we'll stick out for anyone who's looking. Besides, these men aren't going to be taking us anywhere. They'll be escorting us, right boys?"

The man in the middle nodded eagerly, still shrinking under Faron's weapon, but the other two seemed more confused.

"I suppose," Rathan said.

"See?"

Faron hesitated, licking his chapped lips.

"It's the right call, Faron," Synick insisted. "We could search for years in this place and never find her. These men could take us right to her."

"If there's anyone who will know of the slaves coming of age, it's the priestess," the man on the left confirmed. Faron still hadn't learned his name.

"And why is that?" Faron asked.

"Because," Rathan said. "She decides who becomes workers in the fields or the forges. She decides who has mastery of a craft and who will join the Prince's Priesthood. There isn't a man, woman, or child here who isn't where she put them."

Slowly, Faron began to nod. Perhaps Synick was right. Faron had never imagined he'd make it this far and had no idea how to begin his search. The vastness of the city was so mind-numbing that it really would take years to search it all. Hadria didn't have years. He lowered the crossbow. If this turned out to be a trap, he would deal with it. Finding her was worth the risk.

"Alright," he said. "We'll come, but you'll sheath your swords." The man in the center breathed a sigh of relief, and Faron felt a spark of guilt for threatening him but brushed it off.

"And you'll disarm that bow," Rathan ordered.

"I'll wear it on my back," Faron said. "It stays loaded."

"Fine, but you'll surrender it before meeting the priestess. No weapons are to be allowed in her presence."

"Fine," Synick cut in, answering before Faron could have a chance to refuse. "But not until then."

"I can agree to that. Boreth, you and Jeshua take rear. I'll lead." He turned back to Faron. "Now, please follow."

Feeling strangely out of place in the accepted presence of the guards, Faron shrugged the crossbow onto his back and allowed himself to be led away. The wide streets were paved with a fine, smooth cobble, and they made for easy walking, especially when compared to the treacherous terrain they had just crossed for half a month. They walked quickly under a massive archway that must have been at least a hundred feet across and effectively entered the God City. It was appropriately named.

Every building was as grand as an ancient temple from the days before the Supernal Dusk, and it was unclear where one structure ended and another began. Faron and Synick stared up at the massive steeples, flying buttresses, iron-framed windows filled with colored glass, and walls of fine white stone, mouths agape. Faron didn't have the capacity to feel worried about his armed escort. He had made it, and he was coming. Besides, he had been in far worse situations with literal armies at his heels, and he hadn't had Synick then. If Synick didn't have a pair of lock picks in his boot, he would eat his cloak.

Inside nearly every building, a fire flickered, casting light onto the street below. Synick's eyes bulged when the blazing green fire in the sky reflected off what looked like gold-adorning steeples and cupolas atop grand mansions. The air smelled lightly of woodsmoke, and chimneys spouted long clouds from every structure.

They were led down the large paved streets toward the giant temple at the center of the city. It had been easily visible from outside but was obscured by the tall building immediately around him now, but still, Faron's heart fluttered with every step. He had been waylaid time and again and almost lost his lead on his and Hadria's nameday, the day Ulric claimed would be her last, but still, he had made it.

Hadria was alive. She was here, and she was alive.

Faron would take her home. Ulric had asked him not to bring her back for fear of Dageran, but Faron had grown since then. He would kill Dageran, and they could live peacefully in the village they had loved.

Faron felt a pang of guilt as he thought of Ulric. The old man had helped him escape, and Faron hadn't even thought about what the repercussions might be. Ulric had sacrificed himself so *he* might escape and possibly return with Hadria. Faron set his teeth. When he found Hadria, he would return and avenge the old man, and that would be very, *very* soon.

I'm coming.

The Son of Baranor

I t took several hours to reach the central building, and if Faron had thought the city was grand before, it was jaw-droppingly opulent now. Arches, several hundred feet long, soared into the sky, supported by tall stone pillars connecting the surrounding buildings to the palace, creating massive, sweeping grounds.

The scale of it all was mind-boggling. How was it possible something so large could exist—and in the White North, above all? How could such a massive and fine city fall from all living memory in the first place?

Escorted by their white and gold-clad guards, they were led across the grounds. Despite the hour, it was teeming with more of the white and gold men, parading around the massive courtyard in rows of eight by ten. They marched in perfect unison, stomping the ground with every step. It was an impressive display. Faron realized he had not misheard when the woman in the fields had mentioned an army. Certainly, there would be more of these dangerous-looking men.

As they passed under the gigantic arches, Faron realized that the pillars supporting them weren't pillars at all but towers with iron doors at the bottom. It was at one of these that they stopped. Reluctantly, Faron and Synick handed over their weapons, but Faron noticed Synick keep his belt of balanced knives hidden. The lead man pounded a fist on the door. It stayed shut. He pounded again. After a long moment, it swung open on oiled hinges.

A slender woman in a white sleeping dress, draped with lace of black and green, stood inside. Her cold blue eyes adorned the palest face Faron had ever seen, which was impressive considering his subterranean history. Her hair was golden-white, kept up in a brace of gemstones. Faron could practically hear Synick's fingers twitching.

"The hour is early for judgements, Fist of Olsu."

The men bowed deeply. "Begging your pardon, Priestess, but your wisdom is urgently needed."

"What could possibly be so urgent that it couldn't wait until I put a dress on?" She eyed Faron and Synick with a thin brow, arched spectacularly. "I see," she said after only a moment.

"We found them in the southern strip. You won't believe this my lady, but—"

She cut him off with a flick of the wrist. "Yes, I know where you're stationed, Captain Rathan. I put you there, and no need to waste my time. I see what they are."

"But, my lady, Valatha," he said. "They're not workers. They crossed—"

"Be quiet, Captain," the woman snapped. "I know what they are. I've seen those frost burns ten thousand times, and there are no more convoys arriving until the end of the year. Above that, their clothes are ripped nearly to shreds from tooth and claw, and there's a feral look about them as if they've spent the last week sleeping next to their own demons." She looked Faron and Synick in the eye. "You came from across the Veil."

Hesitantly, Faron nodded.

"What do we do with them?" Rathan asked.

"What we do with all the new children," the priestess said, reaching out for Faron's shoulder. He slapped it away and cut her off.

"We are *not* slaves."

She must have seen his willingness to fight to defend the point because she smiled. "I meant, get you *cleaned up*. You're more blood and mud than boy, and you look more than half-starved. Honestly, Captain, you should have taken them straight to the healers."

"We didn't come here to be cleaned," Faron said. "We came to ask your help."

"I wouldn't mind being cleaned up a bit," Synick muttered, but Faron ignored him.

"Well, either way, you won't get what you need out there. Come in. It's far too early to take you to the baths in my office, but I can handle you in here just fine." Something about her tone made Synick grin. Faron followed him inside, and the guards followed. "No," the priestess said, stopping the white and gold guards with a finger. "You can wait outside."

The captain looked for a moment as if he would object but then thought better of it. The bitter air was cut away as the door closed, warmth from a low burning fireplace enveloping them. Somehow, Faron felt more nervous alone with this woman than with the armed guards.

The great circular room was filled with plush furniture and writing desks. Stacks of paper lay on a table that looked to have accumulated a film of dust. In the back was a staircase that turned as it followed the wall. There must have been at least ten more floors up above. Moving with a lithe grace, the priestess filled a large bowl from a basin and set it on the hearth to warm.

"I do apologize for the setting," she said. "This is the first time I've done this in my home. In my offices, there are baths so hot they'll leave you pink, but I'm afraid all I have here is a cold bowl and some rags." She smiled at them. "We'll make do."

"We're not here to be cleaned," Faron reiterated. "We came because we were told you could help us."

"Maybe I can," she said. "But I won't—not if I don't know you."

"I wouldn't mind getting to know each other better," Synick said.

She gave him a tilted smile with eyes that sparkled. She was beautiful, Faron realized. "Oh, we will—trust me. First, though, I'm afraid you'll have to indulge me. I find it so much easier to understand a person when they have nothing to hide behind—words, weapons, clothes—nothing you can use to hide the naked truth."

Faron blushed. "Absolutely not."

She shrugged, exposing one shoulder. "Latrines then. I can always just send you to mire out the sewers for a year and a day. It's where I send the only slaves I can't trust."

Faron's gaze darkened. "We are *not* your slaves." He punctuated each word with heavy slowness.

"Maybe you aren't," she said with a too-casual tone. "How am I to tell? After all, I don't know you."

"Fine," Faron said. "But we're not going anywhere you try to send us, not with even with guards on your side."

"Excellent," she said, wringing out a rag into the warming bowl. "Let's start with you, shall we?" She flicked the rag at Synick.

First, she inspected Synick, pulling at his cold skin, flicking a cheek, and pulling his hood down to run her bare hands through his hair. He managed to form a half-smile with his lips and winked at her. Faron groaned internally. He was always belligerent when nervous, and it only ever served to get him in more trouble.

Unexpectedly, the woman laughed and cupped his cheek in her thin-fingered hand. "I don't care what pit you came from or if you *are* a little overripe, plum; I can already tell you'll see a few years with the breeders before I'm finished with you. With a face like yours, we'll have to put you to use. Atha knows we could use more beautiful servants around here."

"You know," Synick replied. "I've always thought the same thing. If everyone looked more like me and less like *anything* else, the world would be a more beautiful place."

She threw her head back in laughter again. "Oh, you're a tease." Faron eyed the two of them, perplexed. Were they *flirting?* She pulled off his gloves and laid them in his lap, then turned to Faron.

"You, though, you're either a killer or a survivor, by those eyes." She narrowed her eyes and inspected him more closely. "If I send you to Olsu's Fist, you'll make it all the way to commander for certain."

"You aren't sending me anywhere," Faron made it sound like a threat.

"You *are* a bit old," she conceded. "With no chance to have the damage of your formative years undone and too old for the Prince's Priesthood. I'd guess you're perhaps twenty-one"—she pointed at Synick, then Faron—"and nineteen?"

Neither corrected her.

She took off Synick's cape first and immediately revealed

the brown belt of balanced knives he had concealed underneath. Faron clenched his teeth.

"Well, aren't you clever!" she said. She unbuckled it and tossed it to the floor. Her tone seemed to indicate she found it amusing that they had slipped them passed the guard but didn't find them the least bit threatening.

Synick's eyes exuded relief, and Faron was certain his did as well.

She began tugging at the swollen and dirt-encrusted straps of Synick's blacks as if nothing had happened. "It's a complicated scenario; that's certain," she went on. "Everyone in Vam Aranath belongs to the Twinborn Gods, but you came here of your own will and power. I don't know if that makes you slaves, guests, or citizens, but we'll just have to find out, won't we?" She smiled as she freed a strap and loosened Synick's leather.

"Can you help us or not?" Faron cut in, exasperated.

"Darling, I don't even know what you need."

"I'm looking for someone: my sister," Faron said.

"Oh my," the priestess said, freeing another of Synick's buckles. "You came all the way across the Veil for your sister? How absolutely charming."

"Blonde hair," Synick said, "blue eyes, a sharp chin, and a wit to make even a dullard smile." Faron gave him a confused look, and he replied, "You talk about her a lot."

"Her name is Hadria," Faron added. "Can you help us?"

"Blonde hair?" the priestess asked, twirling her own golden locks. "Like this?"

"Not quite so… white," Faron said. "And more yellow—like gold."

She smiled. "From Empyrion, then?"

Faron didn't answer. How *could* he answer?

"Well, I feel as if I'd know a girl like that. It's why I have the position I do, to be honest. I never forget a face. I must admit the name sounds familiar, but I don't remember who it belongs to, and I still don't know if I'm going to help you." She cut off Faron's protest. "It's my turn to ask questions now." She finally extricated Synick from his armor to reveal the woolen fleece that wrapped him underneath. It stank of blood and sweat, but she didn't seem to notice. "My, you're bundled!" she exclaimed in delight. Synick leaned forward as she pulled it over his head and tossed it to the wood floor.

"Now," she said. "You come over the Veil, which shouldn't be possible, in snow cloaks, which you shouldn't know about, to a city that shouldn't exist. Right now, I'm not so interested in *why* so much as *how*." She rang her rag in the bowl of warming water and started to clean the grime from Synick's face. When neither boy answered, she said, "Allow me to restate. How do you know about Vam Aranath? If you came to find your sister, you must know what we intend for her, which is impressive, as even she doesn't. What I want to know is how you learned about all these *secrets*."

What we intend for her. The words rang in his mind. "You mean to kill her and steal her blood," Faron accused.

She smiled. "Well, look who knows how to play the game. Yes, that's exactly what I mean." She pulled over a stool and sat, legs folded to the side beneath her. "I extend you the invitation of honesty. Tell me, young thing, how have you come to know this, and if you do, why have you come like a sheep to the slaughter?"

Both brows raised at the lack of tact. He had expected minced words, not brutal honesty. It caught him off guard.

He shrugged; maybe he could return the favor.

"I killed Jaru'tal Dunestrider."

Her fingers stopped dead on his chest, the line she was tracing cut short.

"Really? How did he die?"

"It's hard to say," Faron said honestly

"And why is that?"

Synick jumped back into the conversation. "Because it may have been from the stabbing, the poison, the arrow through the chest, or the sixty-foot fall out the window, as I hear it."

She raised an arched eyebrow. "So, I was right with the first guess—killer, and thorough too." Despite the words, she seemed impressed. "A pity. He was a pleasure to deal with and reliable in his trade. No matter, though. He was not the first and won't be the last." She resumed her strange affections, unbuckling Faron's gloves and brushing the hair from his face. "You didn't answer my question though, little killer. The Dunestrider doesn't know what happens to the children he brings us, only that he gets paid like a king for each one. What do you know about blood, and how do you know it?"

Faron didn't answer. "Where is my sister?" he asked.

She sighed and began unlacing the sides of his leather armor. It was clawed and scraped half to shreds.

"The things you know are secrets kept safe for centuries. Do you know how many people have come wandering from that forest?" She waited for him to comment but continued when he didn't. "None. Not one—ever. The Lord Pyre has kept this city and its secrets safe for more than three hundred years, and here you are, not only able to travel among the wolves, but able to find us and armed with secrets of blood as well."

When Faron only replied with a cold stare, she moved back to Synick, washing his chest.

"That's alright," she cooed. "We don't know each other that well yet. And what about you, pretty toy? Why are you here?"

Synick took the fat compliment in stride. "I only heard of the striking beauty of the woman of the tower. Knew I had to see her for myself to believe it, and now that I have, I know every word of it is a bold-faced lie. They don't do you anywhere near justice." Faron tried not to groan. That nervous bravado of his was going to get him killed one day.

She traced the thin line of a scar on his jaw and smiled. "I'd offer you the invitation of honesty as well—only I think I like your lies too much to let you stop."

"They're only lies because this city of yours is so snowing hard to get to."

The white rag pulled at a dark area on his skin, thick with filth. When it came away, it revealed Dageran's brand just below his collarbone. She inhaled when she saw it.

"The Ourodurity?" the Priestess asked. "Why do you bear the symbol of the gods on your body?" She seemed genuinely surprised.

"The man who claimed to own us had something of a god complex," Synick said.

"Escaped slaves? You *are* from the Kaor then—but how?"

Faron shook his head. "Not the Kaor. We were slaves to a madman in Blackwood."

Appearing caught off guard, the Priestess asked, "There's a slave trade in Blackwood? I admit it's been a while since I've been there, but last I checked, the practice was outlawed in Alden."

"It is," Faron said simply.

"Well, aren't you fascinating," she breathed.

"Yes," Synick agreed. "I am. And I believe you missed a spot right there." He didn't even bother pointing, instead, trying to lift a single rib on his right side.

Again, Faron shook his head. Synick would flirt with a snow wolf if he thought it would get him anywhere.

"You are positively delightful," she preened. "I might just buy you myself to have you follow me day and night with that silver tongue of yours."

"You'd hardly have to buy me to accomplish that, my lady."

Lips pursed in a half-smile, she flicked water from the bucket on his chest. "Tell me your name, toy, so I might find you in a year if I'm feeling bored."

Faron's ears burned. He felt like he was intruding here, watching something meant to be private, but no, this was about Hadria. He refused to look away.

"They call me Synick, but you can call me whatever you like, and I'll come."

"Don't tempt me, toy," she said. Faron felt as if he was going to be sick. More than that, he felt annoyed. This was a waste of time. She stepped back over to him now and pulled him out of his wool wrappings. She gasped when she saw the extensive scarring across the right half of his chest and shoulder, old reminders of the life Sadagon had stolen from him. Even under a layer of blood, dirt, and sweat, they were an angry red.

"A survivor of fire," she cooed. "Those scars tell quite the tale." Right on top of those scars just above his heart lay the same brand, given to him before his melted skin had even begun to heal. She fingered it with a long, sharp-looking nail. "Even the real gods don't mark their property with a brand," she said. "The Lady Atha will not take well to her mark being used by another."

When Faron didn't reply, she began washing the filth away from his body, the same as she had to Synick. He felt her nails scraping against his skin and was incredibly aware of her eyes on his form. It was extremely uncomfortable.

Faron caught sight of his face in the side of a silver pitcher on the table. It was caked in blood, mud, and who knew what else. The skin on the left half of his nose peeled from burns administered by the wind. He looked terrible—as terrible as he felt, in fact.

"Tell me more about your sister, little killer. The better I know you, the better I feel. I almost feel inclined to help you. You won't be sent to the sewers, at the very least." She scrubbed at his chest, starting with the burned areas and admiring them breathily.

"You won't be sending me anywhere," Faron said.

"Brave little killer," she said, with something resembling affection. "You really don't understand this conundrum, do you?" From beside her, Synick cracked open one eye. "You might not be a slave, as you came here of your own will and power, but neither are you free. You know *far* too many secrets to be allowed to leave."

A long silence passed between them. "Are you threatening me?"

"Yes, and no," she answered honestly. "It's not my place to say you're more convenient dead than alive, but it certainly is Prince Pyre's. Honestly, though, it's not impossible to find this sister of yours and keep her from induction into the priesthood if she hasn't been already. I could see you two digging bulbs together if you please me."

"She's not dead," Faron exclaimed, standing in a rush. The chair fell behind him. "I came in time. Her nameday is still four days off. I came *in time.*"

After another brief silence passed, the priestess said, "What do you know about namedays?"

Faron didn't answer.

"You know what we do with our slaves." It wasn't a question. "That's not a thing the Dunestrider could have told you. You know *when* we exsanguinate, and I wouldn't be surprised if you knew why. That's not a thing the Dunestrider could have told you." She leaned in close, her mask of beauty slipping to reveal the danger underneath. "How do you know the secrets of Vam Aranath?" Her tone was direct.

Searching her deep blue eyes, Faron understood that he had very little left to lose. If she chose, she could keep him here forever or call an army to lock him in a dungeon. He didn't have the advantage of knowing, at least in part, the layout of the city. There was no avenue of escape, and he wouldn't run even if he could. Hadria was here. He had to find her.

"I learned what I know from my father," he finally answered. It was more or less true.

Relieved that he was talking, the priestess resumed her cleaning, wiping away the dead flakes of skin from his face. The rag came away brown with thick layers of dried blood.

"And who in Atha's Iron Halls is your father?"

"Bouren, though you may know him as Baranor."

The rag fell from her hands, and she stumbled back a step, studying the face she had just cleaned. Her eyes were wide and her mouth agape.

"The traitor," she whispered, and her eyes grew even wider. "Captain!" she yelled at the door, all the sultry lowness gone from her voice.

Faron leaped to the side, ready to defend himself, but she didn't seem to notice. Synick jumped to his feet, too; his façade of relaxation completely disappeared.

The door burst open, and the white and gold armored guard jumped inside. He drew his sword in a flash when he saw Faron and Synick on their feet.

"Put that thing away!" she commanded, and Faron stopped in his tracks. He had been ready to put the priestess in a chokehold and use her to make the captain drop his sword, but her words and complete lack of self-defense stopped him. "Captain Rathan, send for General Bairak to escort these two to the palace *at once.* I will write you a permissive and a message for the World Steward, which you will send ahead."

Visibly confused, he nodded.

The World Steward. Faron had heard that title before. It was Jaru'tal's name for Sadagon.

"No!" he exclaimed. "You said you'd help me."

"This is out of my hands," the priestess said. She seemed shaken.

"What does my father have to do with this?" he asked.

"Everything," she crossed to a writing desk and scribbled a few lines with a thin piece of charcoal. She quickly folded it and forced it into the guard's hand. "Have Boreth take this to the palace at once, and send Jeshua for more men; and, bring clothes for these two." When he hesitated, she shouted, "Move!" And he scrambled into action and ran back out the door.

"You lied," Faron said.

"I would never break an invitation to honesty once given," the priestess said, crossing over to cup his cheek.

He pushed her hand away, heedless of the power this woman seemed to wield. "You said you would help me if I let you clean us, so here I sit, after almost three weeks of sleeping with snowbeasts and half dying from the cold; and, instead of helping me find my sister, you send me to the man who killed my father and took her from me."

"Child," she said. "He *has* your sister."

Relief and dread flooded his heart and soul in equal measure. "What do you mean?"

"Do you have any idea who your father is?" she asked.

Faron reflected for a moment. Ulric had said Bouren was an archon, an evil man from Vam Aranath, but beyond that, he didn't know much more besides the false life he had perpetuated in Alhalow. His silence answered for him.

"That bastard Baranor," she said with exasperation.

"Sadagon has my sister?"

"Yes," she confirmed. "He keeps her near. You have no idea the damage Baranor caused him."

Faron wasn't sure he knew enough to defend his father, so he went back to the point. "So he keeps her—like a pet? Like some kind of twisted trophy?" He ground his teeth. "If you send me to Sadagon, I will kill him." His voice was filled with promise.

She actually laughed. "Oh, little killer, for someone who knows so many secrets, you don't seem to understand us at all."

"What I understand is that Sadagon rules this city, he has my sister, and if you send me to him, I will kill him before he kills me or her."

"I have a feeling Lord Pyre would be satisfied with that trade. Either way, this is out of my hands."

Before Faron could recover from his confusion, a knock came at the door, and then it flew open. A man with no helmet and a thick, white beard stepped inside. His armor was white and gold like the others but fringed with red, and his mustache was thick and pointed at both ends.

His eyes flicked between Faron and Synick searchingly, then landed on Faron to stay. "Come with me," was all he said.

"They were to be brought clothes," the priestess said. Another man stepped in with a neatly folded pile in his arms. She distributed them to Faron and Synick.

There was a warm shirt, a pair of black trousers, new boots and socks, and gloves. Faron threw the shirt over his head. Synick wasn't far behind him.

"You're taking me to my sister?" Faron asked the mustached man.

He nodded without expression. "To be presented for the pleasure of Lord Sadagon Pyre."

Faron set his jaw, teeth clenching. Would they put him in a cage with her? Was she chained and half-naked like he had seen in his dreams? It didn't matter. He would go. What choice did he have? Hadria was *here*. He would find her, and even from inside a cage with every spear in the world pointed at his back, he would take her and find a way to escape.

"I will go."

The priestess tried to get him to change his trousers and boots as well, but he ignored her. There was no time. He marched straight out into the frigid North.

"Take me to her," he demanded.

"At least put on your cloak," the priestess said, exasperated. "Jeshua should have brought you new ones, but these are better than nothing." She placed the familiar weight around his shoulders. While fidgeting with the clasp, the length of her sleeve fell away, and Faron saw the exposed skin underneath. Black veins webbed their way from wrist to elbow, marring her perfect beauty. Faron recoiled in horror.

"You…" he said, suddenly alert.

"An archon," she confirmed. "My, you know a lot. Is there anything Baranor didn't tell you?" She stepped away and fastened Synick's cloak before their guards closed in around them. "Remember me fondly in the coming days," Priestess Valatha said as they were marched away. "Dead gods know you'll need it."

Screams

Faron felt the priestess's eyes on him as the escort pulled him along until they rounded her archway tower and made across the beautiful grounds for the massive temple, marching in perfect unison. Even in the dark, it was opulent and rich. Compared to the temple itself, though, the grounds were nothing.

Ice webbed over crystal windows, small piles of snow accumulating in every corner or flat surface. Gold plated every spire, steeple, and cupola on the massive building, which was so large, it could have homed a small village, including the farms. The white stone was a beautifully marbled alabaster, intricate carvings of vines spiraling up the unfathomably tall pillars and spires. The doors were wrought of silver, with white gems forming a half-circle over an engraved throne.

The opulence of it all was put to shame when the doors opened. Blood red carpets ran on opposite sides of the room, forming twin staircases that ran against the walls and met again in a balcony. Underneath the balcony ran a marble path that led into the next room. Compared to the size of the palace, the entryway seemed small, but it was still several times larger than the throne room of any king's castle. The palace in Aru'barrahk could have fit almost entirely within this one entryway. The scale was astounding, but to Faron, it was simply a distance that he had to cross to find Hadria. His heart crashed with an alacrity that sent waves of pain and heat through his migraine, but he didn't care. She was here. She was *here,* and so was he.

Following the armed men under the balcony and into the next room, Faron realized that he had never understood lavishness before in his life. Polished marble floors led up to sweeping arches plated in a white gold, lines of rubies studded up the impossibly tall walls.

Even in the heart of a blizzard, Faron had never seen so much white. The walls, floors, and ceiling were all a gleaming marble or alabaster. The chamber was larger than anything he had previously imagined. It seemed large enough to house an entire mountain. What seemed miles above, massive crystal chandeliers hung from a latticework of archways and supports, glittering with the undeniable shine of diamonds.

At the end of the temple stood a raised dais, a massive staircase that led to two magnificent thrones set before an enormous wall of plated gold. To the side of these thrones sat another, smaller throne, unornamented and unadorned. It was here that Faron noticed the form of a man garbed in an overcoat of a deep blue. The cut was almost militaristic. Long white hair fell over powerful shoulders, gathered behind his head by a white band. At the sides of the black throne were two round pommels, where he rested his hands.

Sadagon.

Screams.

Screams.

SCREAMS.

Faron stopped short, pausing the escort. Yellow light

filled his vision as fire filled his mind. The glimmer of rubies became drops of boiling blood under a dagger in his father's gut. The pillars surrounding him twisted and turned into great bouts of flame that lapped at his skin, hungry to consume. It became hard to see through the smoke. It was hard to *breathe.* Massive arching lattices of stone high above became charred, burning beams that fell upon him, pinning him to stare back at a blackening skull. No shadow protected him from the memory this time. Faron gasped as glowing embers burned through his shirt and dug into his skin, cooking him alive.

Screams.

Pain brought water to his eyes, and he choked on sparks and smoke. He watched as Hadria was torn away, screaming the sound that would come to define him.

Faron stood still, fists clenched, teeth grinding, enduring the hell that had been created for him. Before him, not a hundred feet away, stood the man responsible—the man who burned his home, the man who murdered his father, the man who took his sister—Sadagon.

Hands took him by the shoulders, but it wasn't his guards. Synick held him fast.

"Careful," he whispered. "Be *careful.* Wait for him to play his hand. You can't help *her* if you run straight into a blade here." Synick could see the murder in his eyes.

The guards resumed their march, pulling Faron along with them. The fire never fully left him, but he walked.

He passed over a massive half-circle of studded diamonds encrusted in the floor and came within shouting distance to the white-haired man—to Sadagon. He swallowed hard. The men pushed him closer, and Faron met his gaze.

His eyes were hard and filled with something akin to shock. They flicked over his form searchingly.

Screams.

The procession came to a stop before the white-haired man, all falling to kneel before their ruler. Faron remained standing. The silence inside the great temple was complete, but he couldn't hear it. He only heard screams.

He had dreamed of this moment—never in the same way twice and never here—but he had dreamed of it all the same. He had dreamed of putting a knife in Sadagon's gut, crushing his throat with his hands, and even pushing him into a pit of fire, but he had none of that now. Surrounded by armed men in the heart of a forgotten city, Faron was without weapon or plan of action. He kept his fingers clenched tight to his palm to keep them from shaking, longing to feel Sadagon's neck. Synick was right. He couldn't make the first move.

All was silent in the throne room of the dead gods, and Faron held the blue-eyed gaze of the man who had murdered his father, burned his home, and taken his sister. It was the greatest struggle of his life to remain still.

After what felt like years of this silent exchange, one word slipped from the black throne on the plinth above.

"How?" It carried surprise, disbelief, and a deeply buried emotion Faron could not identify.

Faron breathed hard to calm himself enough to speak. When he did, it was with caustic hate.

"Where is my sister?" he seethed through clenched teeth. There was no cage by the throne, no chains or manacles.

Standing from his throne, Sadagon waved a hand at his men. "Leave us."

"My Lord Pyre?"

"Leave us," he said again, voice thundering through the great chamber.

The men ducked their heads and filed quickly away. Soon, Faron and Synick were alone with the man Faron hated most in the world.

"Where. Is. My. Sister?" Faron said again, biting off the words as they erupted from deep inside him.

Sadagon stepped down from his throne, descending the long stairs. "You're here to kill me." It wasn't a question.

"Where is my sister?!" Faron yelled, stepping forward against his will. Synick pulled him back.

Sadagon stepped onto the diamond-encrusted floor. "It truly is you. I watched you die, yet here you are—whole—despite how I killed you."

Screams.

Synick's arms wrapped around Faron's chest as he struggled to break free and attack the monster before him. Faron fought, but Synick pulled him away.

"Stop!" Synick said. "Faron, stop!" But he couldn't hear him.

"Where is she?!" he screamed, tears touching his eyes. "What have you done with my sister!"

"How you must hate me," Sadagon said, coming closer.

"You took EVERYTHING from me!" Faron clawed at Synick's arms. "WHERE IS MY SISTER?"

Screams. Dead gods, his skin *burned!* His lungs were on fire.

"Safe," Sadagon finally answered. "You will see for yourself." He finally came within inches of Faron, still held back by Synick in a dead grip.

"Let me go!"

"I never thought the damage Baranor caused could be

291

undone, yet somehow, impossibly, you're here and have singlehandedly saved this world."

The air seeped from Faron's lungs as Synick pulled him back harder and harder, and Faron fought with every ounce of strength he had left. He became so constricted he couldn't breathe.

"Stop," Synick whispered in his ear. "Please stop, Faron. He'll kill you."

Faron hyperventilated short breaths, on the verge of passing out. His screams of frustration turned to choking tears as he clawed helplessly at the manifest nightmare in front of him. He was so close.

In a moment of hysteric weakness, his legs buckled, and Synick released him to fall to his knees. Bitter sobs escaped him as his body wracked with the desperation that he had harbored inside for so long.

With only a brief look at Synick, the white-haired man bent down and wiped a tear from Faron's eye. He tried to recoil but was too overcome.

"Come," his father's murderer said. "There is a debt between us, a debt that must be paid."

In a moment of crystal clarity, a voice, more pure and beautiful than a silver bell, rang from behind him.

"Faron?"

Goosebumps rippled along his arms and neck, tears of another kind stinging his eyes. Breath caught in his throat, and he turned his head as Sadagon delicately released it.

His voice trembled.

"Hadria?"

Bloodlines

S he was the most beautiful thing he had ever seen, radiating softness and love like the first warm days of spring. The last time he had seen her, she was a child, but now she was a woman. Her hair had grown long in the lifetime it felt they had been separated, golden curls falling long past her narrow shoulders and nearly to mid-back. Her angular face had become more beautiful than he could have imagined, soft blue eyes brimming with unexpected tears.

With long, pale fingers, she cupped Faron's jaw and held it up for inspection. He gasped, shocked by the power of her presence and the realization of all the goals of his lifetime.

"Gods, Faron. It really is you," she cried in a clear, high voice. Her eyes brimmed over, and two tears slid down her face. She laughed. "I didn't believe it. By what design have you been alive all this time? How have you come to be here?"

She knelt on the ground beside him, grasping a single hand with surprising force and caressing his face with her other. She wore a dress of red velvet, the quality of which had no rival. A necklace of rubies and firedrops adorned her shoulders and neckline along with three gold rings set with flat rubies that stretched nearly from knuckle to knuckle. On her head rested a diadem of white gold and red gems that glittered fiercely as they caught the light.

His breath caught in his throat. "I-I came to save you," he whispered, eyes taking in her clothing and adornment. Feeling numb, he asked, "Haddie…" Her childhood pet name felt strange on his tongue. "What are you wearing? What are you doing here?"

She gasped a small, single laugh. "I live here, Faron," she said.

"Has he been keeping you like some sort of pet?" Anger managed to edge in on the shock in his voice.

The expansive room tinkled with her light laughter. "Of course not! Faron, this is where I live."

Faron shook his head. "No. No, Hadria. You're not safe. He means to kill you on your nameday." Sadagon folded his arms sternly at that.

She laughed softly. "Oh, Faron. There's so much you don't know, and it's *our* nameday." She pulled him into a tight embrace. "There will be parades and feasts all across the city! Of all the gifts I could receive, there is nothing that could have ever brought me more joy than to see you here!" He thought his ribs might crack from the force. "You're alive!"

"Hadria."

"Where have you been? Oh, Faron. I… I watched you die." Her voice was high and filled with emotion.

He shook his head. "I didn't die. I've been… detained."

She sensed the hurt in his eyes and noticed Synick as if for the first time but quickly looked back. "Where have you been? How on earth have you come here?"

He shook his head and cast a nervous glance at Sadagon. "Hadria, we have to leave here." His eyes flicked between them. "Please. He is the man who killed our father, and he means to kill you too." He heard the panic rising in his voice. Did he have to beg her? This wasn't right.

Her eyes softened. "You're wrong, Faron."

"I'm not wrong!" he said, animal desperation rising. She was supposed to flee with him! "Why don't you believe me? He's going to kill you, Hadria! Please. I have to save you from him!"

Her face took on the look of a concerned mother, and she rose, holding both of Faron's hands in her own. She guided him to his feet.

"There is so much to tell you, Faron." She spun around to where Sadagon and Synick stood, Synick shuffling his feet awkwardly. Why wasn't he helping?

"You," Hadria said, pointing. "You brought my brother to me?" Synick only shrugged. "I can never express the debt of gratitude I have to you. There are apartments on the second level. You may choose any that you wish for yourself. They are yours for as long as you live, but please, my brother has been returned to me from death. I wish to speak with him."

Synick appeared to bristle for a moment, then looked to Faron for input. When Faron couldn't tear his eyes away from his sister, Synick flashed his eyes between them, then back to Sadagon.

"He's never been more safe in all of his life," Sadagon said. "Please. Let this be a private moment."

"Not a chance," Synick interjected, giving up on Faron speaking. "I'm not saving him from one wolf only to feed him to another."

Hadria addressed him with surprising sharpness. "He is my brother, and I am no wolf. I watched him die five years ago, and now in the dead of night, he's returned to me and half a step from madness. Please, let him be alone with me."

"You can talk," Synick said. "And I won't listen, but I'll not let him out of my sight." He turned, eyeing Sadagon as he did so. He was half a head taller than Synick and twice as broad. "He's as much my brother as yours." He retreated to a great column to watch.

Consumed in her presence, Faron hardly even noticed the exchange. Hadria took him by the hand, and, in a daze, he allowed himself to be pulled under an archway the size of a Blackwood mansion and through a massive hallway that could have been a councilor's hall. He was so enthralled he hardly noticed Sadagon following a few steps behind.

Diamond-studded mosaics gave way to plush carpets so thick it could have been a giant mattress. Eventually, Hadria pulled him into a great alcove—small compared to the throne room but still far grander than anything he'd seen before today. Red velvet couches and stools lined the walls, blackwood writing tables and dressers dispersed evenly throughout.

Green light filtered through iron-framed windows as tall as Alhalow's snow wall. Faron suspected there were still many rooms above them. A fire behind a fine mesh gate pushed back the chill that seeped through the windows.

Hadria seated him in the light of a wall-mounted lantern on a couch of deep scarlet. Faron had never felt anything so soft in his life. Holding his hands in his lap, she kneeled in front of him, still looking for all the world like a concerned parent.

"What's happened here, Hadria?" he asked, eyeing her finery. Faron remembered the way Dageran would adorn his playthings before he tired of them, dressing them in silks and fine jewelry. His face darkened. "What has he done to you?"

Cold green eyes flashed like burning ice to where Sadagon stood several feet back, hands clasped behind his back. His gaze turned nearly as dark as Faron's.

"You're angry," Hadria said. "Confused."

"Do you know what he plans for you, Hadria?" Faron asked. "About his life spile? Do you know how old he is and what he does to stay alive?"

She looked surprised. "Do you?"

"We have to *go*, Hadria. He means to drain the blood from your veins. Please listen to me!"

A strand of golden hair slipped over her shoulder as she shook her head. "You're wrong, Faron. You don't understand."

His brow furrowed in disbelief. "Are you... are you defending him?" His eyes flicked to Sadagon and then back, confusion stilling his tongue.

"You know I would never lie to you," she said, sounding pained. Suddenly formal for a brief moment, she said, "I offer you the invitation of honesty." There was that strange phrase again.

"What don't I understand?" he asked nervously.

Sadagon, resplendent in a high collared, deep blue suit with gold embroidery, hefted a small stool and placed it near the plush seat. He sat slowly.

"You have come far," he said, his voice thick and smooth. "So I can only assume that you have learned very much about us. You have found our city, so you know many secrets that were lost." In response to Faron's heated glare, he said, "But you do not know all, and you cannot know more without understanding everything. Tell me, Faron." He said the name with a strange distaste. "Who am I?"

Faron wasted no time. "You're the monster who killed my

father and burned my home to the ground, and now you're manipulating Hadria to trust you. I won't let you have her!"

Sadagon nodded. "I can see why, from your perspective, you'd see me in that light. I understand, and I don't hold it against you. Yes, to many, I am a monster. I killed the ancient gods who once ruled from this very city. I did kill Baranor—Bouren, as you knew him—and had a hand to play with the burning of your home, a fact for which I am ashamed." He lifted a thick, strangely rough finger for one wearing such finery, cutting Faron off.

"But there is more to this story, and I would have you understand." He paused a moment. "I killed the gods of this world, and yes, to many, this made me a monster; but, a monster to one man is a savior to another." Suddenly, he stood and stepped a few paces away. "Atha and Olsu were not gods but devils—merely two humans who unlocked the secrets of immortality."

"Slaughtering children," Faron inserted.

Sadagon nodded. "Again, you are right, but you do not know the whole of it." He turned back to face them. "Olsu incited rebellion and wars among his countries, forcing hundreds of thousands of men to their deaths. A war-ravaged land was a religious land and easy to control. Hundreds of thousands of men, women, and children died at his hands so he might tighten his fist over the world. Olsu was the disease that plagued humanity. Atha was no better."

"How is this different from you leeching the blood of children into your own veins? And how is it relevant?" Faron interrupted again. Hadria did not gasp—didn't even blink.

"Olsu was my father," Sadagon said, "and Atha, my mother."

Despite his frustration, that caught Faron off guard.

Sadagon, the white-haired man from his past, was the literal son of deities?

"You are the son of the Twinborn Gods?" he asked, incredulous.

"No," Sadagon corrected. "I am the son of those who pretended to be gods. As I began to grow old, I wondered why they did not." He paced a few steps again. "If they were gods, and I, their child, would I not, too, be immortal? That was when I discovered the god machine and learned of their lies."

"So, you killed them," Faron said flatly.

"I did, and in doing so, I have ended false wars, stopped the burning of libraries and knowledge, the suppression of technologies, the stoning of women impure, and the thousand-year rule held up by the lies of two people." He turned. "I freed the world from false gods—*mad* gods."

Faron's eyes darkened. "This city of yours doesn't seem very free. There are slaves who speak of Olsu as if he were a true god and still alive, too."

Sadagon nodded. "It has taken a hundred years to achieve that, but still, it is a necessary thing that you will come to understand."

"You're little better than the false gods then," Faron spat. "Using his machine to live past your due, killing those who can't defend themselves." The initial shock of seeing Hadria alive and before him was beginning to wear off. She ran her hand over his arm.

"Little better is still better, by definition, Faron." The name sounded twisted as he said it again. "But you say I murdered your father. From your point of view, this is true. But it is also true that Baranor had committed a grave crime against me and my city, and his life was forfeit. I merely collected what was my lawful due."

"He was my father!" Faron spat. "And you murdered him and burned my home to ash!"

"No," Hadria squeaked. Shocked, Faron looked down at her.

"Are you defending him?" he asked quietly. "The man who killed our father, separated us, and sentenced me to a lifetime of misery?"

"She is simply stating the truth as you need to hear it," Sadagon intervened. "A simple truth, which is this: While I did kill Bouren that unfortunate night, I did not kill your father, and I never intended to separate the two of you."

Faron's voice was dangerous. The sickly smiling skull, burned into his vision, grinned behind his eyes, flames dancing all around him. "What do you mean?" he whispered.

Hadria spoke up again, voice straining. "Bouren is not your father, and Faron is not your name."

He stood abruptly. "What do you mean?" he said again, louder.

Hadria's voice matched his for strength but still sounded nervous and strained. "My name, given at birth, was never Hadria, but Atha Vavelt, after our grandmother, and you are Olsu Varek, Son of Sadagon, son of Olsu."

The words struck like hammer blows, reverberating in his head, striking harder and harder as their meaning set in.

"No," he gasped. "No. It's not true. Bouren is our father. Can't you see? He's lying to you, Hadria. He means to kill you!"

"This is our city," she continued as if he had not spoken. "Priestess Valatha recognized you in her tower. The people here are your subjects, and they had given up hope of ever serving their rightful king."

"My subjects?" He felt dizzy.

"We are Father's heirs. You are their king, Faron, prince to an heirdom."

"It's not true," he whispered. "He wants to kill you, Hadria!" He yelled suddenly, pointing at Sadagon, "To *kill* you!"

"I am not Hadria," she snapped, suddenly upset. She stood, stance akimbo. "My name is Atha Vavelt, I am queen of Vam Aranath, and Sadagon Pyre is Lord-Steward over this city and our father."

"Bouren was our father!" Faron yelled, confused fury rising inside him. "Who *he* killed and fed to the flames!"

She slapped him across the face, and it stung—but not nearly as much as the shock and hurt of betrayal it brought with it.

"Bouren—*Baranor*—was a common criminal!" She spat the words harshly. "He killed the Lady Lyss—our *mother*, Faron—and pried us from her chilling corpse at barely a month old, after which he spirited us away as far from our birthright as he could get, which happened to be some backwater named Alhalow where he hid from our father for the better part of thirteen years!"

Faron leaned away from her, stung by the keen blade of betrayal. She truly believed it. He could see that deep down, she really, *truly* believed it, but what scared him far more was that he could feel the truth of it himself.

"When he came to us that night, Faron, he came to find *us*—to reclaim his heirs from the man who murdered his wife." She stepped back so she wasn't so aggressively close to his face. "Hadria was a blade of a name given to me by the man who murdered my mother to conceal me from my father, so you'll forgive me when I take offense at it." She smoothed her dress and lowered her voice. "My name is Vavelt, daughter of Lord Sadagon Pyre, ruler and steward of this city."

Faron felt a deep twisting in his gut. "I can't believe that. Had—" He stopped before he angered her again by saying her name. "He's lying. He's going to kill you on your nameday to fuel his immortality." He felt less certain every time he said it.

It was Sadagon who spoke this time. "Why?" Faron didn't know how to respond. "Why would I want to kill my own daughter to provide the sap of life for myself?" He laid out an open hand, palm up as if it contained the point he wished to make. "Even if she were not my daughter, why would I deceive and lie to gain her confidences only to replenish myself with her blood when there are thousands beyond these walls, and thousands within, who know that that is their fate? If I intended her sap for myself, why would she not be working the fields, the smithies, the stables, or wearing a slave's livery? She is not a slave or a pawn, a pet, or a trophy. She is a queen—and my daughter. And you, Faron, are my son." Unbelievably, his voice almost choked at the end.

Faron hated that he couldn't see the flaw in Sadagon's logic, and he knew he was telling the truth. Hadria was no prisoner.

It hurt worse than he could possibly imagine.

Betrayal and anger mixed in his belly, and he wheeled on Hadria. "Tell me, *Vavelt*." He spat the name angrily. "How have you managed to justify the kidnapping and slaughter of children? How many hundreds have been killed to prolong the life of this one man?" He pointed an angry finger at Sadagon. "How many thousands more will have to die so he can live?"

"It's not what you think," she said, her chin rising slightly. She took on a stately appearance, like that of a true princess.

"There is more at stake than you can imagine."

The hurt he felt at realizing she was not a thing he could save changed from a wounded confusion to a sharp anger. "I have paid *dearly* to learn what I know," he said through clenched teeth. "I learned how the gods lived. I have found orphan halls burned to the ground, hidden slave markets for the buying and selling of children who ultimately end up here. I know what age you let them achieve before letting the blood from them." He stood as his anger grew. "I have run from those who enslaved me, walked through fire and ice, and killed men to find you, Hadria." He used the name he knew her by. As far as he was concerned, it was her real one. "I know more than I would ever care to, and I have paid a terrible price for every scrap of it."

"My name," she said, growing angry, "is Vavelt."

Sadagon stepped between them. "Enough," he said, keeping them apart with the force of his presence. "Vavelt, Hadria is the name he knows you by. He doesn't know it for the weapon that it is, and you cannot expect him to give it up so readily. You yourself took years to answer to it, even after you accepted the truth of your parentage." He turned to Faron. "And yes, this is another thing you are not wrong about. I am surprised how much you know, but again, you don't know everything."

"What could possibly justify the slaughter of innocent children?" Faron challenged. "How could you ever make that right?"

"It is a simple trade," he countered. "My men and those under their employ find the sick, wounded, dying, and impoverished children all across the empire. Orphaned children are a clear example of this. Their guardians are dead or happily missing, and the many would rather they starve than confront the issue. I take these into my fold.

"Here, I raise them, give them food and shelter—a family. I give them a life that they otherwise could not have until their nameday when they give that back to the city." His eyes grew soft. "I'm not killing children, Faron. I'm taking the disenfranchised who are already doomed or dying and giving them an extension on life, one that they could not find any other way."

"You're still killing them!" he screamed. "Say whatever you like to soften the load, but in the end, they're alive until the moment you put the blade to their throats. You are immoral." He turned to see Hadria, who seemed nearly as angry as he was. "What you are doing is still immoral."

Sadagon replied for them both. "And what have you learned about morality, Faron? How many people have you killed in your quest to bring you here?"

He raged at having the issue flipped on him, but the question struck hard. He had killed two: Garad and Jaru'tal. He cringed. Jakal had also died at his hand, even if he had deserved it; and Haka'een, the man in the desert; and the two men he had thrown from the palace window in Aru'barrahk. His heart thumped as he thought of Ulric and the blame that certainly lay at his feet. He supposed Jakab and Badune's deaths were somewhat attributed to him as well, and what of the man who had been executed for failing to stop him from killing Jaru'tal Dunestrider, slave master of Aru'barrahk? Synick had almost been killed because of him too.

Their souls weighed on him like anvils. He had vowed to carry them because it led him to Hadria and the injustice she suffered, but now...

How was he to carry the weight of these souls?

The tally made him sick as he realized its scope. "That's not the same thing," he defended. "I have only stained my blade with the blood of slavers and those who would kill me."

"And why is that any different?"

He stammered. How could it not be? "Because you kill to further your own goals, and I seek to protect someone!" His eyes glared daggers at Hadria. She had betrayed him. He had come all this way to find that not only did she not need to be rescued but had joined the very man who had ruined them.

"So, it's justified," Sadagon explained, "because you believe in the cause you're killing for?"

Faron said nothing, heartbeat escalating as he waited for Sadagon to explain away his crimes.

"Then you understand that sometimes some need to die so others may live."

"They were criminals!" Faron shouted. "Slavers!"

"And are you an executioner? Are you sent by a governor to carry out the law?" He let the silence stand for an answer. "If you are not acting within the law, then you cannot use it as leverage for justification. You killed because it was expedient—because it furthers a greater goal." He peered into Faron's seething eyes. "In this, we are the same. I offer life to those without lives—as long as I can—until their sacrifice is required to protect not just one person but the whole of the world." He nodded sadly. "They die, yes, but not for selfish goals, Faron. Their sacrifices will protect all mankind."

"By keeping you alive?" Faron mocked. "Are you really so self-important?"

"No," Sadagon replied, shaking his head. "By keeping you alive."

Shock swept over him. That was not an argument he had expected. "What are you talking about?"

It was silent for a few moments until Hadria, who had been quiet for several minutes, chirped, "Tell him." She met Faron's stare, eyes soft once again. "Or I will."

"It is your fate to save the world, Faron—yours and Hadria's both."

"What nonsense are you spewing now?"

Sadagon sat back on his blackwood stool, fire roaring in a massive open fireplace behind him. "When I learned of my father's lies, I was outraged. I have seen death on a scale you can only imagine and all without purpose. City turned against city, father against son, as Atha and Olsu pitted them against one another. Wars were fought over promises never kept, from glory in a supposed afterlife to favors for one city in detriment to another, and that was before the religious wars when Olsu tried to gain power over Atha and nearly shattered the world.

"I have seen entire cities burned to ash, not a single stone left stacked on another." He actually seemed to shudder as he recalled the memories. "Mountains of corpses—man, woman, and child—over the petty struggles between two immortal beings. How many women Olsu raped only to watch executed afterward, I cannot count. Petitioners for aid or mercy who came before him were tortured and fed to his wolves as a rule." He turned to Faron.

"When I learned that they were not the gods they pretended to be, I cast them upon a pyre and threw down their rule. They were mortal. I hoped that when the world learned, they would overcome the differences set upon them and forsake their old ways, but I was wrong. Not only did the wars continue, filling an immense vacuum of power, but the religion they had created lived on as well."

To Faron's great surprise, he found himself hanging on to Sadagon's words. Despite himself, he was intrigued.

"A lie grows deep roots in a thousand years. My followers and I spent decades traveling the world, burning books, erasing the names of Vam Atha and Vam Olsu from the world, but it held firm all the same. If anything, we only helped erase the memory of their cruelty and corruption."

"What does this have to do with me?" Faron interrupted.

"Everything. You are the thread from which the world hangs."

"Listen to him, Faron," Hadria said but threw a pitying look at Sadagon.

"In the end," the white-haired man continued, "salvation would come despite my efforts, not because of them. Centuries after the fall of the gods, when their death was long known but their names not forgotten, I learned of a new threat, one that my parents had not shared."

Whatever it was, it couldn't be worth the mass murder of the young, but Faron asked anyway. "What?"

"The world is dying."

Faron narrowed his eyes. "That doesn't mean anything. A world does not die."

"No," Hadria offered. "But the creatures that live upon it can."

"What do you mean?" He was getting very tired of asking that.

Sadagon picked back up. "Many have seen the signs, but few understand. The seasons are changing. It is a pattern of millennia and one that is coming to a head."

"Speak clearly," Faron demanded.

"Every year, the Veil falls sooner and farther. If not this decade, then the next, the Veil will grow so large that it will not recede past even the southernmost regions of our world. Winter is consuming us, Faron. It is beyond our power to stop, and soon, it will freeze the earth."

Faron's brow furrowed. "That can't be true, and even if it were, how am I to stop it? You said yourself there never was and never will be such a thing as gods."

"It is true, Faron, and there is a world of proof. You certainly have seen some of it yourself in your time above the Veil."

"How's that?"

It was Hadria who spoke next. "Forests where they cannot grow, great lakes where water cannot flow, cities buried under ice—the truth is clear, Faron." It echoed ominously in his mind. Did they know that winter had already come to Anveil? A winter more than a month early.

"You've seen the signs," Sadagon said, reading his expression. "You know the truth."

"I can't keep the world from freezing," he said weakly.

"No," Sadagon said. "But when the crops do not grow and cities have no wood left to burn, you can feed them, warm them. When the pillaging armies come to rape and to ravage, you can stop them. When the walls are buried in mountains of snow and the dire wolves fill the streets, you can protect them. You cannot keep the world from freezing, but you can save the people that live upon it when it does."

"How?"

"By unifying them under one banner. Smash the divisions that separate a man against his neighbor, crush the wars of survival before they begin, and teach them to endure, one with another."

"How?!" Faron yelled.

"By taking up the mantle I tried to destroy centuries ago. Rekindle the lie that I could not extinguish. This is why you were born, Faron: to save mankind from the coming frost and themselves."

"What are you saying?" Faron whispered.

Sadagon stood and clasped his arms behind his back. "You are named for more than just your grandfather, Varek. You were born to become him."

Faron leaped to his feet. "No."

"You, Olsu Varek and Atha Vavelt, were born to be the gods of this world."

Epilogue

Sadagon watched as Varek, his only son—returned from the dead and forged harder than steel—teetered on the edge of falling into hysteria. His chest rose and fell dangerously, unruly and matted hair framing his dark eyes in the faint light of the rising sun. The next few moments were critical.

Varek shook his head violently. "No. No, it isn't true. I am no god, and you are not my father. You're the man who *killed* my father, and you've poisoned my sister with your lies. Get away from her!" He wheeled on Hadria. "Can't you see how he's turned you from reality? He means to kill you, Hadria! His life depends on the blood in your veins."

She shook her head, a piteous look on her face. "No, Faron."

Inwardly, Sadagon exhaled in relief. Varek spoke strong words, but he didn't believe them. He was responding to the panic that welled within him, his doubt pouring out like water in a cracked vase.

He would be convinced.

"I am sorry," Sadagon said. "It is not a burden I would wish on anyone. You were meant to be raised under my tutelage, groomed for the position from your first steps, but I failed you. Now, impossibly, you've been returned to me, and I must ask you to accept your rule with no period of guidance or grace."

"I don't believe you," he whispered. Sadagon could see the lie on his lips.

"I know that you do not want to believe, but search your heart, Faron." The name pained him to say, and he cursed Baranor for it. "After everything you've learned, how can you doubt?"

"After everything you've done, how can I trust you?"

"Trust is a thing earned over a long period of time, my son. I vow to try and be worthy of yours."

"Don't call me that! I'm not your son."

"You are," Vavelt said, speaking up. "Look in a mirror and see yourself in him."

"Fear cannot change the truth of your heritage, Faron. It can only distort the way you perceive it. The blood that runs in your veins is eternal, descended first from Atha and Olsu, then from me. In time, you will come to accept your place beside your sister."

"You're lying," Varek said. "You're a murderer and a thug, and I won't let you manipulate her into sacrificing herself for you."

Vavelt stood, releasing her brother's shoulders. "No one is manipulating me, Faron. Please, can both of you just stop this? For five years, I've had nightmares about what happened to you, felt guilt for surviving when you did not, and missed you terribly. Now, out of nowhere, you're alive, in good health, and whole before my very eyes, and all you want to do is fight!" She stared them both down. "Can we please stop to appreciate this miracle? Tell me how you came across the Veil. How did you survive? Where have you *been*?"

Varek cast his eyes at Vavelt, who returned his look with the utmost sincerity. He loved her more than anything—it was clear to see—maybe even more than his own will to live. Seeing her here, associated with the man who represented all the evil in his life, must have been a difficult thing indeed. Choking down his own protestations, Sadagon ran a hand through his daughter's hair.

"I know it isn't easy—seeing her like this. In a way, I suspect it would be simpler for you to see her in a cell as a thing you could save and escape with." He could see his words' effect like a hammer upon molten iron. Varek's breathing began to shudder, and it was obvious he agreed. Pity filled Sadagon's heart. Varek was a man of passion like his father, not a boy ruled by the dictations of his heart. In time, he would learn to control his passions instead of being controlled by them, but until then, he needed help.

"Vavelt is right. The unexpected joy of finding you is near overwhelming. Let me prove to you that I am no monster, as you understandably believe. Let me prove that your sister and I take no pleasure in the cost of uniting the world. Stay with us and let us show you the truth."

Varek took a breath to cool himself. "Am I a prisoner here?"

"Of course not. You are a god and a king."

"Then would you allow Hadria and me to leave?" He invested the word with pointed doubt.

"Do you wish to leave, Vavelt?"

She shook her head. "This is my home, Faron. This is our role in the world."

"Then will you let *me* leave?" he snapped, directing his gaze back to Sadagon.

"Would you want to? After how far you've come to find

your sister, you would leave her after learning her home is not a cage? As god of this world and ruler of this city, I will be one of your subjects come your ascension. There is nothing I could make you do."

Vavelt spoke. "Without you, there is no hope, Faron. Selfishness and evil and cruelty will destroy everything when men are hungry and cold. By coming here, you've given them a second chance."

"No person should be enslaved to another, let alone an entire world, Hadria!"

Sadagon nodded in agreement. "Worship and right of rule are not the same as slavery. Men will be free under your guidance, free from hunger and free from the swords of others."

"So long as they accept my rule."

Sadagon didn't let it show on his face, but he smiled to himself. The argument was reframing. Not a moment ago, Varek had claimed not to believe a word of what was said, fighting back against the very idea of being a ruler and god, and now he was arguing the morality of that rule. He didn't see it, but he had legitimized Sadagon's position.

"True enough," he said. "But is that so bad a thing? The people already accept rule from the ever-shifting seat of Empyrion. They would only shift it to you."

"The empire doesn't sacrifice their children," Faron spat.

"But they do," Sadagon replied. "The same children, only in different ways. They sacrifice them to their economies, letting them starve in the streets. They sacrifice them to their lusts and vanity, in dark circles far worse than their fates here. Adults, children—people die in droves by the fists of apathy and neglect. They would not end up here if this weren't so.

This is only one thing that your rule will put an end to."

"By killing children."

"Please," Vavelt interdicted again. "Don't yell at him. He's helping you to understand."

Sadagon sighed. "You should know, Faron, my son, there are fates far worse than death. To live a tortured existence is far bleaker than the absence of life." Despite his starved-looking frame, Varek's gaze smoldered with intensity and showed no signs of burning out. He seemed to know the truth of that statement firsthand. "But your sister is right. Let us not diminish the blessing of your arrival. You argue like your mother, Faron. She, too, was so righteous—so stalwart." He let the silence hang for a moment. "But that cannot change the fact that the world needs you. Whatever I might say, it is not an easy sacrifice that I've asked you to bear, but it was for this purpose that you were born. You will unite the world under a righteous banner, and to do that, you must be a god."

Varek only stared. He was resilient, but he was convinced, even if he didn't know it yet. He had broken down the boy's walls as much as he could. Any more and he would become belligerent. What he needed, now, was a soft hand and time to process. Vavelt could give him those.

"You will see, my son, in time. For now, this needs to suffice. I can only imagine the trials you overcame to come here and the state you must be in. You need rest." He appeared to be conscious through force of will alone. It pained Sadagon to think of how he earned the ice burns on his face and the exhaustion he must be enduring. "Vavelt, will you show him to his chambers? Vam Olsu's old rooms, I think."

She grinned at that.

"I will appoint a servant to watch over you," Sadagon

explained. "Speak for anything, and it is yours. Food, wine, and rest will be a good start, and I suspect you will want some time to think."

Varek stared at him with an unreadable expression. What was he thinking behind those smoldering eyes? There was hatred, certainly, but also pain, desperation, and fear. He seemed beyond words because he didn't reply. Sadagon wanted nothing more in the world than to stay and shower questions upon his son—*his son*—but he had already over-stayed. Varek was not yet ready for that.

He stood, more alive than he had been in a hundred years. "Rest, Faron, and when you are well, we will hold a celebration, the likes of which hasn't been seen in Vam Aranath for three hundred years. Take care of him, Vavelt." He strode from the foyer, overcoming his desire to stay. His son was returned from death and had singlehandedly restored his ability to unite the world.

It was time to ready the army.

* * *

Faron watched in complete numbness as Sadagon walked away. The man he'd sworn to find, sworn to *kill*, and nearly lost himself hunting, turned around and left without even a single word of protest. Was it true what he'd said? Could this monster of a man truly be his father? He worked it over in his mind for the hundredth time but still felt no clearer. It didn't matter. He would kill the man anyway.

His mind fell on Hadria. How might she react if he assassinated her father? Somehow, against all odds and reason, Sadagon had won her over to his side. They were alone now, though. Perhaps she would lean over and whisper how Sadagon had been controlling her, forcing her to say those things. She would take him by the hand and run away with him. The world could be simple again.

The words he waited on didn't come. He tried to think of what to say to her, what might convince her to take his side, or at the very least, express the knot of emotions that pulled him a hundred different ways. There was nothing but silence. There were no words that could adequately convey the frustration he felt at Hadria's siding with his mortal enemy, no words to explain the joy that nearly lifted him off his feet at seeing her face, no words for the relief knowing she was still alive, and no words for the betrayal he felt at seeing her here. Instead, there was silence, and it stretched through a long moment.

"I know what you must be thinking," Hadria said, searching his eyes, but how could she? She didn't know how she'd haunted him these past years.

The quiet was impossible to break.

"Please," Hadria said eventually, blue eyes flitting back and forth between his green. "Don't be upset."

Faron finally found his ability to speak. "He murders children, Hadria."

Her lips pulled slightly at the use of that name, but she didn't comment. "He *saves* children, Faron. He gives them years of life they couldn't otherwise have."

"That has the sound of a practiced argument," Faron accused. "Something you tell the mirror to make yourself believe."

"Because it is!" Hadria said, taking him off guard. "The life spile is a terrible thing and one that I need daily help to tolerate. I *hate* it, Faron. I hate it so much I want to destroy it every time I see a new batch of young girls or scared eyes, but I know how important it is. As much as I loathe the thing, it's *necessary*."

Contrary to the point she was making, her words brought a bitter comfort to Faron. Could she perhaps be swayed to his side? Faron went on the offensive.

"Dead gods, Hadria, how are you a part of this? Even if you believe every word of what he says, which I don't think you do, it's still drastically unjustified."

She didn't rise to the bait, keeping her cool and speaking in a soft voice. "You know what I'm going to say, Faron. 'You don't know yet. You don't understand yet. You'll see soon.' Can we set this aside for now? I know with every fiber of my being that you'll come to see things my way, just as you undoubtedly know I'll see things from yours." Faron felt a slight prick of guilt at the accuracy of her words.

"Please," she continued. "Let's put this down. You don't have to be a god right this moment." A smile crossed her lips. "Or a butcher, or a bard's guard and underpaid traveling companion." She nudged him as she spoke the last, eliciting a wan smile as he too remembered the late-night conversation they'd had so long ago as children. The nostalgia of the moment was so thick he almost choked on it.

"For now, the only thing you need to be is my brother. You don't even have to be Sadagon's son if you're not ready for that. We'll just hide all the mirrors so you can't see it for yourself." Faron's small smile slipped at that. "Just my brother," Hadria said, correcting her misstep and wiping away her own smile. "Do you think you can do that?"

"I'm sorry," Faron said. "Yes, I'd like that." He felt a heavy weight lift off his chest. "More than you know."

"I daresay I know quite well, actually," Hadria countered. "You've been dead for five years, Faron. There are no songs or sweet words that will do to tell you how amazed and overwhelmed I am to see you again—to have you back for myself." Emotion colored her voice.

She slipped off the padded bench and knelt before him. "Gods," Hadria whispered. "Even now, I don't believe it. It *really* is you."

The look she gave him seemed to dissipate the exhaustion and pain that bore down on him, sustaining him through the sheer warmth of it. She pulled him into a tight embrace, and Faron melted into her. That one simple motion was enough to overwhelm the defenses he'd spent years building up, and he broke down, crying into her golden hair.

"I found you," he said through bitter tears. "I really found you."

"I know," she whispered back. "You're safe now. I'll take care of you."

"You're alive."

She stroked the back of his head and held him close.

"You're alive," he said again as if he could hardly believe it, and the events of the past few hours were only beginning to register.

She held him tight, unsuccessfully trying to make up for the lost years between them. Softly, without gasps or shakes, she cried as well and held her brother late into the morning.

Later, half delirious from fatigue and emotional exhaustion, Faron was led by a tall, thin man to a place where he could sleep. He entered the rooms without seeing them, falling onto an overstuffed sofa and staring at the ground.

Alive—Hadria was *alive*. That knowledge filled him with

joy every bit as much as the knowledge of her alliance with Sadagon filled him with dread. She was happy, and her joy was radiant; but, that tore at him too. On one hand, she was healthy, beautiful, and happy. On the other, she was happy *here*. She didn't want to leave.

That didn't even touch on the topic of Sadagon. Thoughts tore away at his sanity in a maelstrom of terror as he grappled with this new reality, staving off sleep in an attempt to process this new world of information. Faron felt someone sit next to him and turned numbly to see Synick watching him carefully. With no words between them, Faron looked back at the floor.

There was a long silence before Faron spoke. "I found her," he said simply. Synick didn't respond, for he didn't know the right words to say. Instead, Synick put his arm around his friend and let him cry.

THE END OF BOOK TWO
of
THE GROWING VEIL SERIES

I hope you enjoyed reading *A Gate of Wolves and Winter*.

Please consider leaving a review at one of the sites below to support my craft as an independently published author:
   amazon.com/author/ts.howard
   goodreads.com/tshoward
   bookbub.com/profile/t-s-howard

To continue on Faron's journey, read *A Pyre of Men and Mountain* at:
   tshoward.co/apomam/

To stay updated on any future releases, join my mailing list, or order signed copies, visit:
   tshoward.co/

Thank you,
   T.S. Howard

BOOK THREE OF THE GROWING VEIL

A PYRE OF MEN AND MOUNTAIN

T.S. HOWARD

The Veil descends with monsters in its wake, swallowing the world in wolves and white. Starvation and the promise of monsters threaten humanity as the Veil grows, heralding eternal winter, and if Faron does nothing, everyone will die. Armed with secrets to forever change the world, Faron must choose between abandoning humanity to certain extinction, or slaughtering thousands of innocents and subjugating all who remain to save them.

Harrowed by the truth of his family and the weight of nations, Faron must become the thing he hates most if there's any chance of saving humanity from the growing Veil...

Even if it kills him.

Find A Pyre of Men and Mountain at *tshoward.co/apomam.*

About the Author

I'm T.S. Howard, and I am, above all else, a storyteller. I see stories with my two children, who I love unreasonably, with my wife, who is a grand adventure by herself, and in my daily duties. I see stories in the world around me and feel them burn inside until I can put them to page. I see stories in the faces of those I pass who I don't know and in the lives of those I do. Stories are my life, and it is my undying goal to make them a part of yours.

Ever since the second grade, I knew what I wanted to be: a bestselling author, and I dedicate most of my time to that pursuit. It isn't a vanity or desire to be a household name that drives me, but that same desire for my characters, their names, and their stories.

Still, we aren't only defined by our largest goals. When I'm not writing, I'm tending to my family, obsessing over the quality of coffee and various cheeses (I am, after all, a millennial), and playing as a hobbyist geologist. I am untenably obsessed with garnets and other gemstones and almost always carry one with me. Similarly, if you see me without my headphones, you can safely understand that I'm having an off-day. Finally, when I'm not writing, reading, cooking, cleaning, looking for something shiny, or listening to music, I'm probably getting my ass kicked in an FPS game online.

www.ingramcontent.com/pod-product-compliance
Lightning Source LLC
Chambersburg PA
CBHW030556180626
46816CB00005B/1560